Praise for the Midnight Breed series by LARA ADR

BOUND TO DAI

"While most series would have ended
Midnight Breed series seems to have picked up steam. Lara
Adrian has managed to keep the series fresh by adding new
characters . . . without having to say goodbye to the original ones
that made the series so popular to begin with. Bound to
Darkness has all the passion, danger and unique appeal of the
original ten books but also stands on its own as a turning point
in the entire series with new pieces to a larger puzzle, new friends
and old enemies."

—*Adria's Romance Reviews*

"Lara Adrian always manages to write great love stories, not only
emotional but action packed. I love every aspect of (Bound to
Darkness). I also enjoyed how we get a glimpse into the life of
the other characters we have come to love. There is always
something sexy and erotic in all of Adrian's books, making her
one of my top 5 paranormal authors."

—*Reading Diva*

CRAVE THE NIGHT

"Nothing beats good writing and that is what ultimately makes
Lara Adrian stand out amongst her peers.... Crave the Night is
stunning in its flawless execution. Lara Adrian has the rare ability
to lure readers right into her books, taking them on a ride they
will never forget."

—*Under the Covers*

"...Steamy and intense. This installment is sure to delight
established fans and will also be accessible to new readers."

—*Publishers Weekly*

EDGE OF DAWN

"Adrian's strikingly original Midnight Breed series delivers an abundance of nail-biting suspenseful chills, red-hot sexy thrills, an intricately built world, and realistically complicated and conflicted protagonists, whose happily-ever-after ending proves to be all the sweeter after what they endure to get there."

—*Booklist (starred review)*

DARKER AFTER MIDNIGHT

"A riveting novel that will keep readers mesmerized... If you like romance combined with heart-stopping paranormal suspense, you're going to love this book."

—*Bookpage*

DEEPER THAN MIDNIGHT

"One of the consistently best paranormal series out there.... Adrian writes compelling individual stories (with wonderful happily ever afters) within a larger story arc that is unfolding with a refreshing lack of predictability."

—*Romance Novel News*

Praise for Lara Adrian

"With an Adrian novel, readers are assured of plenty of dangerous thrills and passionate chills."

—*RT Book Reviews*

"Ms. Adrian has a gift for drawing her readers deeper and deeper into the amazing world she creates."

—*Fresh Fiction*

Praise for LARA ADRIAN

"Adrian has a gift for drawing her readers deeper and deeper into the amazing world she creates."

—*Fresh Fiction*

"With an Adrian novel, readers are assured of plenty of dangerous thrills and passionate chills."

—*RT Book Reviews*

"Nothing beats good writing and that is what ultimately makes Lara Adrian stand out amongst her peers . . . Adrian doesn't hold back with the intensity or the passion."

—*Under the Covers*

"Adrian has a style of writing that creates these worlds that are so realistic and believable . . . the characters are so rich and layered . . . the love stories are captivating and often gut-wrenching . . . edge of your seat stuff!"

—*Scandalicious Book Reviews*

"Adrian compels readers to get hooked on her storylines."

—*Romance Reviews Today*

Praise for Lara Adrian's books

"Adrian's strikingly original Midnight Breed series delivers an abundance of nail-biting suspenseful chills, red-hot sexy thrills, an intricately built world, and realistically complicated and conflicted protagonists, whose happily-ever-after ending proves to be all the sweeter after what they endure to get there."

—*Booklist (starred review)*

"(The Midnight Breed is) a well-written, action-packed series that is just getting better with age."

—*Fiction Vixen*

Look for these titles in the *New York Times* and #1 international bestselling

Midnight Breed series

. . . and more to come!

Hunter Legacy Series

Born of Darkness
Hour of Darkness
Edge of Darkness *(forthcoming)*

Other books by Lara Adrian

Contemporary Romance

100 Series
For 100 Days
For 100 Nights
For 100 Reasons

Run to You *(forthcoming)*

Historical Romance

Dragon Chalice Series
Heart of the Hunter
Heart of the Flame
Heart of the Dove

Warrior Trilogy
White Lion's Lady
Black Lion's Bride
Lady of Valor

Lord of Vengeance

HOUR OF DARKNESS

A Hunter Legacy Novel

LARA ADRIAN

ISBN: 1727535618
ISBN-13: 978-1727535617

HOUR OF DARKNESS
© 2018 by Lara Adrian, LLC
Cover design © 2018 by CrocoDesigns

www.LaraAdrian.com

Available in ebook and trade paperback. Unabridged audiobook edition forthcoming.

HOUR OF DARKNESS

CHAPTER 1

Cain sank his fangs deeper into the brunette's neck, closing his eyes on a low snarl as bitter, coppery red cells filled his mouth. Seated beside him on the sofa of his palatial Miami hotel penthouse suite, the female he'd met only minutes ago clung to him and whimpered as he drank from her opened vein.

He was rough about it, eager to take his fill and be done. Cain made no secret of what he was. In the twenty years since humans had learned of the existence of the Breed, it wasn't unusual for his kind to mingle among their mortal neighbors. Some, like the blood Host he'd hired to service him tonight, seemed to find the open coexistence of the past two decades not only an acceptable arrangement but a profitable one too.

Cain gave the small punctures a brisk, businesslike swipe of his tongue to seal the wounds and conclude the transaction. Unfortunately, his Host didn't seem to grasp the limitations of his interest in her. As he drew away, her moan held a whining edge of complaint.

"Mmm, don't stop now, lover. Let's move to the bedroom and keep this party going." She reached for him, licking her cherry-red lips in invitation. "Look, I know you're only paying me for blood, but if you want something more—"

"Your cash is on the table in the vestibule."

Cain was already on his feet, wearing nothing but a pair of dark jeans. He reached for the black dress shirt he'd removed before sitting down to feed a few minutes ago. He slipped it on, not bothering to button it as he turned to meet the disgruntled face staring up at him.

Although the female was pretty and he wasn't the type to deny himself pleasure or sustenance, he rarely mixed the two. Repeat performances weren't his thing. He kept to a strict one-and-done policy, even when it came to the human women who offered him their veins. Life was simpler that way, cleaner.

No strings.

No complications.

No exceptions.

He lifted a black brow, impatient to be done now. "There's a bathroom down the hall if you need to clean up before showing yourself out."

The female frowned, muttering something under her breath as she stood and grabbed her purse off a nearby chair. Her spiked heels clacked sharply over the beachfront suite's polished tile floors in her swift march into the foyer. The hotel door closed behind her with a bang.

Cain blew out a breath, glad for the return to his solitude.

He had been in Miami for more than a week now, having eventually drifted to the very edge of the East Coast after leaving Las Vegas and a job that had been slowly devouring his soul. He'd assumed all he needed to clear his head—and his conscience—was enough time and miles put behind him. Now, a couple of months on the road, with nothing to keep him busy outside of feeding and fucking whenever the urge arose, about the only thing he was feeling was bored.

And restless.

Turns out, he wasn't built for idling. None of his kind were, but especially the Breed boys and men born into the infamous Hunter program. Twenty years of freedom from that hellish enslavement was hardly enough to erase the brutal discipline and training that had made Cain and the rest of his assassin half-brothers bred inside that laboratory anything close to civilized.

As much as Cain enjoyed life's endless luxuries—all the things his mercenary existence provided him—inside he was still shackled to the program. There had been a time, once, when he'd longed for a different life. A simpler, normal life. But those dreams belonged to better men than him.

Deep down, he was still the cold, detached killer his master had made him. Still the solitary predator existing on the shadowed fringe of the real world.

And lately, every one of his Hunter instincts was beginning to tell him it was time to move on.

He hadn't survived this long by ignoring them.

Strolling barefoot across the expansive living area of his suite, he pulled a bottle of whiskey from the fully stocked bar and poured a glass. As Breed, he couldn't drink the liquor but he swished it around in his mouth

3

to erase the metallic tang left over from the human's blood then spit it into the wet bar's polished steel sink.

On the other side of the ultraviolet-blocking shades that covered the floor-to-ceiling glass doors overlooking the beach and ocean beyond, the sun had finally dipped below the horizon. Blue hour. The fleeting moments between day and night when he could stand outside with no threat of searing his Breed skin and eyes.

Cain walked to the sliding doors and opened them wide. He stepped out to the terrace ten stories above the hotel pool and courtyard below. Warm salty air stuck to him, carrying the drifting aromas of blooming flowers and grilled foods. Just off the blanket of white sand still littered with beachgoers, an old reggae song being sung live in one of the tiki bars competed with the pulse and racket of a dance club down the street.

Christ. He'd left the nonstop glitter and noise of Las Vegas for some peace and solitude, but had only traded one circus for another.

He shook his head. Hell, maybe he'd roll out tonight yet. He'd already gone about as far south as he intended. Nothing but swamplands and a lot of bad memories in that direction, anyway. Instead, he thought he might venture north for a while, eventually end up in the Dakotas or Montana. As one of the Breed, he needed living human blood every few days for sustenance, but the idea of getting far away from people—even his own kind—was beginning to sound like a damn good plan.

He turned to go back inside, but paused when he glanced down at the hotel pool. A woman swam alone in the glowing turquoise water, slender arms and legs propelling her with effortless grace and speed across the Olympic-sized length. She wore a skimpy black bikini, with her thick blond hair bound in a long ponytail and floating like gossamer waves over her back as she swam.

Her gorgeous body alone would have been enough to make Cain pause to admire, but it was the delicate body art that decorated her limbs and torso that drew him to the railing for another look. That and the fact that it was next to impossible for anyone to have the entire pool to themselves no matter what hour of the day.

And now that he was looking closer, he realized she wasn't exactly alone after all.

Four big men in dark suits were positioned around the vacated pool and courtyard garden. Their grim faces alternated between watching her swim and scanning their surroundings. Cain didn't have to see the faint outline of firearms holstered beneath their jackets to know they were professionals.

So, who was this woman?

Whoever she was, the female was a knockout. Curves and lean muscle in all the right places. Smooth, alabaster skin that only made the contrast of the ink even sexier. Twisting vines and blood-red roses wrapped her upper arms and long legs, the unbroken chain continuing all the way around her ankles. Each movement of her body made the roses appear alive, begging to be touched.

Cain angled for a better view of her face as it dipped in and out of the water with her sleek strokes, but all he could discern was the hint of high-cut cheekbones and a lush mouth.

It was plenty for his libido to take an interest. Arousal coiled inside him as he fixated on her gliding trek back and forth across the pool. He watched her face lift out of the water in rhythmic motion, her parted lips taking in air between each fluid stroke of her arms.

The illuminated water licked every inch of her body the way he suddenly wanted to do. Each fluttering kick of her strong legs made him hunger to have them wrapped around his hips as he drove inside her. He'd just fed, and yet hunger coiled in him. The urge to feel her throat giving way beneath his sharp fangs was nearly overwhelming.

He closed his eyes on a growl, entertaining a swift and powerful image of the two of them tangled together in his bed. His cock went heavy and hard at the thought, his fangs erupting from his gums.

Fuck.

When he lifted his lids a second later, his eyes burned with unearthly heat. He watched her pivot at the end of the pool and begin another lap. Her loose blond hair undulated around her shoulders and down her spine, and Cain's fingers clenched with the desire to feel those silken strands clutched in his fist as she writhed naked beneath him, begging for everything he gave her and more.

He let the fantasy play out as he watched her swim, trying to ignore the bulge growing more unbearable behind the zipper of his jeans.

He was so transfixed, he hardly registered the quiet pop that sounded from somewhere nearby. But in that next instant, a bloom of red erupted from the back of the woman's head.

Blood. It streaked into the pale blond tendrils of her hair, a growing stain that grew and grew, swirling around her like scarlet tentacles.

Her strokes stalled. Her body went instantly limp, collapsing lifelessly under the water.

Holy shit.

She'd just been shot in front of his eyes. Executed. The massive wound in her skull erased any doubt about that.

Ten stories below him, her corpse began to sink to the bottom of the pool as her security detail scrambled in to retrieve her.

"Son of a bitch." Cain closed his lids in disbelief.

When he opened them again, the blood was gone.

The blonde was still swimming her lap, alive and well. Totally unharmed.

At least she was for now.

Because the killing he'd just witnessed hadn't happened yet. What he'd seen was a sixty-second glimpse of the future. Her future, coming to a violent, watery end.

It wasn't the first time he had experienced a sudden flash of precognition foretelling someone's death, but it had been years since the last one. His unique Breed ability had been with him since he was a boy. He hadn't learned to hate it until he was a man and his cursed gift had failed him when he'd needed it the most.

Failed not only him, but someone else too.

Cain bit off a dark curse, refusing to let the memory—or the shame—take hold of him. He had buried that part of his life and moved on. He'd been damn glad his unwelcome gift had seemed to abandon him altogether in recent years.

The visions had been gone so long, he assumed they'd never return. And good riddance, so he had thought. Yet as much as he wanted to ignore what he'd just witnessed in his mind's eye, he couldn't.

If he didn't do something, his vision would become

LARA ADRIAN

reality and she would be dead.

The last thing he wanted was to get involved. He shouldn't care what happened to a random woman he had no business craving, let alone thwarting destiny to protect.

But none of that stopped him from palming the railing of his tenth-floor balcony and leaping over the edge.

He sailed down in a flash of motion, faster than any human eye—or sniper's sight—could track him. Feet first, he plunged into the water and grabbed the woman into his arms.

She screamed. One of her bodyguards jumped in from the side of the pool, but Cain was already well out of reach, moving her out of the bullet's path just as the assassin's round tore into the water where she'd been only seconds before.

Cain swiveled his head and glanced up toward the roof of the hotel, scanning for signs of the sniper. The would-be killer was already gone from his post, not a trace of a weapon or a hunkered shooter anywhere above. Meanwhile, the woman struggled to get loose.

Her body was lean and strong in his arms, and warm. She twisted around in his grasp, crushing her curves against the front of his body in her efforts to break free. Everywhere her bare skin touched him, he burned with awareness of her.

She fought the firm bands of his arms, finally shoving him away on a shocked curse. Long-lashed eyes in an arresting shade of warm burgundy stared at him in confusion and fury. "What the hell are you do—?"

Her voice, tinged with a Slavic accent, cut off as she looked at him. She glanced from the sharp points of his elongated canines to the Breed skin markings that covered his wet torso. The tangle of multi-hued *dermaglyphs* prickled everywhere her gaze touched him. He couldn't hide what he was, even if he tried. His fangs were bared in battle-readiness, and in response to the feel of her curves having been pressed against him.

"Are you okay?" he asked her.

She didn't answer, merely looked around his shoulder to where her guard now sagged lifeless in the pool, his blood staining the water instead of hers. Cool and collected in spite of what just happened, she returned to Cain's gaze.

"You saved my life." She swallowed, her intelligent wine-dark eyes searching his face. "But how did you— where did you come from?"

He shrugged, unsure how he would explain what just happened. Not that he was going to have the chance. Two of her men were at the edge of the pool, lifting her out of the water while the remaining one held his pistol on Cain.

"Yury, *nyet*." Her voice was crisp with command. She held up her hand, giving the gunman a tight shake of her head. She said something more in their language, orders that had all of the guards snapping to attention.

God, she was beyond attractive. Those sharp cheekbones and pouty lips were even more striking up close, but combined with her burgundy gaze and delicate bone structure, her beauty was both angelic and exotic. Her attitude was pure confidence, though, and Cain had hardly seen anything hotter.

The weapon trained on him lowered immediately and the third man moved to her side, adding his bulk to the human shield surrounding her. Without another word, she and her guards were moving hastily away from the pool. Cain watched her go, standing in the waist-high water along with the corpse that might have been her if he'd allowed fate to have its way.

And the question that had intrigued him from high atop his penthouse terrace only deepened now.

Who the hell was she?

The woman glanced back at him only for a moment, a silent connection of their gazes that shot through Cain like a physical caress. He saw the curiosity in her eyes too. And the flicker of awareness that made the memory of her bare, wet skin against his burn even more intensely.

She blinked once, then turned around and hurried into the shelter of the hotel surrounded by her bodyguards.

CHAPTER 2

Marina Moretskova accepted the glass of cold water from the captain of her security detail with a faint nod and only a slight tremble in her fingers. "Thank you, Yury."

It had been more than an hour since the attempt on her life in the pool, but the grim soldier's face was still drawn with concern. Deep lines bracketed his mouth and creased his brow, a look mirrored by the other bodyguards her uncle in Russia had sent to accompany her on her trip to the States.

It seemed strange that Kirill wasn't standing there with the other three. Just a few hours ago he had been cracking jokes with Ivan and Viktor, and now his lifeless body was on its way to the local morgue. Tonight they had lost one of their own, but the remaining men charged with keeping Marina safe had taken their comrade's death in stride, her life being their sole priority.

Uncle Anatoly would have it no other way.

Especially on this trip.

Yury stepped away from Marina's seat on the delicate chair in the presidential suite's living room, but he didn't go far. With his large hands clasped in front of him, the big man took a protective position at her right while Marina continued her conversation with the pair of law enforcement officers who'd been dispatched to the hotel to interview her shortly after the attack.

"Forgive us for taking up so much of your time tonight, Ms. Moretskova. After what you've been through, answering all of these questions can't be easy. But before we wrap up here, can you think of anything else that might assist with our investigation?"

Marina took a sip of her water and slowly shook her head. "What more can I tell you? I was simply enjoying a relaxing swim in the pool when suddenly everything turned to chaos."

The two uniformed officers from the Joint Urban Security Taskforce Initiative Squad—one human, one Breed—exchanged a look from where they sat across from her on the silk-covered sofa. The older of the two, the human, scratched his whisker-shadowed jaw. He had been asking the most questions since they arrived, but now it was the ginger-haired Breed officer who leaned forward with his forearms resting on his knees as he addressed her.

"I think what my partner, Officer Powell, is trying to say is, do you have any reason to believe this wasn't a random shooting?"

Although he posed the inquiry in a casual tone, only a fool would mistake it as such. And Marina Moretskova was no fool. Nor were her uncle's men. She felt Yury's tension ratchet beside her. He and his two comrades stood still as statues in their positions around the room. Marina kept her expression mild as she held the Breed JUSTIS agent's probing stare.

"I have no reason to believe anything of the kind." She tilted her head. "Do you, Officer Jonas?"

"We'll know more as we investigate further," he said, neither confirming nor denying.

The officers had informed her that no evidence of the sniper had been found from their search of the hotel rooftop, but that hardly gave Marina reassurance. Someone wanted her dead. Failure and escape tonight only left the shooter free to try again.

And while Marina mourned the loss of a man who had served her family faithfully for years, she owed her life not to her uncle's hand-picked team of bodyguards, but to a stranger who had appeared out of thin air to pull her to safety.

The whole incident was a confusing blur, but she would swear her unlikely savior had her in his arms even before the sniper had fired his weapon.

"You have our word JUSTIS will do everything in our power to get to the bottom of this," the officer continued. "We've got a decent start between our interview with you and the other witness to the shooting, your neighbor in the penthouse down the hall."

"He's staying in the penthouse?"

The question blurted out of her before she could hold it back. She didn't intend to sound so curious about the man who had leapt into the pool and saved her life, but he hadn't been far from her thoughts for a moment since the attack. Those piercing, laser-intense silver eyes beneath inky brows and close-shorn ebony hair were branded into her memory.

And it hadn't escaped her notice that her rescuer was more than simply a man. A Breed male. Sharp fangs had gleamed diamond-bright behind a sculpted, generous mouth. She'd never been so close to one of his kind, let alone held in powerful, inhuman arms.

She could still hear the stranger's deep growl of a voice echoing in her veins.

Are you okay?

She was, but only thanks to him.

Like a dark angel, he'd swooped down out of the night sky in silence. She had been terrified at first when those *dermaglyph*-covered arms had wrapped around her like warm bands of iron, caging her against an immense body carved of solid muscle. Then she heard the shot.

Unmistakable, sharp.

Lethal.

And despite what she told JUSTIS, Marina knew to her marrow that the bullet clearly had been meant for her. Instead, it was Kirill's corpse that had been removed from the water, dead from a single gunshot wound to the head.

The older JUSTIS officer studied her, his eyes glancing off the tangle of tattoos that wrapped around her biceps and down onto her forearms. The vines and roses continued around to her back and twisted along the length of her legs. She knew he wanted to ask about the delicate body art, just as he'd not-so-subtly eyed the black Vory stars on the backs of Yury's and her other bodyguards' hands when the officers had first arrived.

Marina waited out the silence, until finally the man cleared his throat.

"This Breed male who pulled you to safety," Powell prompted. "You say you never met him before tonight?"

"That's right. I'd never seen him before. I don't even know his name."

"It's Cain," said the Breed officer. "Cain Hunter, according to the Nevada ID he's got on file with the hotel. We ran a quick background on him, just a routine thing. He's been here in Miami for about a week, but until a couple of months ago, he was working security for one of the big casinos in Las Vegas."

"Speaking of IDs," said the other man. "Ms. Moretskova, we couldn't help but notice you hold dual citizenship. Russia and the United States."

"That's right." She blinked mildly and took another sip of her water. "I was born in New York. My mother was Russian. She studied in the States and played the cello with the city symphony before she became pregnant with me. We returned home to her family soon after I was born."

"You and your mom still spend a lot of time in this country?"

Marina held the expectant stare. "This is my first time here. My mother never returned, as far as I know. She died when I was three years old."

"Ah, I'm sorry." The officer's brow furrowed in sympathetic regard. "That must've been rough on you . . . and your father?"

He phrased it like the probing question it was, though whether he was seeking confirmation of something he already knew or probing for further detail, she wasn't sure. "I never met my father. From what I understand, my mother never told him about her pregnancy and she never spoke of him to anyone."

"Not even to your uncle?" asked Officer Jonas, his Breed gaze pinning her like lasers.

Marina stiffened. At her side, Yury practically vibrated with violence, as did the rest of his comrades. "Excuse me?"

"Are you any relation to Anatoly Moretskov?"

Her heartbeat sped, even as she rationalized that it should hardly come as a shock that her uncle would be on international law enforcement's radar. The fact that he was only made her business in the States all the more urgent.

She schooled her expression into one of bland indifference. "It seems to me that you already know the answer to that question, Officer Jonas. Are you here to ask about the shooting or my personal life?"

The older JUSTIS man cleared his throat. "To be perfectly frank, Miss Moretskova, we're trying to assess if the two might be connected."

"I'm not sure I follow your meaning."

"You strike us as an intelligent young lady, so I'm sure we don't need to dissect your uncle's reputation. Anatoly Moretskov has ties to organized crime going back decades. He's got some very dangerous friends. Probably more than a fair number of enemies too."

No, Marina didn't need any reminders. She was well aware that her uncle made his living managing the financial interests of criminal oligarchs and corrupt politicians. Her uncle had laundered countless billions of dollars over the years, including a sizable fortune for Boris Karamenko, one of the most ruthless mafia bosses in Russia. Uncle Anatoly was no saint, but he had been the closest thing to a father Marina had ever known from the time she was an orphaned toddler. Good or bad, he was all the family she had and she loved him with all her heart.

If these JUSTIS men thought she would betray any of her uncle's secrets to them, or confirm anything they purported to know about him or his business dealings, they were deeply mistaken.

"Personally, I find that reputations are often grossly exaggerated, if not outright lies," she said, keeping her expression schooled, her voice level. "My uncle Anatoly has managed a small bank in Saint Petersburg for thirty years. Perhaps if you have specific questions about his work you should ask him yourselves."

The Breed officer leaned back. "Maybe we will."

As he spoke, his phone buzzed and he immediately brought it to his ear. While he listened to the information being relayed to him, Marina caught Yury's sidelong glance. The guard was tense for a fight, a low snarl building in his barrel chest.

She gave him the faintest quelling look, a silent command he knew better than to defy. All of these questions from law enforcement were troublesome enough. It would serve no purpose, least of all her uncle's, to allow the interview with the JUSTIS investigators to escalate toward a confrontation.

She needed time to think, to regroup and decide how best to proceed now that it seemed obvious that someone was aware that she was in the States. Someone who very likely still had her in the crosshairs of a sniper's rifle.

But who?

Her uncle had many enemies; that much was true. The list was long, but there were few who would dare invite his wrath by harming her. And that list shrank even more when it came to the number of people who were aware she had left Russia two days ago.

And absolutely no one, not even her bodyguards, knew the true purpose for her trip.

No one but Uncle Anatoly and her.

Lifting her glass of water to her lips, Marina took a drink and held the JUSTIS officer's studying gaze as he grunted an affirmative to the person on the other end of the line. He slipped the device back into his pocket.

"We're needed on another investigation downtown, so that will be all for now, Ms. Moretskova." The two officers stood. "If you'd be more comfortable, I'm sure we could arrange for a unit to keep an eye on you for the duration of your . . . vacation, is it?"

She smiled. "Yes. I'm here on a brief holiday, as I mentioned." More than once, in fact, and she was certain neither of the officers had been so careless with their documenting of her statement that they needed clarification. "As for your kind offer of added security, thank you, but I'm sure that won't be necessary."

Measuring glances slid from Yury to the other guards. "Yes. Well, if you think of anything you'd like to add to your statement, or if there's anything you think we should know—anything at all—don't hesitate to get in touch."

"Of course," she replied, having no intention of doing either.

She walked them to the door. Her breath didn't leave her lungs until the panel was shut and locked at their backs.

"I thought they would never leave," Ivan muttered, crossing tattooed arms over his broad chest.

Viktor nodded in agreement. So did Yury, but he

sent a reassuring glance at Marina. "You handled them well. Your uncle would be proud. Perhaps one day he'll crown you boss of the Moretskov banking empire, eh?"

"Perhaps." Her smile felt anxious, although not for the reason the men might think.

She had no designs on her uncle's dangerous business. Although he strove to keep her insulated from the ugly realities of his work, Marina knew enough. And every day she worried for him more and more.

For years, she had urged him to leave his dangerous life. She could hardly believe it when he came to her two months ago and told her that he had finally decided to get out, to seek an escape from all of his risky entanglements and retire in exile. Marina had been overjoyed—and determined to do whatever she could to help make it happen. Although her uncle had been reluctant to involve her, in the end he had relented. That alone told her just how desperate he truly was to leave his old life behind.

No one but Marina knew her uncle's intentions, not even the team of loyal soldiers pledged to protect her on what they understood to be a private banking matter in the States.

No one could know her actual purpose, or the truth of all that she carried with her. Uncle Anatoly's life depended on it.

Not to mention her own.

"Trust no one, my darling girl," he had cautioned her before she left.

It was a lesson he had drilled into her for as long as she could remember. And so she had arrived yesterday in Miami with his secret held close, waiting to be instructed about a meeting with a powerful contact of

Anatoly Moretskov's from Cuba who, for a price, had agreed to provide safe exile for them.

"Take this," Yury said, breaking into her thoughts as he pivoted away from the fully stocked bar. He had poured some chilled vodka into a cut-crystal glass and now held it out to her. "You look like you need something stronger than water."

"Thank you." She accepted with a nod, hoping it would take some of the edge off her jangled nerves. With the drink in hand, she headed for her private bedroom suite, pausing at the door to glance back at her men. "Have the vehicle ready to leave in ten minutes. I'm not going to wait around and give someone the chance to take another shot at me. We're changing locations."

Yury held her in a grave stare, then nodded. "I'll make the necessary hotel arrangements."

"No," Marina said. "I will make them myself."

Entering her quarters, she closed the door behind her then padded into the dressing room to begin collecting her things. Inside the large wardrobe was a personal safe provided by the hotel. It contained a locked aluminum briefcase and a burner satellite phone, both brought with Marina from Russia.

She picked up the phone and held it for a moment, wishing she could call home to Uncle Anatoly for comfort or advice after the incident tonight. But he had forbidden contact for any reason so long as she was away, not only for her own safety but for that of her mission. The satellite phone was to be reserved incoming calls. More specifically, it was intended for a single use—the call that was to come from Ernesto Fuentes once the meeting time and place with the Cuban crime boss had been secured.

As much as Marina wanted to take comfort in hearing Uncle Anatoly's familiar voice offering reassurances, she refused to give in to the weakness. As for the attack at the pool, there was nothing to be done now except regroup and move forward. Troubling her uncle with the details would serve no purpose but to make him doubt her ability to see this mission through for him. And she would not fail.

Marina could hardly fathom the kind of courage it must require for him to decide to risk everything in exchange for his freedom. It would take more than a sniper's errant bullet to shake her determination to help him finally taste that freedom.

She took the phone and briefcase out of the safe and set both on the bed, then fetched the small suitcase she brought on the trip. It was packed with just enough clothing and travel supplies to make her short holiday overseas seem believable. Before the JUSTIS officers had arrived, she had changed from her black bikini into a creamy silk tank top and caramel-colored lounge pants.

Her black bikini was still damp from the pool, but she retrieved it from where it hung in the bathroom and packed it anyway. She should probably toss it in the trash instead. As much as she enjoyed her daily exercise, after tonight she doubted Yury would ever permit another round of laps no matter how stir-crazy she got being cooped up in a hotel room. She had been shocked when the overbearing guard had agreed in the first place.

Marina was starting to feel a bit of her claustrophobia returning. They needed to clear out as quickly as possible, but right now all she wanted to do was breathe in some fresh air and try to cool the rising heat that was beginning to bloom in her temples. Sipping a bit more of the crisp vodka, she walked across the spacious bedroom to the wall of sliding glass doors that faced the ocean.

Cautiously, she stepped outside. All she needed was a moment or two, just long enough to clear her buzzing mind and try to purge the painful images of Kirill's death. She gazed in silent awe at the vast blackness of the night sky and the sparkling, dark water of the Atlantic.

Fresh salt air filled her lungs and lifted the loose strands of her hair. Waves rushed to shore in a soothing rhythm, a wordless roar that drowned out all of the doubts and uncertainties that had been clamoring in her head even before she left Russia.

This was freedom. Her chest ached with the glory of it, the longing for it.

Marina closed her eyes on a deep, unfettered sigh, savoring the purity and serenity that didn't seem to exist back home in Saint Petersburg. It never would as long as her life and her uncle's belonged to Boris Karamenko and the criminal syndicate he controlled.

She had come on this journey out of love for her uncle, but there was a part of her that craved an escape too. She would die for the chance to be free.

Earlier tonight she nearly had.

A shiver racked her as the whole thing played through her mind for the dozenth time. The shooting chilled her veins, but it was the recollection of firm, warm arms wrapped around her, pulling her out of harm's way, that had shocked her just as deeply.

She wanted to tell herself it was merely the heightened emotion of tonight's ordeal that made her feel so off-kilter. But the buzzing in her veins was something more than that. It was because of him. The stranger. The vampire who'd saved her life.

"Cain," she whispered, testing the name the JUSTIS officer had given her.

Cain Hunter.

That unusual last name gave her more than a moment's pause, even now.

Although Uncle Anatoly had no use for the Breed as a whole and made sure Marina knew how he felt, it was impossible for her to have lived twenty-five years of life among dangerous men and cold-blooded killers and not be familiar with the term Hunter.

They were beyond lethal, even more so than any Vory soldier or Russian mobster's enforcer.

Part of an experiment that raised Breed boys and men as highly skilled, emotionless assassins, Hunters were reputed to be savages, even after spending two decades away from the hellish laboratory that had created and trained them to be more machine than flesh and blood.

And now she owed her life to one of them.

Good Lord. She could only imagine what a beast like that might try to demand in return. Fortunately, Marina was confident she would never lay eyes on Cain Hunter again.

In just a few minutes, she and her bodyguards would be miles away from Miami and tonight would be just an unfortunate detour in her quest to secure a safe future for her uncle and for herself.

Downing the remainder of her vodka in one swallow, Marina pivoted away from the terrace balcony and returned to her bedroom suite to finish packing to leave.

CHAPTER 3

He didn't move, not even to exhale, until after she went back inside.

When Cain finally let go of his breath, it gusted out of him on a muttered curse. The sharp, rough sound was the exact opposite of the way the lovely Russian rose on the terrace next door had sighed his name to the moonless night just a moment ago.

Obscured by the darkness that spilled over his terrace balcony, he pushed away from his lean against the exterior wall of his unlit suite and prowled to the railing. Maybe he should have made his presence known when she slipped out of her suite to stare at the dark ocean beyond. Instead he had melted into the shadows like the predator he was and simply . . . watched her.

Wanted her.

Then she'd whispered his name and it was all he could do not to leap across the distance and pull her against his body again.

Damn. Not good.

Lust punched into his veins, even in her absence.

Her scent lingered in the air, delicate and yet more potent than any perfume. Fresh and sensual, the unique combination of roses, rain, and sandalwood had been branded into his senses from the moment he first touched her in the pool.

Cain inhaled deeply and scowled, raking a hand over his jaw.

He had no business craving this woman. He had no business wondering who the hell might want her dead either, but that hadn't stopped him from looking for answers. He'd started his own investigation immediately after the shooting.

While she was being escorted back into the hotel by her bodyguards, Cain made a swift search of the roof and the surrounding structures. The sniper was already long gone, not a trace of evidence left behind. Which meant the bastard was no amateur. And that meant the odds of his pretty target being just a random mark were reduced to exactly zero.

How long before the son of a bitch tried again?

Cain would have bet the bulk of his sizable bank account that another attack was coming sooner rather than later.

Despite his efforts to covertly collect some information about the female from the investigating JUSTIS officers during their brief interview with him, the two men only dodged his questions and stonewalled every attempt he made to get even as much as her name. He could understand protecting a victim's privacy, but his instincts were telling him this was different.

Did JUSTIS view her as a victim or something else? More to the point, which was closer to the truth?

Cain wouldn't deny he was relieved to see her walking around unharmed. Hell, he'd only be lying to himself if he tried to pretend he hadn't delayed leaving Miami tonight because he wanted to see her one more time. If only to confirm that she was alive and well.

That for once, his damnable gift had done some good for someone.

No problem when it came to strangers or people that didn't mean something to him. But the minute he started to care . . .

On a growl, he thrust the reminder of his failure years ago to the far corners of his mind. In all this time since, he hadn't been able to get free of the painful memories—or his guilt—but he refused to let those emotions own him.

Not ever again.

As for Blondie next door, she'd better hope her bodyguards did a better job keeping her safe than they had so far. Considering the men bore more than a few Russian mafia tattoos, not to mention the serious firearms they were packing, it seemed clear that someone had hand-picked them to watch over the female. Letting her take a swim in the open, even with the group of them standing nearby, was a stupid risk. Either her team had been unaware she was under surveillance by a sniper and marked for death, or they were worse than incompetent.

The only other alternative was so heinous it set Cain's molars on edge.

Not his problem, damn it.

And it was long past time he put Miami in his rearview mirror.

Stepping away from the balcony railing, he headed

back inside. His packed leather duffel bag sat on the floor of the vestibule where he'd left it a short while ago. Grabbing the key fob for his car in the hotel garage, Cain picked up his bag and opened the door.

He didn't take the first step out to the corridor before the hair on his nape prickled. Something was off. All of his Hunter instincts lit up at once, sending oil into his veins.

Faint sounds of a scuffle carried to him from the suite down the hall. Not just any suite.

Hers.

Then gunfire. Two sudden, staccato shots. They were muffled by a silencer, but to his acute Breed hearing, they rang out as loud as cannon blasts.

So did the answering thump of a pair of heavy bodies hitting the floor.

Holy fuck. So much for the return of his precognitive gift. It was already starting to fail him.

Then again, he didn't need an ESP vision to know the female next door was likely only moments away from death for the second time tonight.

The only question was, what the hell did it matter to him?

Cain didn't have that answer. Nor did he have answers for the dozen other questions jamming his brain when it came to the mysterious Russian beauty with an apparent target on her back.

He only knew that whoever wanted her dead, the bastard would have to come through him first.

~ ~ ~

Marina's hands froze, her body registering the odd

sounds she'd just heard, even while her mind struggled to accept the truth.

Gunshots.

Two of them.

And now . . . silence.

Worse than that. Outside her bedroom the rest of the suite was eerily, utterly quiet. As still as a tomb.

She let go of the silk blouse she'd been folding, the last of her clothing to be packed into her small suitcase on the bed. As desperate as she was to call out to Yury and her other bodyguards, she didn't dare alert an intruder to her presence.

No, not merely an intruder.

An assassin.

From the sounds of it, one who had just taken out two of her bodyguards in the room outside.

Alarm exploded in her breast, panic icing her veins. She waited in dread to hear a third shot split the quiet, but it didn't come. As she pivoted to glance at the closed door of her private quarters, the handle slowly turned.

"Marina?"

Thank God. Yury's low voice sounded so welcome to her ears, she almost ran to him as he entered. But every muscle in her body clenched tight with shock when she noticed the pistol gripped in his hand. A pistol equipped with a silencer.

Yury's dark, cold eyes found her. His expression was flat, his face harder than usual as he stepped toward her and raised his weapon. He gave a vague shake of his head, but there was no mercy in his gaze. "I didn't want it to go this way. Now, I don't have a choice."

His words sank in like talons. No, this couldn't be happening. But it was. Yury had just killed his comrades—his friends—and now he was turning on her.

Marina swallowed and took a hesitant step away from the bed. She had nowhere to go. Yury and his gun blocked her escape from the suite. Across the room, nothing but the glass doors and a ten-story drop to the ground below.

Yet instead of pulling the trigger, Yury's glance flicked away from her and toward the metal briefcase lying on the bed beside her luggage. She frowned, confusion and shock swamping her. She had to stay calm. Had to keep her head even though the captain of her security detail had evidently lost his.

"What are you talking about, Yury? What do you mean, you don't have a choice?"

He didn't answer. Using the nose of the pistol, he gestured at her. "Open it." When she didn't move, rage flashed over his tight expression. "Open it now, goddamn you!"

She jolted, her own fury tasting futile, as bitter as acid on her tongue. Returning to the edge of the silk-covered mattress, she worked the combination lock and freed the twin latches on the case. They opened with a pop.

"Empty it," he instructed her. "Dump everything out on the bed."

She obeyed him, not that she had any room to refuse. Two million dollars in neatly secured stacks of U.S. currency spilled onto the fluffy duvet. Marina stared at the piles of bills, feeling sick at this betrayal, sick over her stupidity in trusting even a man as steadfast and loyal as Yury had seemed.

"This deal you mean to broker for your uncle," Yury muttered as he drew closer. "It's not going to happen. Anatoly shouldn't have sent you to do his dirty work. Or maybe you didn't need much convincing."

Marina felt some of the blood drain out of her face. Yury knew about the meeting with Fuentes. How? She wasn't sure, but everything in her seized with the understanding that somehow, someone had leaked her uncle's plan to buy his way out from under Boris Karamenko.

Oh, God. Did that mean Karamenko knew too?

If he did, Uncle Anatoly might already be dead.

No, she refused to think that. And if there was a chance to warn him, she had to try. Unfortunately, the odds of being able to do that dwindled with every second. Although she had avoided one attempt on her life tonight, the murderous look in her bodyguard's eyes told her she wasn't going to survive this time.

"The sniper out at the pool tonight," she murmured, glancing up at Yury in bleak understanding. "You arranged for it. That's why you didn't argue when I wanted to take a swim tonight. You practically encouraged me to do it."

"It would've been over quickly for you, Marina. Which is more mercy than either you or your uncle deserve."

So, he was working for Karamenko. That statement all but confirmed it.

"How much is he paying you to do this, Yury?" She scoffed, indignant despite the control her traitorous guard held over her. "Or is this two million to be your reward?"

Another wag of the pistol served as a wordless command for her to step away from the bed. As soon as she did, Yury walked closer and sifted through the stacks of money with one hand while still holding her at gunpoint with the other.

"This isn't about money and you know it." Yet he shuffled the bills around on the bed intently as if counting his new fortune.

Or looking for something more among the case's spilled contents.

Marina's dread deepened as he continued his search. "It's not here." He shot a glare at her. "Where's the file?"

Her heart skipped a beat. "What file?"

Yury raised the pistol, aiming it right at her face. "The file, Marina. Where the fuck is it?"

Cold panic bled into her veins. The situation was even worse than she thought.

Feigning ignorance would only speed her demise now that she was certain Yury knew the briefcase full of cash wasn't the real item of value she carried. Two million dollars was only a fraction of what her uncle intended to trade for sanctuary away from Karamenko and the rest of the Russian mafia.

The file Yury demanded was worth many hundreds of millions more. Upwards of a billion, if she had to guess.

Uncle Anatoly's grim face and solemn words the day she'd left for the States played through her memory in an instant.

"Are you sure you want to do this, moya radost?*" he'd asked soberly, placing the small flash drive in her hand. "You must understand how dangerous this information is, Marina. Karamenko's entire financial empire is encrypted on this device— bank accounts, passwords. Everything." He closed his hand over hers, curling her fingers around the flash drive he intended to sell to one of Karamenko's many rivals for enough money to secure a long*

future somewhere far away from Russia. "The only way I can ever be free is by destroying him first."

It seemed so risky to her, using the greed of one criminal ringleader to weaken another. But Uncle Anatoly had been resolute that it was the only way.

Marina understood the gravity of her mission, and she had left Saint Petersburg without a single doubt about undertaking it.

Even now, she refused to feel defeat. But she couldn't deny that staring into the barrel of Yury's weapon had her terrified that she had not only failed, but put her uncle's life in jeopardy as well.

"The file," he snarled, nostrils flaring in his anger. "Don't make me ask again, or I promise I will make you suffer."

Marina bit her lip. The flash drive was concealed within the inner construction of the briefcase, not six inches from his free hand. But she wouldn't give up the information, no matter what Yury did to her. And she'd rather die right here and now than surrender her uncle's only means of freedom.

She couldn't fight him, but she could stall him a bit. Maybe formulate a plan or wait for a chance to make a break. Everything was risky, but what choice did she have?

"All right," she relented, letting her shoulders sag. "It's still in the safe inside the dressing room."

Yury jabbed the gun in the general direction. "Go get it. *Now.*"

She walked cautiously, feeling him hulking a few paces behind her. Now that she was in the smaller space of the dressing room, she wondered if she had just sealed her doom. With no clear option to get around him, she was trapped. And the likelihood of overpowering a big man like him was less than nil, especially with no weapon at her disposal.

Well, almost no weapon.

She did have one small, unusual advantage she could tap.

But in order to activate it, she would have to touch Yury skin-to-skin.

"Move faster, Marina. Keeping me waiting will only try my patience."

She crouched in front of the safe, anxiety clawing at her as her fingers hovered over the keypad. Yury's threat left no doubt that she would be shot dead as soon as she opened the safe and he saw it was empty.

Her fingers trembled as she pressed a number on the pad. At first, she tried to ignore her nerves, but then thought better of it. Maybe her actual fear was all the excuse she needed.

She fumbled the combination lock a couple of times, exhaling a short breath. "I'm sorry."

Yury swore harshly. "Damn it, open the fucker now!"

"I'm too nervous," she murmured, which was truer than she wanted to admit. "Yury, please. I can't do it. Let me tell you the combination instead. Then you can open the safe yourself."

As she spoke, she ventured a glance over her shoulder to where the traitorous guard loomed, huge and imposing at her back.

But Yury wasn't alone now.

Standing behind him in predatory silence was an even bigger man. Immense. Black-haired. Silver eyes ablaze with sparks of glowing amber, and fangs bared in a feral, menacing sneer.

Cain.

Marina must have gaped. Yury frowned, then started to turn and look behind him.

Time froze in that same moment. Or perhaps it sped up instead, everything moving as fast as lightning, too swift for her to process what happened next.

Cain moved with inhuman speed—and pure lack of mercy. One large hand shot out, seizing Yury by the wrist. Marina heard the savage crack of bones breaking, then the sharp, answering howl of a man in agony. The gun dropped to the carpeted floor, smoothly kicked away by Cain's foot at the same time he smashed his fist into the center of Yury's face.

The big Vory soldier sank to his knees, blood and broken teeth raining from his open mouth as he choked and sputtered. But Cain still radiated violence, and the snarl that erupted from him was nothing short of murderous.

Grabbing Yury's skull in his bare hands, the Breed male wrenched his head to one side, instantly breaking his neck. Yury's lifeless corpse sagged to the floor. Cain glanced up, meeting Marina's stunned gaze.

"Get your things. You can't stay here."

She hesitated, still shaken, and not at all certain she should put her life in another man's hands. Least of all this Hunter who had just demonstrated how easy it was for him to kill someone. He reached for her and Marina took a step back, mutely shaking her head.

"I'm not going to hurt you." His deep voice was edged with impatience, even annoyance. "If you want to live, you need to come with me. Now."

Trust no one, her uncle had warned her. Marina's eyes

strayed to Yury's bloodied, broken body. Betrayer. Not even Uncle Anatoly could have guessed how prudent his advice to her had been.

"Hey." Cain's fingers were beneath her chin, strong and firm against her skin. He guided her gaze back to his grim stare. "Your guard is dead, but he wasn't the shooter out at the pool. Someone still has you marked for death. You need to get out of here, go somewhere you'll be safe."

He was right. Marina swallowed, torn between the panic still leaching into her veins and the logic that urged her to accept the facts. She had a target on her back. Uncle Anatoly might be in the same kind of danger now.

She needed to contact him, warn him that somehow his plan appeared to have been compromised.

She stared into the amber-flecked silver eyes of the lethal stranger who had just saved her life a second time in the same night. She would have to be the biggest fool in the world to imagine she could be safe with a demonstrated killer like Cain.

Unfortunately, she had to take her chances, because he was all she had.

"All right," she replied. "Let's get out of here."

CHAPTER 4

For a woman who had come within seconds of death twice in a matter of a few hours, Cain had to give her credit. She was holding herself together with nerves of solid steel. No emotional breakdowns as she swiftly collected her belongings and repacked the briefcase with what appeared to be easily a million-plus in cash.

Her only falter came as Cain ushered her through the main living area of her suite where two of her bodyguards had been shot execution-style by one of their own. He heard her breath catch when she saw the fallen men. The quiet inhalation sounded very close to a sob, the first crack he'd seen in her armor.

He touched her arm, fighting the urge to let his fingers rest for more than a second on her soft, warm skin. She may be shaken by the killings, perhaps mourning these men who had served her, but Cain had other, more pressing concerns now. "Come on," he said, impatient to get her out of there. "Quickly."

After grabbing his duffel from his own suite down the hall, he hurried her down to the hotel's underground garage. His black Aston Martin rumbled to life as he hit the remote starter, the doors unlocking with a chirp. He tossed their bags and the aluminum briefcase behind the seats of the sleek Vanquish, then helped her slide into the passenger side before he dropped behind the wheel and roared out to the busy street.

She sat in a prolonged silence once they were moving, her cheeks slack and drained of color. Cain had seen that kind of shell-shocked look before, and he steeled himself to the pang of sympathy that jabbed him as he glanced at her.

"Did he hurt you?" he asked, his voice more curt than intended. She gave him a mute shake of her head, loose blond strands sifting over her shoulders. Cain grunted. "Good. Because you've got a lot of questions to answer. You can start with your name."

"Marina." She blew out a slow breath. "Marina Moretskova."

Definitely Russian. He was hardly surprised by the confirmation. Her accent out at the pool had left little doubt in his mind. Neither had the Vory tattoos on her security detail.

"What kind of business brings you to Miami?"

"Business?" She turned a frown on him. "I don't know what you mean. I came here for a brief holiday and suddenly I'm living a nightmare."

Christ, she almost sounded convincing. The nightmare part was accurate enough, but as for the rest, he wasn't buying it. "Here on holiday with a team of armed bodyguards and a briefcase full of large denomination currency? How much are you carrying? A fucking fortune, from the looks of it. More than enough to get you killed—twice, in case you've lost count."

She didn't answer. Her silence and mistrust was almost as infuriating as her lie. Cain scoffed as he navigated the city's nighttime traffic and kept an eye on their surroundings.

"Let's get something straight, Marina Moretskova. I may have saved your life back at the hotel, but that does not mean I won't dump you out of this car right here and now. I don't need your problems. I'm sure as hell not the kind of man you want to play games with or try to bullshit."

"I know what kind of man you are, Cain Hunter."

He caught the pointed way she said his name, leaning the heaviest on his uncommon surname. The last name he and so many other former Hunters had adopted after they escaped the infamous program. Before he could ask how she knew even this much about him, she folded her arms across her breasts and shrugged.

"The JUSTIS officers mentioned your name during my interrogation with them."

Interrogation. Interesting way to describe her interview with law enforcement. Marina seemed every bit as cagey and suspicious about JUSTIS as the two investigating officers had been when Cain tried to probe for information about her.

"Tell me what's going on, Marina." When he flicked another glance at her, he found her arresting burgundy-colored eyes fixed on him, studying him. Measuring him. "I've seen enough to form my own conclusions, but I want to hear it from you. If you want my help getting out of here tonight, you need to trust me."

"Trust?" She said the word like an accusation. "I trusted Yury and he almost put a bullet in my head tonight."

"Yes," Cain said, needing no reminder. Christ, he was still vibrating with rage over the scene he'd walked in on a few minutes ago. "But I'm not Yury. I'm not the sniper who tried to take you out, either. The way I see it, I'm your best chance of survival now. Possibly your only chance. So, I'll ask you again. What the fuck is going on?"

"I told you—"

He shook his head. "The truth, Marina, or you're on your own right here and now. Yury and your other bodyguards were sporting some impressive Vory ink. Criminal henchmen like that don't get hired to watch over innocent civilians. Especially not beautiful female civilians. Are you involved with someone in the Russian mafia?"

"No." A quiet, but firm denial. One he didn't quite believe.

"You sure about that? Because the way I see it, I've got more than a million reasons to doubt every damn word that comes out of your pretty mouth."

Her lids lifted, giving him another shot of that smart, but guarded, wine-dark gaze. "I'm not involved with anyone. Least of all someone who belongs to the Bratva."

Finally, an admission he sensed was the truth. Hearing that she wasn't involved with one of the dead men back in her vacated hotel suite or any other mafia thug gave him more satisfaction than it should. As for Yury, Cain only wished he could have delivered a slower, more fitting death for the traitor who would have shot her in cold blood.

"The money in the case," Cain prompted. "It's mafia money, isn't it?"

She didn't deny it, not that she could. He'd seen too much and he could tell she was too intelligent to think she could continue feeding him lies. But her stubborn silence was equally frustrating.

"Did you steal the money? Or maybe you're here to launder it for someone back home? Someone willing to send you to the States on a reckless errand. One that might still get you killed."

Oh, yeah, he was definitely getting warmer.

She licked her lips, an anxious reflex that drew his gaze to her mouth against his will. That small flick of her tongue wetting her lower lip sent a hot coil of lust twisting through his veins. It was virtually impossible to be seated this close to her and not be acutely aware of how staggeringly beautiful she was.

Long-lashed, luminous eyes dominated the delicate, fine-boned oval of her face. But her mouth was the where the innocence ended. Lush and ripe, her lips made Cain think of hundreds of wicked possibilities, each more carnal than the last. None of which he intended to act on.

And he was done playing her game.

He found a break in the traffic and swerved hard to the right, coming to a halt at the curb in front of a complex of tall buildings. He swiveled to face Marina.

She flinched as the passenger side door lock popped open. Cain reached over and freed her from the seatbelt.

"What are you doing?"

"Bringing you to someplace safe."

She looked out the window and stilled when she saw

the lighted JUSTIS sign in front of the building. When her face swung back to him, she stared at him as if he'd just delivered her to a firing squad.

"No one in there can help me."

"Why not?"

She swallowed. "Because they've already judged me. The two officers who came to the hotel tonight made that pretty clear. They think I'm some kind of criminal."

He thought back to the guarded demeanor of the officers when they interviewed him, the way they pumped him for any and all observations about the shooting at the pool, yet refused to give up a single bit of information about Marina.

"So, are you a criminal?"

"No." The word rushed out of her, vehement. Earnest. "I don't expect you to understand, Cain."

"Try me." He leaned forward, crowding her against the inside of the door, giving her nowhere to run unless she wanted to get out of the car. "Tell me what I've stepped in by saving your life tonight."

She let out a shallow breath, her gaze searching his. "My uncle is Anatoly Moretskov. He's a banker in Saint Petersburg. He is also one of the top men in a very powerful branch of the Bratva."

Cain clamped his jaw tight, holding back the curse that was boiling at the back of his throat. "You're not in love with a Russian mobster, you're family to one of them. Jesus Christ."

She didn't look the least bit ashamed. All he saw in her face was devotion, and a fierce resolve. "My uncle wants out of the organization. That's why I'm in the States. I'm supposed to meet with one of his Western allies who's agreed to help Uncle Anatoly gain his freedom."

"For a healthy price." Cain grunted. "How much is in the briefcase?"

She glanced away from him, staring down at her lap. "Two million dollars."

Although the sum was substantial, it seemed like a pittance where the Russian mob was concerned. He didn't much care about the specifics of the deal at the moment. He was more troubled by the delivery method. "Why send you to the front line? If your uncle's so powerful, doesn't he have any other soldiers willing to sacrifice themselves for him?"

She frowned, looking defensive. "I offered to go. Uncle Anatoly has been like a father to me from the time I was three years old. He's the only family I have, and I'm the only person he trusts completely. I would do anything for him, just as I know he'd do anything for me."

Cain leaned back in his seat. "Anything except stop you from risking your neck on the chance you might spare his."

She scowled, lips pressed flat. "Like I said, I wouldn't expect someone like you to understand."

"Someone like me. Because I'm a Hunter?" When she didn't elaborate, he chuckled low under his breath.

Let her keep her assumptions about him. After all, he had nothing to prove to her. The sooner he could make her someone else's problem, the sooner he could be on his way somewhere else.

Anywhere else, so long as it was far away from lovely Marina Moretskova and the vipers that seemed to be on her trail.

Still, something was bothering him about what he

saw in her suite tonight. "So, Yury got greedy. Decided to take you out and steal the money?"

"Evidently," she murmured, avoiding his gaze.

Cain thought back to what he'd walked in on seconds before he disabled the traitorous bodyguard and snapped his neck. "If the money was dumped on the bed, why were you trying to open the safe?"

Her mouth went a bit slack, but only for an instant. She blinked those shrewd, burgundy-colored eyes and shrugged. "I had to do something. I had to try anything."

"What was in the safe?"

"Nothing. It was empty. It was only a bluff, a stall for time."

Something in her tone made him believe she was telling the truth. About that much, at least. Still, there was something guarded in her careful stare as she looked at him now. Secrets she was trying to keep hidden.

"Stalling a man holding a gun at your head?" He uttered a sharp curse. "To what end, Marina? What the hell did you think it was going to buy you, other than a skull full of lead?"

She seemed to struggle deciding whether to tell him anything more. Finally, she shook her head and let go of a short sigh. "I needed Yury to get close enough for me to touch him."

Cain growled. "Tell me you didn't actually consider trying to fight him off."

"No. I knew I couldn't do that."

"Then what?"

"I could do something . . . else. I could change his mind." She turned her palms over, staring at her open hands. "If I touched him, I knew I could bend his will."

A dark understanding bled into his veins. Cain

frowned. "You're talking about an ESP ability? You have a psychic gift?"

She lifted her gaze to him once more and nodded solemnly. "I was born with the mark. The teardrop-and-crescent-moon birthmark."

Ah, fuck. He knew what that meant.

She wasn't Breed like him; over time there had been only a handful of females born with fangs and *dermaglyphs* and eyes that turned fiery amber in blood thirst or in moments of intense emotion.

But Marina Moretskova wasn't merely a human female, either. She was something more. Something rare and precious.

A Breedmate.

"Prove it." Cain snarled the demand. "Show me your mark."

Bad enough that saving her life was a problem he never should have accepted, but if what she was saying could be believed—if she had the birthmark that all Breedmates bore somewhere on their bodies—then his night was about to get a hell of a lot more complicated.

And there were few things he hated more than unwanted complications. Especially when they came in the form of a secretive, knockout blonde that already had his blood simmering with arousal.

When she didn't jump to obey his command, he bared his fangs and pinned her with a harsh glare. "Show me the fucking mark, Marina."

On a soft huff, she slowly pivoted to face him. Bending her left knee, she lifted the hem of her linen lounge pants and tilted her ankle so he could see the inside of the delicate joint.

And there it was, all but hidden among the tattooed

vine of blood-red roses that twisted around the full length of her leg.

A tiny scarlet stamp in the shape of a teardrop falling into the cradle of a crescent moon. Unmistakable. Undeniable, no matter how much he wanted to think otherwise.

Marina Moretskova was a Breedmate.

"Goddamn it."

He reeled away from her on a growl, raking his fingers over the top of his head. When his hand came down, he made a fist and struck the top of the dashboard. What he wanted to do was drive his entire arm through something.

Because now that he knew this about Marina, keeping her alive just became his top priority.

With the exception of a few demented or diseased individuals, all of the Breed lived by a strict code of honor when it came to Breedmates, the only females capable of carrying their offspring. They cherished them. Honored them. Would die to protect them.

Even Breed males born Hunter, like him.

Cain glared out the windshield at the glowing JUSTIS station sign. Dumping Marina on law enforcement was no longer an option, not that he was even certain he had intended to go through with the threat.

Marina was keeping secrets.

Secrets that had nearly gotten her killed twice already tonight.

She had a target on her back, and until Cain figured out how to eliminate that danger, her life was in his hands.

He only hoped he wouldn't fail her too.

"Put your seatbelt back on," he muttered.

She slid back and quietly clicked the restraint closed. "Where are we going?"

"I haven't decided yet." But even as he said it, he knew where he had to go. Back to the nearest shelter he could think of, the only safe place he'd ever known.

And back to a past he'd hoped he would never have to face again.

CHAPTER 5

After an awkward two-hour drive south from Miami—one that was heavy with silence and the simmering menace of the vampire behind the wheel—Marina was starting to wonder if she had lost her mind getting into the vehicle with Cain.

Outside the speeding sports car, the nighttime landscape was nothing but dark wilderness on both sides of the narrow two-lane highway through the Everglades. They had been on this same remote stretch of pavement for nearly half the time they'd been on the road, the Aston Martin's headlights the only sign of civilized life for miles since they had entered the heart of the vast swamplands.

Without warning or explanation, Cain slowed the vehicle then turned onto an overgrown dirt lane that didn't appear to have been in use for decades. That didn't seem to faze him. He navigated the unmaintained path as effortlessly as he'd managed Miami's busy streets, obviously familiar with this area in spite of its forbidding location.

Marina wasn't half as confident that this was a good idea. She swung a wary glance at him as they jostled and lurched over the uneven terrain. "Where are we going?"

"We're already here." He cut the headlights and killed the engine. "It's not safe for the car to go any farther into the swamp."

"Not safe for the car?"

What about them? She peered out the darkened windows, seeing nothing but bramble and thick vegetation crowding in from all sides. Cain opened the driver's door and the low, eerie call of an animal carried over the swamp.

He pivoted to look at her. "Leave the bags and the money here. I'll come back for everything later."

"Later, when?" Suspicion shot through her, cold and dank like their surroundings. "You mean you'll come back for the money after you dump my body out here where no one will find it?"

"Jesus." He scowled. "Do you really think that's what I'm going to do?"

She crossed her arms. "I have no idea what you're going to do. After everything that's happened today, I don't know what to think about anything or anyone. And I don't like this feeling of not knowing what to believe. I don't like being afraid."

Dammit. She hadn't intended to be so candid, but the admission slipped past her lips too quickly for her to hold it back. Weakness was unacceptable under any circumstances, but particularly in times of crisis or uncertainty. She was Anatoly Moretskov's niece, after all.

She had learned early on in life to face her fears head-on, with her chin held high. Yet here she was, telling this virtual stranger that she was afraid.

She wanted to dissolve into the seat as he stared at her for a long moment, saying nothing.

Then he slowly reached toward her and popped her seatbelt open. "I'm taking you somewhere safe, Marina." His deep voice was low and gentle, soothing in spite of his dark expression. "I don't give a damn about the money in that case. I've got plenty of my own without stealing yours. And if I wanted to get rid of you, do you think I'd go to all this trouble?"

No. She knew he wouldn't. She had seen this Breed male kill tonight. His methods were cold and precise. Efficient. He hadn't tried to conceal what he was, and as crazy as it seemed to her, she understood on an instinctual level that she was safe with him. At least, for now.

His body lingered too near hers. Marina felt trapped in his pale gray gaze. She had registered that he was an attractive man when he leaped into the pool to save her from the sniper's bullet. After the adrenaline overload during Yury's attack and her escape from the hotel, this was the first opportunity she'd had to truly drink in every detail of Cain's rugged face.

Although the moonless night cast much of him in dark shadows, there was less than a foot of distance between them in the confines of the car. It was enough for her to realize she had been wrong.

Cain Hunter wasn't attractive.

He was gorgeous. Unearthly handsome. Strong cheekbones and a bold, square jaw. Skin that had a tawny tone in spite of the fact that it had never known the heat of the sun.

Even his mouth was beautiful. Broad, sculpted lips that had seemed unforgiving and harsh on first glance but were far from either of those descriptions when he held her in the kind of stare that was locked on her now. How would his lips feel pressed against hers?

Would he kiss her with the same kind of aggression that seemed to radiate from him every time she'd been near him so far? Or would he be as careful as his pale silver eyes seemed to be holding her now in the all-too-close quarters of a vehicle parked in the middle of a vast, forbidding patch of swamp?

God, what was wrong with her?

Marina blinked to break the almost tangible hold his gaze seemed to have on her. Evidently, two near brushes with death in the space of one night had rattled more than just her nerves. It must have shaken loose her good sense, too, because she had to be out of her mind to be sitting there fantasizing about what Cain's kiss might feel like when her first priority—her only one—was staying alive to deliver on her promise to Uncle Anatoly.

She cleared her throat, then lifted her chin and spoke as if she were dispensing orders to one of her bodyguards. "My belongings can stay in the car, but I'm not leaving the briefcase behind. Not for any reason."

"Suit yourself." He smirked, and the crooked tug of his mouth sent a slow lick of heat through her body. One she didn't want to acknowledge. "Watch your step out here, and stay close to me."

He got out of the car and closed the door.

Marina reached behind her seat for the aluminum briefcase, her gaze rooted on Cain as he rounded the front of the vehicle and waited for her to join him. She climbed out gingerly, her progress slowed by the mucky ground under her sneakers and the hindrance of having only one free hand for stability while the other gripped the handle of the briefcase.

As soon as she reached the spot where Cain stood, he grabbed the case from her grasp. "I'll carry the damn thing. Can't have you slipping into an alligator nest because you're too stubborn to listen to me." He started walking. "Better keep up."

She swore under her breath and fell in behind him. Cain walked briskly, but cautiously, his long legs eating up a lot of distance with minimal effort. At five-foot-eight, Marina had grown up accustomed to being taller than many of her schoolmates and a good many of her uncle's men, but she had to hurry to meet Cain's pace.

"Are there a lot of alligator nests out here?"

He grunted, sounding somehow amused. "This is the Everglades, sweetheart. It's crawling with gators and pythons and a hundred other things that will try to eat you if you give them half a chance."

Oh, God. She winced, trying not to imagine the scores of predatory eyes watching them in the darkness. "I assume you have a good reason for marching us out here on foot, then?"

"Right now, it's the only way for us to get where we need to go. And don't worry about the alligators and snakes. They know they're not the top of the food chain in this particular stretch of swamp."

"What is?" She was almost afraid to ask.

Without pausing, he glanced behind him, shooting her a quick grin that flashed the razor tips of his fangs.

As if she needed any reminders of what he was. Then again, maybe she did. After all, she was trudging willingly through the dark swamp toward a location known only to the Breed assassin in front of her and her most troubling thought about being with him was her lunatic curiosity to kiss him.

Instead, she ought to be trying to memorize the path in case she needed to escape. Not that she stood any chance of making it back to the vehicle ahead of Cain or any one of the other predators he so lightly dismissed.

He continued walking. "Like I said, stick close to me. We don't have far now."

Marina closed the distance between them, refusing to slow down or give in to the exhaustion that had been pulling at her from the moment they left the hotel.

She'd be damned if she let Cain think of her as weak. She had spent most of her life trying to prove herself in a world that favored and rewarded strong men. Even Uncle Anatoly insisted on shielding her from reality more often than not. From the time she was an orphaned little girl, she had been surrounded by bodyguards and nannies. Over the years that cloying protection had started to grate on her. That was part of the reason she had been so eager to help when her uncle needed someone he could trust to assist him in breaking free from the Bratva.

Thinking of Uncle Anatoly only made her more anxious to get in touch with him. As soon as she had a chance, she needed to find a few minutes of privacy and phone him with the news of Yury's betrayal. If Yury truly had been aware of the information on the flash drive Marina had in her possession, she could only hope she reached her uncle before Boris Karamenko did.

Her thoughts gone dark with worry, she trudged along after Cain, watching the ground and his hulking shape in front of her, concentrating on putting her feet precisely where his had been. The farther they trekked, the louder the sounds of the swamp became. All manner of animal croaks and chatter filled the space all around them, punctuated by an occasional howl or screech or splash that raised the hair on Marina's nape.

Cain led her on a winding path that seemed random and forbidding, yet he never faltered. She followed at his heels as he took her through the overgrown thicket and bramble while avoiding the worst of the marshy loam and the pools of treacherous, deep black water that spread out in all directions.

He navigated the harsh terrain as if he knew it by rote. As if it were as familiar as home to him.

"How long have you lived in Las Vegas, Cain?"

She nearly ran into him when he stopped in front of her. "How the fuck do you know that?"

"The JUSTIS officers told me they ran your ID. They said you worked security for a casino there."

He scowled. "Used to. I'm finished with Vegas. I haven't been back there for a couple of months."

"Why did you leave?"

"Because if I stayed any longer, I knew I'd never leave."

He bit off the words, clipped and evasive. She knew a stonewall response when she came up against one. Living with her uncle had been excellent training where that was concerned. Unfortunately for Cain, Marina's curiosity was equally as strong as her need to drown out the noise of the swamp with whatever conversation she could.

"What kind of security work did you do in Las Vegas?"

"The expensive kind."

"Mercenary work, you mean."

"If you're wondering if I killed people for money, the answer is yes." He stared at her, almost daring her to flinch. "I did the things I know best, and I got paid very well to do them."

"But then you left," Marina pointed out. "You quit."

"Yes. Because I finally got tired of cleaning up other people's messes."

And now here he was, helping to clean up hers. She glanced at the briefcase in his hand, wondering how well-paid he had to be for two million dollars in cash to pose nothing of a temptation to him. For that matter, how expert of an enforcer was he to command the kind of compensation he implied he received? How heartless must he be to have made his living spilling blood and taking lives?

Marina grew up around hard men, dangerous men, but Cain was something altogether different and not only because he was Breed. Menace radiated from every immense, honed inch of him. She should be wary. Part of her was. Part of her understood on a visceral level just how devastating this powerful man could be.

And yet the tremor that raced through her was less about fear than it was something else. Something deeper, something even more threatening to her peace of mind.

Desire.

The silence between them stretched and he let out a low grunt. "I never said I was one of the good guys, Marina."

"Then what are you?" She raised her chin, if only to meet his glower head-on. "Bad guys don't go around saving random women's lives."

He scoffed. "Neither do I."

For what wasn't the first time, her mind replayed everything that had happened tonight—starting with the unknown sniper's gunshot that would have certainly left her dead in the hotel swimming pool. She could still hear the high-pitched zing of the round as it ripped through the air so close to her. She could still feel the heat of Cain's strong arms as he pulled her safely out of the bullet's path seconds before it would have struck her.

"Why did you do it?" she murmured. "What made you jump down and save me?"

He blew out a harsh grunt. "I've been asking myself that same question all night."

"What I mean is, how did you know it was going to happen? You were in the pool moving me out of range even before the shooter squeezed the trigger." She watched Cain's expression harden, a response not even the darkness of the swamp could hide. "How did you know I was in danger if the sniper hadn't even fired yet?"

"I saw it happen."

"You saw it?" She shook her head. "You mean, you saw the shooter?"

"No. I saw you, Marina. Your blood in the water, your lifeless body sinking below the surface. You were dead. I saw the last sixty seconds of your life play out in my mind as if it were happening in real-time. Or, rather, what would have been the last sixty seconds of your life."

Despite the unsettling description of her own demise, she couldn't hide her amazement. "You're talking about a vision? An ESP gift? I know the Breed have psychic abilities and unique talents. This is yours?"

Cain seemed less than enthused to admit it. He gave

a begrudging nod that may as well have been a shrug.

Marina's ability to mold another person's mind was invasive. So much so, her uncle not only disapproved but forbade her to use it from the time she was a child. Cain's ability, on the other hand, was nothing short of miraculous.

"Is that how you knew about Yury too? Did you see everything that was going to happen tonight?"

"No." The hard lines in his face grew even more rigid now. "My ability doesn't work like that. It's . . . unreliable."

"What do you mean unreliable?"

"I mean it has limitations. Flaws."

"Mine does too," she confided. "For instance, it doesn't work on anyone who's Breed. I tried it once at a symphony concert my uncle took me to for my eighth birthday. A Breed family with twin boys were at the reception. One of the boys kept making faces at me from behind his father's tuxedo tails, so when I had the chance, I touched his arm and told him to sneak back inside the auditorium and steal the conductor's wand. Instead, he told his father and I ended up grounded for two weeks."

Cain grunted, still scowling at her. "You were a brat."

She wouldn't deny it. "Headstrong, according to Uncle Anatoly. Tell me more about your ability. Why do you think it's unreliable?"

"Because I know it is."

As if the conversation was over, he pivoted away and started walking ahead of her into the dark. She hurried to keep up, refusing to back down now.

Since she owed her life to his ability, she wanted to understand it as thoroughly as possible. But as she stared at Cain's broad, retreating back, she also wanted to know why she was getting the sense that he not only mistrusted his Breed gift, but despised it.

"What happened, Cain?"

He didn't answer. His pace went from brisk to aggressive, his long legs chewing up several yards of distance as if he couldn't move fast enough, couldn't get far enough away from her. Or from her questions.

Something must have happened to make him believe that. Something that had caused him a great deal of pain if he was still carrying the weight of it with him.

"Did you lose someone you cared for?"

Up ahead of her, he hissed a low curse but didn't slow his pace. That's how she knew she was right. That, and the fact that she knew what it was like to live with an empty ache in her heart for someone she loved.

"I'm sorry, Cain," she whispered, not even sure he was listening now. "I know what that's like. My mother died when I was three years old. I still miss her every day."

He swore again, more viciously now. Before she realized what he was doing he stopped abruptly and rounded on her, fury flashing in his eyes. He dropped the briefcase on the path between them and seized her by the upper arms.

"There's something you need to understand. I didn't sign up for this job. I don't want to be here. I don't give a fuck about you or your uncle or this fool's errand he's sent you on, Marina. The only reason I didn't leave you parked on the curb outside JUSTIS is that damn mark on your ankle. We clear?"

Rage poured off him, hot and dangerous. She knew it couldn't be wise to challenge him, especially when his eyes were lit up like burning coals and his fangs were gleaming like diamond-bright daggers with every angry word he spat at her. But Marina had never been the kind of woman to shrink away in fear. She sure as hell wasn't about to start now.

"I never asked for your help. I never asked for your protection, either. I don't want it. If I thought a silly birthmark would make you feel somehow obligated to me, I never would've let you see it."

He thought *he* was furious? She was livid—at herself even more than him. She knew better than to trust a stranger and yet she'd allowed herself to sink into the comfort of Cain's strength. She'd been an idiot, and now she was hundreds of miles away from any trace of civilization and stranded in the middle of the Everglades with a man she suddenly couldn't wait to get away from.

"I'm not going any farther with you," she told him, wrenching out of his loose hold. She reached down to grab the handle of the case. "I'll find my way back to the car on my own."

He scoffed. "What are you going to do once you get there?"

"Call my uncle. He's got connections in the States. He will send someone out to find me and take me somewhere I'll actually be safe."

"Like hell you will."

She ignored his tight reply. Pivoting in the opposite direction, she took a couple of steps back on the darkened, nearly invisible path.

Cain appeared in front of her, moving so fast she had no idea how he'd done it. He blocked the way, a dark shadow against the night. Dark, except for the fierce glow of his transformed eyes.

"Who's your uncle going to send, Marina? Another loyal comrade like Yury? You think your uncle's people will be able to reach you before the shooter from the pool catches up to you?" Cain slowly shook his head. "For all we know, your uncle's got a target on his back too. Hell, he could be dead already. Either way, that still leaves you in the crosshairs."

Marina's breath sawed out of her lungs. Although her heart refused to consider that Uncle Anatoly might not be alive, she knew Cain was right about everything else. There were countless risks in trusting anyone now. Yury's betrayal had proven that much. And she couldn't forget the fact that Yury hadn't been working alone. Until the sniper was identified and eliminated, she couldn't afford to let down her guard.

But staying with Cain didn't feel like any sort of acceptable option, either.

"I'm not afraid to finish this on my own."

She tried to shove past him, but the path was narrow and the edges of it were slippery with muck and wet vegetation. For an instant, she lost her footing on the soft, uneven ground. She started to pitch to one side, but Cain caught her.

"Marina," he growled tersely.

He didn't let her go. Not even when she had righted herself on the path.

His arms wrapped around her, one braced against her back, the other circled around her shoulders. The briefcase hung limply in her hand, the only thing keeping their bodies from pressing against each other in the dark.

A strange silence drew taut and heated between them as Cain's unearthly gaze caressed every inch of her face. Her heart pounded relentlessly, awareness throbbing in her veins.

Every wild imagining she had about kissing this dangerous Breed male came rushing back to her again as his eyes lingered on her mouth. Her breath raced shallowly through her parted lips, and to her utter shock, she heard herself whisper his name like a plea.

As angry and confused and uncertain as she was about everything else that had happened in the past several hours, this much she was sure of. She wanted Cain to kiss her.

She needed it with an intensity that rocked her.

Slowly, with fury and torment etched in every harsh line of his face, he bent his head toward hers.

Then he went still.

Even his breath seemed to pause in that same instant.

A growl built in his chest, a wary, defensive sound that vibrated so powerfully she could feel it in her bones.

"We've got company."

No sooner had he said it than a large figure peeled away from the shadows of the surrounding thicket. Then another, and another.

Cain released her, but kept her close. Three immense Breed males hemmed them in, two in front and one in back. Their eyes crackled with bright amber sparks, and their bared fangs glowing stark white against the night.

One of them, a tall male with a mane of thick, copper hair and a trimmed beard, expelled a sharp breath.

Then he stepped forward as the leader of the group and clapped Cain hard on the shoulder. "Son of a bitch. What the fuck brings you back here after all these years, brother?"

CHAPTER 6

They say you can never go home again. For the past eight years, Cain had been certain he'd never have to test the theory. He had stayed far away, determined he would never step foot anywhere near the sprawling, secret sanctuary hidden in the middle of the Everglades.

He didn't want to be here now, either.

So much for best laid plans. Since he'd first set eyes on Marina Moretskova, he'd been doing a lot of things he knew he damned well shouldn't.

Not the least of which being the fact that he had nearly kissed her a moment ago. If not for the interruption of the three Breed males who surrounded them on the path, he'd probably have his mouth locked on hers right now.

Big mistake, letting her get under his skin.

One he had no intention of repeating.

He couldn't allow himself to care. Especially if he

meant to keep her safe and alive.

He only hoped returning to this place tonight wasn't a mistake too. But that decision wasn't about him. It was about her, about ensuring whomever had her in the crosshairs would never be able to reach her.

"I wouldn't have come," Cain told the trio of vampires, all former Hunters like him. "I need a safe house. This is the only place I know I can trust."

"Sounds urgent." Bram, the behemoth Breed male with the crown of thick, red waves falling to his shoulders had been first to speak when they arrived. Now, he grunted in acknowledgment, his grim gaze assessing. "What kind of trouble are you in, brother?"

"Not me." Cain glanced beside him. "This is Marina. Someone tried to kill her tonight in Miami."

"Jesus." Bram scowled, the low curse hissing past his teeth and fangs. He looked at Marina, who stood ramrod straight at Cain's side, as indomitable as a queen in spite of all she'd been through the past several hours. "Are you hurt?"

She shook her head. "I survived. I wouldn't be able to say that if not for Cain."

He steeled himself to her praise, and to the tender gratitude he heard in her quiet voice.

The other big male standing next to Bram, a mountain of dark brown skin and lethal power named Logan, cocked his head as he looked Marina. "I'm guessing that accent's not local."

His broad mouth quirked, then he spoke in what was clearly fluent Russian. The male's unique gift was an instant, endless understanding of any language. Right now he was charming the hell out of Marina in her native tongue, eventually hooking his thumb in Cain's direction. Whatever he said made her dart a glance at Cain, then smile.

The curve of her lips was faint and brief, but it was also the first sign of relaxation he had seen in her since they'd met. He'd spent several hours with her—had saved her life not once, but twice—and yet she'd met him with mistrust and resistance at nearly every turn.

It took Logan less than a minute to pull a gorgeous smile out of her. No doubt by cutting on Cain. Not that he hadn't earned a lot of scorn and denigration the last time he was here.

"What'd he say to you?"

Logan ran a hand over his skull-trimmed black curls and winked at her. "Just saying hello, brother."

"Yeah, I'll bet," Cain replied. He didn't like being left out of the joke, but he had bigger problems than trying to mitigate the other male's easy charm around Marina. He looked over at Bram, the de facto head of the group. "She's got the mark. That's the only reason I brought her here. Marina's a Breedmate."

"Yours?" The question came from behind Cain, voiced in a deep, smoky rasp.

He turned to look at the Hunter in black jeans and a matching T-shirt who was studying Marina with more than a little intrigue. Razor's tousled light-brown hair was longer than he recalled, beachy tangles adding to the big male's untamed aura. His steady, calculating gaze refused to release Marina.

Cain took a step, placing himself between his Hunter brother and her. "No, Raze. She isn't mine."

Although the statement was true, he couldn't explain the jab of possessiveness that sank into him as he faced down Razor. He wasn't a threat to her. None of the

Breed males living here would do anything to hurt her. Cain trusted that much as surely as he trusted himself.

Hell, probably more.

Bram rubbed his bearded chin. "Tell us what happened in Miami. Last we knew, you were living in Las Vegas."

The newsflash that his old friends had somehow been keeping tabs on him took him aback. Not that he should be surprised, considering the group of former Hunters had turned the art of intelligence-gathering and high-value private security operations into a lucrative business after they'd walked away from Dragos's lab.

Still, considering the circumstances surrounding his absence, the pain he'd left in his wake, Cain didn't think anyone would give two shits about where he'd ended up. He sure as hell wouldn't have, if the tables had been turned.

"I left Vegas a couple of months ago. Been on the road taking a breather before I decide where I'll settle next."

Razor grunted. "Did you leave town before or after that lowlife casino owner you worked for took his swan dive off the roof of his own building?"

Even Logan picked up on the thread. "I don't know about that, Raze. I've heard rumors saying another Hunter had a hand in ending Leo Slater." He crossed his arms over his massive chest and eyed Cain. "You ever cross paths with Dragos's enforcer while you were in Vegas?"

Cain felt Marina's gaze on him as the other men spoke. He shrugged off all of the speculation, figuring he could fill in the blanks about Slater, Asher, and the rest of his time in Vegas later on—if he stuck around that long.

Bram seemed to be on the same page as him. "Let's save the twenty questions for another time. There's only one important thing we need to know right now. Who the hell is trying to hurt this woman?"

"We can't be sure yet," Cain said, glancing her way and giving her a reassuring nod that she was in safe hands here. "Earlier tonight, someone took a shot at her in the swimming pool of the hotel where we both happened to be staying."

Logan exhaled a sharp expletive. "Someone tried to kill her in a public place? Damn. That's a serious move."

Cain inclined his head, grave. "I made sure the sniper missed his mark, but the bastard got away without leaving a trace. Then a few hours later there was another attempt. This time by someone Marina knew and trusted."

"One of my bodyguards," she interjected. "I knew him for more than ten years. None of that mattered to Yury tonight."

Her voice was steady as she spoke, but Cain could still hear the edge of disbelief in her tone. He could still hear the hurt, as much as he tried to pretend otherwise.

"I heard the scuffle in Marina's suite. When I found her, she was staring down the barrel of her bodyguard's pistol."

Bram listened in silence, but Cain saw the male piecing things together in his mind. "Public hits. Bodyguards turning traitor. A beautiful Russian Breedmate marked for death and in need of asylum. Got a feeling I probably don't want to know what's in that briefcase."

Cain held his old friend's sober stare. "If there was

anywhere else I could take her, I'd already be there."

"I don't doubt that, considering how long you've stayed away." Bram rubbed his bearded chin, then he nodded. "Come on, then. We can talk some more inside."

The term among the Breed for family mansions and private compounds was Darkhaven. The shelter they approached now, hidden deep in the swamplands, was somewhere between a fortress and a communal estate. Enclosed within a secured perimeter wall lay more than twenty-thousand square feet of living space. All of it surrounded by acres of wilderness and marshes, impassable except to the small group of former Hunters who had built the sanctuary together and settled here after escaping the program two decades ago.

This Darkhaven had been the only home Cain had truly known.

Memories crowded in as he and Marina walked the rest of the way with the others through the swamp toward the hidden sanctuary. The Breed males leading them into the compound had been his closest friends, his only family. Half-brothers, in fact. As was the case with all of the Hunters, each of them had been born from a different Breedmate mother but sired from the same Ancient otherworlder imprisoned in Dragos's labs.

Cain hadn't realized how much he'd missed the place until he strode inside the main residence with its exposed timber beams and crisp white walls. Beams and walls he'd helped to put up alongside his brothers.

Including the one former Hunter he hadn't seen yet tonight.

Bram led the way into a spacious, open-concept living room. Leather chairs and earthtone-upholstered sofas situated atop an autumn-hued rug had replaced a Spartan hodge-podge of rustic furnishings on bare wood floors.

Cain noted other numerous improvements to the overall aesthetic that had been lacking when he'd last been there, too. Tasteful artwork on the walls. Beautiful handmade pottery bowls and urns perfectly placed around the room and in the entryway. Framed photos and filled bookcases beckoned a closer look, while accent pillows and soft woven throws invited casual gatherings and long conversations. All of it spoke of a comfortable, feminine touch.

At his side, Marina took in every inch of the room too. Although Cain had come to think of her as guarded when it came to showing her emotions, she didn't even attempt to hide her awe. "It's so lovely. I didn't expect to find such a beautiful place here."

Bram smiled. "My brothers and I merely built it," he said, gesturing to Cain and the others. "All the credit for turning our man-cave into a proper Darkhaven home goes to my mate, Lana. She's in her studio throwing some new pottery, but I'm sure it won't take her long to come and find us."

Cain could hear the adoration in the male's deep voice. If anything, it had only deepened over time. That a cold assassin like Bram was able to find a love like the one he shared with Lana was something of a miracle.

But Cain knew all too well that it could also be a curse.

One that could pit brother against brother, as it had between him and the male everyone seemed careful not to mention in front of him now.

"Where's Knox?" He glanced at his brothers,

figuring it was as good a time as any to address the elephant in the room. "I assume if he was here, he'd already be trying to put a knife in my back."

Not without good reason, although no one said as much now.

"Who's Knox?" Marina asked, wariness furrowing her brow.

"A former Hunter, like the rest of us," Cain told her. "We all escaped together when Dragos was killed and the lab was destroyed. Knox is my half-brother, same as these other men."

"Why would he want to kill you?"

A reasonable enough question, but one that carried more weight than she could possibly know. Cain couldn't hold her searching gaze. "Long story. Not important. Where is he, Bram?"

"That's anyone's guess. He still crashes here on a semiregular basis. But even when he's around, it's not unusual for him to disappear for stretches of time."

Razor smirked. "Probably a good thing for everyone that he's gone, now that you're here. Knox hasn't exactly been fit for company these past several years."

Since the accident, he meant.

Since the death of the woman Knox loved more than anything else in the world.

Regret pressed down on Cain as the memory of the horrific wreck looped in vivid detail in his head. He had been haunted by those memories all this time. He didn't want to imagine the kind of torment Knox had endured since that terrible night.

Logan slowly shook his head. "Knox's problems go deeper than losing Abbie. He's heading for disaster the way he's going. It's not like we all don't see it coming."

"You want to be the one to tell him that?" Raze scoffed. "If you poke the beast, brother, you better be damn ready for the fight."

"What's all this talk about disasters and fighting?" Bram's Breedmate entered the room and stopped short, a big smile breaking over her pretty face. "Oh, I don't believe it—Cain!"

Petite and dark-haired, with deep brown eyes and smooth olive skin that hinted at her Seminole roots, Lana was even more beautiful than Cain recalled. She was also heavy with child. That didn't stop her from rushing across the room with a happy cry to greet him.

She threw her arms around Cain's neck in a welcoming hug. "God, it's been so long! What are you doing here?" Letting him go, she turned that bright, warm smile on Marina. "I'm sorry. Hi, I'm Lana."

"This is Marina," Cain said. "We just drove down from Miami."

"Oh." Lana's eyes went wide. "How interesting."

Bram cleared his throat. "There was some trouble up there tonight, love. Cain and Marina are in need of safe shelter."

"Well, you have it," she told them resolutely, zero hesitation. Her glance moved back to Cain, going uncomfortably tender on him. "This is your home, after all. It always will be."

Her kindness humbled him. Eight years ago Knox had lost a lover when Abbie died, but Lana had also lost her best friend. Where Cain's brother put the blame squarely—and aptly—on him, Bram's Breedmate still looked at Cain with the same care and compassion she always had.

It made him twitchy, feeling the undeserved warmth

of her regard.

"We won't be staying long. A day or two at most." At least, that was his plan. Whether he left Marina in his brethren's care while he hunted down whomever wanted her dead, or if he would personally see her returned home to her family in Russia while he eliminated the threat to her life, he hadn't yet decided.

"You must be exhausted, Marina," Lana remarked to her. "I'm sure you'd like to relax somewhere and freshen up. Maybe have something to eat or drink?"

"Yes," Marina said. "That would be nice. Thank you."

Cain frowned, realizing only now how drained she looked and sounded. Shit. And he hadn't even thought to pause and offer her something as basic as water or a moment to catch her breath.

She'd been through hell on repeat tonight. First by the two bastards who tried to kill her, topped off by a long drive and a trek through the muck of the swamp with Cain snapping and snarling at her at nearly every turn.

That is, when he wasn't fighting the urge to kiss her. Even now, his veins still thrummed with the force of his attraction to her. Not good. Not for him, and most certainly not at all good for her. Letting desire cloud his focus could be deadly. Hadn't he already learned that lesson in spades eight years ago?

If he needed any reminders that he was singularly unsuited to be responsible for someone else's well-being, he had plenty as he watched Marina turn and leave the room with Lana.

As for the mistake he'd nearly made earlier tonight when he'd been less than a second from claiming her luscious mouth, it wasn't going to happen again. It had been a momentary weakness, one that would only jeopardize her safety and his own sanity if he gave in to it.

No, Cain assured himself. He was qualified for one thing in this life—dealing death.

The sooner he could get busy doing that, the better.

CHAPTER 7

Clutching the handle of the aluminum briefcase, Marina followed Bram's beautiful Breedmate out of the room where Cain and his brothers continued what seemed to be a somewhat uneasy reunion.

Although everyone had been kind enough to her since she'd arrived, she didn't know what to make of the guarded mentions of the missing Breed male, Knox, or the bad blood that obviously existed between him and Cain. Honestly, she wasn't sure what to make of anything she had seen or heard since her life had taken such an unexpected detour earlier tonight in Miami.

Being around Cain didn't help.

It was hard to think clearly about anything when he was near. God, sometimes the intensity of the man made it hard for her to do so much as breathe.

She had never been the kind of woman to melt at a man's feet or surrender her good sense just because her body craved something it shouldn't want and wasn't going to get. She was used to calling the shots when it came to sex and relationships, not that she'd had either one—and certainly nothing lasting—in quite a while. She felt that lack more than ever being forced into the company of a powerful, darkly attractive man like Cain.

Which made the idea of staying under the same roof with him a bigger problem than she cared to admit.

He didn't seem any more enthused with their current situation than she was. His surly mood had only intensified once they had arrived in the Everglades and met up with his fellow Hunter friends. *Brothers,* she mentally corrected. Brothers who hadn't seen or heard from him in several years, from the sounds of it.

Marina couldn't help but wonder why. An inexplicable softness opened up in her breast as she considered the hard male who had saved her life for no good reason other than he could. She wanted to believe that any tender emotion she may be feeling for him was merely gratitude, that her curiosity was perfectly natural and meant nothing. But deep down, she felt a yearning to know more about Cain.

As Lana led her farther into the heart of the sprawling residence, it was impossible not to imagine him living there. What had his life been like then? It was clear that he'd been close to Bram and the others, so why would he choose to avoid the people who were his family and the home he had helped build with his brothers? Whatever the cause, it had been enough to make him leave and not look back until he'd been forced to return because of her.

Lana's glance lingered on her as they walked. "How long have you and Cain been together?"

"Together?" Marina nearly choked on the word. Lana couldn't possibly think they were anything close to a couple, could she? "We are most certainly not together. We're not anything to each other. We only just met a few hours ago."

Hours that already seemed like days, and not only because of the shocking attempts on her life. Being forced into close quarters with him—being wholly reliant on him for her safety at the moment—was not something she accepted easily. All the less when the man she owed her life to was a surly, dominating Breed male who was no doubt every bit as lethal as the danger she'd barely escaped in Miami.

"Oh. I'm sorry to assume," Lana said, tilting her head as though studying Marina in her silence. "It's just the fact he brought you here, of all places. And the way he looks at you, I suppose I thought . . . well, never mind what I thought."

She swept her hand through the air as if to dismiss the idea, but it had already taken root in Marina's subconscious.

She had felt the heat of Cain's stare on her as she walked away from him to leave the room with Lana. That stormy, kinetic energy stirred an answering turbulence inside her every time he looked at her. It awakened an unsettling sense of anticipation inside her, even when his gaze was dark with menace or flashing with aggravation.

Even worse, when those thunderhead-gray eyes were lit with smoldering heat as they had been out on the path through the swamp. Just recalling it made her blood run hot all over again.

She nearly groaned. What was wrong with her that

she couldn't ignore the man and his disturbing effect on her for as much as a moment?

She drew in a centering breath, then pushed it out on a short sigh. "Cain brought me here only because he said he had no choice. Someone tried to kill me tonight. If not for him, they would've succeeded."

Lana sucked in a gasp. "Oh, my God. Bram mentioned some trouble in Miami, but I had no idea it was something as serious as that. I'm so sorry, Marina. Do you want to tell me what happened?"

No, she didn't. She wasn't the type to confide every little trouble to the nearest sympathetic ear. She solved her own problems and she never, ever complained. It was the Moretskov way, after all. Yet as she looked at Lana, the automatic denial of her offered friendship didn't come.

Something about this warm, doe-eyed Breedmate made her feel safe, not only within the walls of the Darkhaven, but safe to share a part of herself as well. "I've come here to help my uncle in Russia. He's involved in some . . . bad business back home. Dangerous business, involving some very bad men."

"Oh." Lana paused, a grave understanding tempering her gaze. "You're talking about the mafia?"

Marina nodded. "Uncle Anatoly manages the finances for one of the most powerful factions of the Bratva. He's been a part of it for as long as I've been alive. But he's done with all of that now. I've been trying to persuade him for years to find his way out of the life, and he's finally agreed to walk away. It's not an easy thing. I'm the only one he trusts to help him escape."

"How are you supposed to do that?"

"By trading what's in this briefcase for his safe exile."

It was the truth, right down to the secret data file concealed inside.

Lana glanced at the silver case. "Trade it with whom?"

"One of my uncle's allies. The contact is supposed to call me with the meeting information once everything is agreed upon and in place for the exchange." Marina frowned. "If my uncle is still alive, that is. I can't be sure of anything now. One of the men who tried to kill me tonight was the captain of my own security detail."

"One of them?" Lana's dark brows lifted. "How many others were there?"

"The first was a sniper who fired on me while I was in the hotel pool. Cain jumped in from the tenth floor and pulled me out of the bullet's path."

"Did he now?" There was a note of curiosity in her response. Almost disbelief.

"He said he saw a vision of me being killed in the pool. He saved my life," Marina admitted. "A few hours later, it was Yury who turned on me. He shot the rest of the men on my team, then held me at gunpoint. Apparently, he was working covertly with the sniper who escaped. Yury said he wasn't going to let me make the exchange for Uncle Anatoly, even if he had to kill me to stop me. One moment I was staring into the barrel of his pistol, and the next I was watching Cain take Yury out with his bare hands."

Lana let out a breath. "What an awful ordeal you've been through. I'm sorry, Marina."

"It's okay." She shrugged, but her shoulders felt heavy. "I am alive and unharmed. I only hope the same can be said for my uncle."

"I hope so, too," Lana said. "Do you have some way

to get in touch with him?"

"I have a satellite phone in my bag. It's with the rest of my things in Cain's car."

Lana nodded. "I'll send Bram to bring everything in for you. In the meantime, let's get you comfortable in one of the spare rooms, then I'll fix you something to eat."

"Thank you." Marina smiled, feeling grateful not only for the hospitality, but also Lana's easy demeanor. To her surprise, a good deal of the night's stress and exhaustion was lifting simply for being in the other woman's company.

She followed her new friend on an abbreviated tour of the expansive home, which appeared to be laid out in a hexagon shape with various gathering places and social rooms spoking off a central corridor with tall windows that encircled a pretty, moonlit courtyard outside.

"All of the windows in here are equipped with UV-blocking shades during the daylight hours to avoid roasting any of the guys," Lana explained with a wink as Marina slowed to look out at the dark palm trees and night-blooming flowers that beckoned on the other side. "Pretty, isn't it?"

Marina nodded. A pair of carved-stone benches sat at the center of the lush garden space, providing a romantic alcove under the canopy of towering palms and the endless night sky overhead.

Lana walked over, resting her hand atop the large swell of her belly. "Bram made this little courtyard for me as a gift to celebrate the first year of our blood bond. It's one of my favorite spots in the entire Darkhaven."

Marina smiled. "I can see why."

"The residential wings are this way," Lana said after

a moment, gesturing ahead. "We always keep a couple of guestrooms open, so you can have your pick."

Marina murmured her thanks as they resumed their walk along the corridor. Timber beams elevated every soaring ceiling of the sprawling, single-story compound, lending both a sturdy architectural beauty and an airy openness to a residence that had obviously been constructed for security and function, as well as entertainment. She and Lana passed a large theater room, then a library stocked with countless books and a fireplace situated in front of a cozy sofa and chairs. In another room was a billiards table and an old-fashioned jukebox. In the next, a sleek computer room and security operations center.

To Marina's surprise, there was even an indoor lap pool.

"I didn't expect everything here to look so . . . normal."

Lana glanced at her. "How else would it look?"

"I don't know. I've never been inside a Darkhaven. I suppose I imagined something grim and lightless. Cold. Menacing." She was thinking about how she'd been raised to think about the Breed, but all of those same words could just as easily describe her life back home in Uncle Anatoly's house, where the Bratva was an insidious and constant danger in their lives.

"I was saving the tour of the coffin room and torture chambers for later," Lana said, her smile wry with amusement.

Marina winced. "I'm sorry. I don't mean to sound rude and ignorant."

"You don't." Lana tilted her head. "You're a Breedmate, but you don't know many Breed?"

"None. I've lived with my uncle since I was a little girl and my mother died. It's hard to meet people outside your own social circle when you're surrounded by nannies and tutors and bodyguards. Uncle Anatoly is overprotective, even now."

"Ah." Lana lifted her chin. "I grew up in one foster home after another, so I never had those kinds of problems."

"How long have you lived here?"

"Not quite nine years. I had a little art studio on Key Largo. Bram came in one night as I was getting ready to close the shop. He bought a few pottery pieces I'd made, and we talked for two hours. The next night he came back and bought more. On the third night, he invited me to the Darkhaven on the pretense of needing my help deciding where to place everything he picked up. It didn't take much convincing for me to stay overnight. By the morning I realized I never wanted to leave. We've been together ever since."

It was a sweet story, one with a happy ending that was only going to deepen with the arrival of the baby Lana carried. Marina couldn't deny that she was touched, even a little envious, of the simple, yet idyllic life the other Breedmate seemed to enjoy.

She had never longed for a husband and babies, especially not when having either one meant having them under the yoke of the Russian mafia. And regardless of the birthmark she bore, when she thought of sharing her life with someone, she had never allowed herself to imagine it might be with a Breed male who would want to bind her to him with an unbreakable blood bond.

A vision of Cain's enormous fangs bared in battle

rage as he ended Yury's life sprang to life in her mind. Those diamond-bright daggers could tear out her throat in an instant. The thought chased a shiver through her veins, followed by a rush of heat she refused to acknowledge.

"Was Cain also living here when Bram brought you home?"

Lana nodded. "Cain, Bram, Knox, Razor, Logan. This has been their only true home since they escaped their collars."

"Sorry?" The term was unfamiliar. It also put a knot of ice in her breast. "What do you mean, collars?"

Lana gave her a sober look. "You probably don't know about that, either." Her tone was tender, yet edged with a hatred that still simmered beneath the surface of her steady calm. "All of the Hunters were fitted with unbreakable polymer collars as soon as they were old enough to walk. The collars were equipped with ultraviolet light in order to prevent any of the Breed boys and men in the program from trying to escape the laboratory, and to make sure they stayed obedient and emotionless. If a Hunter tried to run, if he disobeyed or rebelled in any way, Dragos or his enforcers would detonate his collar."

"My God," Marina murmured, the cold knot turning into a leaden weight on her heart. She couldn't picture someone like Cain—a massive, lethal force of nature—being shackled to a collar that could kill him on a whim. How had he and the other Hunters managed to exist under the conditions Lana described? How had any of them not gone mad or simply given up? Horrified, she drew in a shallow breath. "And I thought the Bratva were merciless monsters. This Dragos sounds far worse."

Lana nodded solemnly. "He was. Thankfully, he's been dead for two decades and there were many Hunters who found their freedom once the program's command center was destroyed and their collars fell away."

"All of them half-brothers like Cain and Bram and the rest of the men who live here?"

"Yes. Hunters all share the same father, an otherworlder who'd been held captive by Dragos in his lab. He used the captive Ancient to father Breed offspring on dozens of Breedmates who were also being held prisoner by Dragos until they were rescued and he was killed."

Marina exhaled a strangled sound, disgusted by each new detail and overwhelmed with pity for all of the lives Dragos had destroyed in his madness. "Where are the others? You said there were more Hunters who escaped the program. Where have they all gone?"

"No one knows for sure. Some may not wish to be found. Not all of them will be able to adjust to life on the outside of the lab. To hear Bram describe it, there were many Hunters who had little hope of reclaiming any of their humanity even after they were freed. Others fled the program like wild animals, dangerous and unhinged."

Walking alongside Lana, Marina wondered where Cain fit on that troubling spectrum. He was no monster, of that she was certain. But he was a hard, lethal man. Forbidding and detached. Cold and emotionless, especially when it came to her.

At least, he had been until the moment they almost kissed out in the swamp.

Her entire body still felt strangely electric following

that charged instant when Cain's lips had started to descend on hers. Warm heat licked through her veins even now, uninvited. Unwanted.

As for him, all he appeared to feel toward her from the moment they left Miami was enraged. If possible, after their near-kiss on the path outside, he seemed beyond furious, and even more regretful that he'd stepped into the midst of her problems.

Not that she had asked him to.

And not that she wanted him continuing to insert himself into her troubles now, either.

Lana paused outside the open door of a spacious guest room decorated in calming neutrals and sumptuous, soft furnishings with an elegant, yet casually tropical feel. "Here's the guest room I think you'll like best. What do you think?"

Dominating the room was a king-size bed with a woven-rattan headboard and a cushioned bench at the foot of it. Crisp white linens and mounds of fluffy pillows looked like heaven to her tired eyes and weary body. Marina stepped inside, practically sighing as she soaked up all of the inviting details.

"The room is beautiful, Lana. Thank you for letting me have it."

"You're welcome. There's an en suite bathroom over there, and the closet is yours too. Please, make yourself at home, Marina."

She nodded, setting the briefcase on the little bench as she strode further inside the room. On the walls were a handful of framed photographs and art. One painting in particular drew Marina in for a closer look. It was a whimsical piece, rendered in bright, bold strokes.

Marina couldn't help but smile as she looked at the

folksy mermaid seated on a rock beneath a crescent moon and an indigo sky pierced with stars. Long, curly red hair spilled all around her pale skin and fish-scaled turquoise tail. Sweet freckles dotted an impish face with big blue eyes and red lips fashioned in the shape of a heart. No one would mistake the work for anything but amateur, but there was something special about the playfulness and charm of the artist's eye. Whoever painted it had a natural, compelling talent.

"I always smile when I see this painting, too," Lana said, drawing up beside her. "My best friend made it. We went to one of those silly wine and watercolor places one night as a joke. My painting was as terrible as you might expect after three glasses of Chardonnay, but Abbie's . . . well, as you can see, she had a gift."

"Abbie." The conversation between Cain and his brothers upon their arrival replayed in Marina's head as she glanced at Lana. "I heard Bram and the others mention her name tonight, before you came into the room. Your friend and the Hunter who's not here now, Knox, were together at one time?"

Sadness moved over Lana's expression. "Abbie and Knox were madly in love. She was a Breedmate, too. Like us." Marina flinched inwardly at the reminder of the birthmark she wasn't quite ready to acknowledge, but she said nothing as Lana continued to speak. "I'd never seen him so happy. She was too. They were practically inseparable, and everyone knew it was only a matter of time before they announced they were going to be blood-bonded. Knox had all of these plans for a romantic getaway as a surprise to her."

Marina frowned, trying to reconcile this version of Cain's brother to the one who'd been described as a menace, even a threat, to those around him. According to the other Breed males here, losing Abbie had done that to him. "What happened, Lana?"

"One night there was a terrible storm. It came up unexpectedly while Abbie was leaving the hospital where she worked. Her car broke down on the highway. A tractor-trailer lost control in the rain and high winds. There was no visibility that night. The truck driver didn't see Abbie's car in time to avoid her. She died on the scene."

"Oh, no." All the air left Marina's lungs on a weighted sigh. "How awful. I'm so sorry. For you, and for Knox."

Lana gave a wobbly nod. "Abbie's death impacted all of us, especially Knox. But I feel for Cain too."

"Cain?" Marina couldn't hide her confusion. "Why him?"

"Because after Abbie's death, things were . . . different between him and Knox. They'd been as close as any brothers could be after they'd escaped the lab, but all of that changed after Knox lost Abbie. He was filled with so much anger. Cain was too. He left the Darkhaven a couple of nights after the accident. Knox was already gone. He went out that night to look for Abbie and he didn't come back for six months."

"And Cain?"

Lana slowly shook her head. "He's been gone all these eight years since . . . until tonight. Until you."

The words settled heavily on her. No wonder Cain's mood had grown increasingly dark the closer they got to the Everglades. No wonder he acted as if he'd rather be anywhere else tonight, with anyone else.

Now his anger toward her made a little sense.

So did the pain she saw in him out on the swamp path.

"I'll go see about warming up something for you to eat," Lana said as she headed for the open door of the guest room. "Make yourself at home. I'll be back in a few minutes and we can talk some more in the kitchen over a bowl of chicken stew and biscuits."

"Thank you, Lana. That sounds lovely."

Marina smiled, but her face felt as if it were made of clay. Her empty stomach growled in approval of the meal she definitely needed, but her appetite had all but dried up.

Because now she knew she was right. Cain had lost someone he cared about, even loved.

The problem was, that woman hadn't belonged to him.

CHAPTER 8

Cain moved the Aston Martin off the swamp road to the Darkhaven's secured garage. He'd parked it on the path when they arrived, unsure how he would be greeted if he drove right up to the gates and demanded to be let in.

Returning inside now with his small duffel and Marina's luggage, it felt strange as hell to be walking in and out of the place as though he'd never been gone. As far as homecomings went, his tonight was smoother than he deserved—even if the only other person who could truly understand his reluctance to be there had yet to make his appearance.

He'd have to cross that bridge with Knox eventually. He owed it to his brother. He only hoped the confrontation, when it came, wouldn't end with one or both of them torn to shreds.

As for the rest of the former Hunters, after Marina

and Lana had left the room, he'd brought everyone up to speed on the situation in Miami, starting with his vision of her would-be assassination and the subsequent attack on her life by Yury. To a man, his brothers agreed that protecting Marina was a duty that could not be refused.

Whether that meant Cain would accompany her to the eventual rendezvous with Anatoly Moretskov's contact or that he would instead pack her ass up and sending her back home to Russia at the earliest opportunity, he hadn't yet decided. He'd take whichever scenario seemed to be the least likely to get the Breedmate killed on his watch.

Right now, neither option felt right. He had precious little intel to go on apart from Marina's word, and the prickling of his instincts warned him not to take the female on face value. No matter how staggeringly fine the face in question happened to be.

Fuck.

His fangs pulsed in his gums as he strode through the vacated great room on his way to the hexagon-shaped Darkhaven's interior corridor with the two bags in his hands. Bram and Logan's deep voices carried from one of the many gathering rooms that spoked off the connecting hallway. But as he turned toward the residential wing, it was the low thump of growling rock music and the accompanying clack of computer keys that slowed Cain's steps as he approached Razor's living quarters.

The door was open just wide enough to see the big male seated at his workstation in near darkness, but for the light of a single desk lamp and the glow emanating from a pair of open monitors on his desk. One of the screens was filled with code and open browser panels. The other displayed a live video feed of the exterior of a small cabin on a pine-studded mountain. Based on the sunset, Cain guessed the location had to be about three time zones west of the east coast.

Without noticing he had company standing silently behind him in the doorway, Raze typed commands on his keyboard and the focus of the drone's camera overhead tightened. The feed sharpened with laser clarity on an open-air Jeep that was just making its way up the mountain toward the cabin. A curvy brunette in faded jeans and a gauzy white peasant top hopped out from behind the wheel and began to unpack a bunch of groceries and supplies.

Raze leaned forward in his chair and homed in even closer on the young woman, until her sun-kissed, freckled face and bright green eyes filled the monitor. The focus lingered on her as she went about her business, carrying items into the cabin unaware she was being watched.

"She's pretty."

Razor hit a key and the surveillance went black. For a male who was damn hard to rattle, he looked more than rankled to realize he had a witness to his cyber spying. "Just keeping an eye on a situation for a friend."

Cain grunted. "Good thing. Otherwise the whole long-distance stalking scenario might seem creepy."

Ordinarily, Raze would have chuckled at a brotherly jab, or at least broken a smirk. Instead he killed the music, then pivoted in his chair and watched Cain stroll inside the room uninvited. With the pair of bags stowed at his feet, Cain crossed his arms and eased his shoulder against the wall.

"I need your help, Raze." He gestured to the computers on his brother's desk. "I need to know whatever you can dig up on Anatoly Moretskov."

Razor hated to be called a hacker, but he was remarkably adept when it came to chasing down a target, either online or in person. And if he needed more specialized computer skills than his own impressive abilities, Cain knew the male had a network of contacts all around the world that he could tap for assistance at a moment's notice.

A sly tilt kicked up the corner of Raze's broad mouth. "I'm about ten minutes ahead of you, brother. I started pulling data on the bastard as soon as my ass hit the chair."

Cain approached the workstation as Razor began opening browsers and files on the bigger of the two monitors. "Question number one, is Moretskov still alive?"

"As of a few hours ago, he was. Here's a photo from a State dinner he attended in Moscow last night." On screen was an image of three men in tuxedos holding cigars and glasses of sparkling champagne. "Moretskov's the balding penguin on the right."

Cain studied the grinning, portly man with the dark eyes and thinning ring of salt-and-pepper hair. The smile and laughing eyes didn't seem to belong to a man who'd just sent his niece on a life-and-death errand for him five thousand miles away.

Then again, Moretskov likely had no idea yet that Marina had run into danger. Since leaving Miami, she'd been desperate to get in contact with her uncle. Cain had her satellite phone in his pocket, which he intended to deliver along with her other belongings once he was satisfied with the intel he got from Razor.

"Who are the other two men with Moretskov?"

"Dude in the middle is a multi-billionaire who also happens to be married to the Russian president's cousin. And the big-nosed ox on the left is none other than Boris Karamenko, head of a particularly nasty group within the Bratva. Arms trading, narcotics, human trafficking. He's got his chubby fingers in all of it. He's also got a reputation as a beast to his enemies, well-deserved by the sound of it. Nobody crosses Karamenko and lives to tell."

"And Moretskov? Is he as bad as his boss?"

Raze glanced at him. "No one's as bad as Karamenko. As for our man Anatoly, he reports directly to Karamenko as his personal banker. According to rumor and speculation, Moretskov's bank in Saint Petersburg has been laundering mob money and managing various other financial interests for Karamenko for about thirty years."

"And now he wants out," Cain said, staring at the men in the photo. He shook his head. "If Boris Karamenko is as bad as you say, it's going to cost a hell of a lot more than two million dollars to get out from under him."

"You think she's lying to you?"

Cain frowned. "I think she's protecting her uncle and nothing else matters to her. I think she'll say or do anything for him." Even risk her own life, evidently. "What else do you have on Moretskov?"

Razor brought up another file. "Here's the basic bio. Fifty-eight years old. Rumored net worth of half a billion by U.S. numbers. Never been married. One younger sibling, a sister, Ekaterina. She died twenty-two years ago."

Cain nodded, recalling that Marina said she had lost her mother when she was three. He didn't want to recall the pain he'd heard in that confession, the vulnerability in her voice when she'd admitted that she understood the pain of loss.

He cleared his throat. "What about the rest of the Moretskovs? Do they come from a long line of mobsters and oligarchs?"

"Not at all," Raze said. "His parents were middle class. His father was an accountant who later worked his way into management of the bank in Saint Petersburg. Anatoly's mother was a music teacher. They made enough money to send their son to the United States for college. Sounds like he might've stayed in the U.S. indefinitely, but when Anatoly was in his late twenties his father had a stroke and had to retire from the bank. Anatoly returned to Russia and assumed control of the family business. In two years, he'd increased the bank's worth to over one-hundred billion in holdings. Mostly rumored mafia business."

"And it only took him thirty years to find his conscience." Cain scoffed, still skeptical about Moretskov even though he had no right to be sanctimonious. He'd spent a number of years in Las Vegas working for a man who wasn't much better than Moretskov, or even Karamenko. He had a bank account that was fat with blood-stained money earned by delivering pain to his employer's enemies.

He was far from a saint, but he'd rather walk headlong into the sun before he'd even consider allowing someone he cared about to brush up against the filthy edges of his profession.

Meanwhile, Marina was standing front and center in the midst of some of the most dangerous and powerful players in the world.

Cain braced his hands on the edge of the desk. "What can you tell me about Marina?"

"What do you want to know?"

"Everything." He watched impatiently as Razor typed on the keyboard and brought up a number of files and documents. Public record information, society articles translated from Russian, a handful of old photographs from assorted events Marina had attended. One social announcement and image was dated nine years ago, on the night of her society debut in Saint Petersburg.

Cain scanned it all while Razor provided a verbal summary. "Born twenty-five years ago in New York City, father unknown. Dual citizenship, but it doesn't look like she's spent any time in the States other than now. Educated in Russia, fluent in both languages, as we know. Not a lot to tell here, man. Private tutors, expensive finishing schools, some equestrian awards when she was a teen. Just the basic rich bitch stuff you'd expect."

Cain pointed to an old article that mentioned her mother's name. "What's that one about?"

"Death notice for Ekaterina Moretskova." Raze ran it through a translator then hit the highlights. "Only sibling of Anatoly Moretskov, Ekaterina died twenty-two years ago while on a boating holiday in Spain with a male friend, a young literature professor from Moscow. Medical examiner ruled the drownings accidental due to the presence of alcohol and narcotics in both victims' bloodstreams."

"Jesus." Cain exhaled the curse low under his breath. He knew Marina's mother's death couldn't have been natural based on her age when she'd passed, but he hadn't been expecting something this tragic.

Neither Cain nor any of his Hunter brothers produced in Dragos's labs knew what it was like to have actual parents. They didn't know that kind of love. They didn't know the kind of hurt it might inflict to have a parent's love only to lose it.

For a three-year-old child like Marina had been, it must have been devastating.

All she had left was her uncle. Even now.

Anatoly Moretskov wasn't going to win any Man of the Year awards, but could Cain really fault Marina for clinging to the only family she had?

He didn't fault her, but he didn't care, either. He couldn't allow himself to care, he reminded himself sternly.

The only truth that mattered was the damned birthmark on her ankle and the moral obligation he had to keep her alive. Even that was made of flimsy matter. For what wasn't the first time, he wondered how low of a man he'd have to be to leave Marina in the care of Bram and the rest of his brothers here at the Darkhaven, then be on his way.

He had no doubt she'd be better off without him. Safer.

Christ, without him, she'd be safer on more levels than he cared to admit.

"What about boyfriends or lovers?" he blurted. "Any of those articles or documents mention any men in her life?"

Razor slanted him a flat look. "You've been eating

her with your eyes all night, but you haven't worked up the balls to ask her that basic fact? You're slipping, Cain."

He glowered. "I'm not asking because I'm interested in the female."

"Whatever you say, man." His brother had the nerve to chuckle.

"It called due diligence," Cain drawled. "Besides, she's not my type."

Raze arched a tawny brow. "Didn't realize you had one."

Cain grunted. "Anyone without a Breedmate mark, for starters. And no one I'm supposed to be protecting." He gestured to the blackened screen that had been trained on a mystery woman when he walked in the room. "You might want to adopt a similar policy."

The other male lifted his chin, then blew out a short chuckle. "Yeah, fuck you, too, brother."

"As for Marina," Cain said, "I want to be sure she's not part of the Bratva along with her uncle."

"You got reason to think she is?" Razor swiveled toward him, folding his *glyph*-covered muscled arms over his chest. "You think her story about Moretskov seeking asylum is bullshit?"

Cain shook his head. "No. I don't think so. But I know she's not telling me everything. She's protecting some kind of secret and I don't like it."

"Hell, we've all got secrets to protect, man."

Cain wasn't going to deny that. But whatever secret Marina was hiding had likely already put a target on her back. It might put one on anyone else near her, too, including the people he cared about in this Darkhaven.

And if it did, that meant Cain and his unwanted

charge were going to have serious problems.

Problems far bigger than the impossible desire that he couldn't seem to shake whenever she was around.

CHAPTER 9

Marina ran a soft terry washcloth under the cold water tap in her en suite bathroom, then wrung it out and scrubbed the cool, damp cloth over her face. Exhaustion leaked away on her sigh, but the face staring at her in the mirror still looked weary. Worse than weary, she looked scared and uncertain.

All accurate, no matter how much she wanted to deny it.

And she was hungry too. The appetite that had abandoned her when Lana left a few minutes ago had come back with a vengeance by the time a short knock sounded on the guest room door in the other room.

"Come in," she called, drying her hands. "The door is open, Lana."

But as Marina stepped out of the bathroom, she found it wasn't the other Breedmate who entered the room. It was Cain. Hard silver eyes locked on her as he walked in holding her suitcase. It was easy to forget how big he was, how just the sight of his muscled bulk and stern dark looks radiated unearthly menace and power. Even the air seemed to make way for him, growing thinner and hotter every second he remained in the room.

Marina crossed her arms under her breasts and raised her chin as she struggled to hold his unnerving stare. "Lana said she would send Bram to retrieve my bag from the car."

Cain grunted. "Sorry to disappoint." His tone was anything but apologetic as he set the suitcase on the foot of the bed. She saw his gaze flick briefly, distractedly, to the cheery mermaid painting on the wall. Abbie's painting. His brow furrowed with a deep scowl. "I trust Lana is seeing to it that you're comfortable and have whatever you need."

"Yes. She seems very nice."

"She is."

A monotone reply, accompanied by a cold, impersonal stare that took her aback even more than the fury that seemed to bubble so close to the surface of the lethal former Hunter. Something was different about Cain now, a subtle yet unmistakable change in his demeanor since the last time she'd seen him.

Starting in Miami, he'd been irritable and broody toward her. Half the time she'd been with him, she hadn't been sure if he wanted to shake her until her teeth rattled or strip her naked and make her scream for an entirely different reason.

Now she felt a cool detachment stretch between them, as if she were looking at a stranger, not the man who saved her life. Not the man who had ignited a desire in her that still smoldered even in light of his chilly aloofness now.

Marina ignored all of it, focusing instead on what truly mattered. Her uncle and her promise to help him.

"Thank you for bringing the rest of my things," she said, crossing to the bed with brisk strides. She opened the suitcase and sifted through the clothing with her hand. She frowned. "There was a satellite phone in here."

"Yes." Cain's deep voice drew her gaze to him. He reached into the pocket of his black jeans and withdrew the device.

"You went through my belongings?"

He didn't answer. Not so much as a shrug, let alone an apology or excuse. "This Darkhaven is off the grid. All communications going in or out are monitored and controlled."

"Monitored and controlled by whom?"

"As far as you're concerned? Me."

Marina faced him and held out her hand. "I need to call my uncle." Emotion threatened to clog her throat, but she held fast to her anger instead. "You don't own me, Cain Hunter. No man does. Now, give me the phone so I can call and make sure nothing's happened to my uncle. For all I know, his enemies could have killed him just as they tried to kill me."

"He's alive." Cain's low voice was practically a growl. "As of last night, he was living large at a black-tie soiree in Moscow along with Boris Karamenko and a bunch of other Kremlin boot-lickers."

Uncle Anatoly was all right? She didn't know whether to feel relieved or suspicious that Cain sounded so certain. "How do you know that?"

"Raze and I did some internet recon. I can't say we found anything that improved my opinion of your uncle. He's a career criminal, one who made a fortune washing the blood off Karamenko's dirty money. He's also a fucking coward, since he's willing to put your neck on the line while he's out drinking champagne and sucking on cigars. That makes him worse than a coward in my book."

She wanted to fire back in defense, but the words wouldn't come. Maybe she was too weary. Or maybe Cain was saying something she didn't want to acknowledge, not even by refuting it with a hot retort. "You don't have to like him. He's my family and I would die for him."

Cain's eyes darkened. "Not if I have anything to say about that."

Marina reached for the phone and he let her take it, although he made no move to leave and let her make the call. "You don't expect to stand there and listen, do you?"

His expression left no doubt of that. "Nothing you do is private now, Marina. Not while you're here. Make your call. I'll wait."

She glared at him, but the need to reach her uncle was stronger than the pride that made her want to throw the phone at Cain and refuse to let him handle her as though she were his prisoner. He didn't trust her. She saw that truth in his eyes as he watched her enter her uncle's private number on the satellite phone.

He answered with a single word. "Marina?"

"Uncle." She sagged onto the bed, awash in relief to hear his raspy voice. Oh, thank God he was all right. She whispered those same words to him in Russian, unable to hold back her relief.

Cain scowled as she spoke, giving a grim shake of his head. "In English. I know he's as fluent as you are. And keep it short. No mention of where you are or anyone besides me."

She hugged the phone to her ear. "Uncle Anatoly, I can't talk for very long. I just . . . needed to hear your voice."

"Marina, who was that speaking to you?" He followed her lead, switching seamlessly from Russian to English. It was barely six in the morning in Saint Petersburg, but he was instantly alert. Alarm bled into his tone. "Something is wrong. What's happened? Are you okay? Who are you with? Are you still in Miami?"

She didn't know which of his rapid-fire questions to answer first. "I'm . . . I'm fine, Uncle. There were some problems earlier tonight. I was attacked, but I'm okay. Everything is under control, so please don't worry."

"Don't worry? *Moya radost.*" His endearment gusted out of him, ripe with concern. "What do you mean you were attacked? Goddamn it, put Yury on the phone at once, Marina."

"I can't. Yury is dead. He is the one who attacked me tonight. He betrayed us, Uncle. He shot Viktor and Ivan, then he came after me." She glanced at Cain. "Fortunately, I was able to escape. I'm fine, and I have the briefcase with me."

He went silent for a moment, and she knew that he had picked up on her cautiously worded statement. "The briefcase. And the contents?"

"Yes, Uncle Anatoly. It's safe with me. All two million dollars are right here."

"Good," he said slowly. "That is very good to hear."

They both understood that she was also talking about the data file, the true item of value he had entrusted to her. "But you are . . . not alone, Marina? There is a man with you. I heard his voice. It is not Kirill."

"No. Kirill is dead too. He was shot earlier tonight by a sniper who had evidently been working with Yury. They both failed because another man helped me." She let out a shallow sigh. "The man I'm with saved my life. He helped me get away from Miami to somewhere safe."

The answering silence was heavy with skepticism, even suspicion. "Tell me his name, this man who saved your life."

She glanced at Cain. He inclined his head in permission, those stormy gray eyes leaving her no place to hide. "His name is Cain Hunter."

"Hunter." He uttered the word in an airless, toneless murmur. A low curse, spoken in vivid Russian, spilled into her ear. "That's a Breed name, Marina."

"Yes." If he hadn't been so horrified by all the rest that she'd told him, she knew her uncle would be livid to hear this further detail. "I'd be dead if not for him, Uncle Anatoly. I am safe with him."

"Safe?" He scoffed, a brittle scrape in his throat. "You couldn't be less safe, girl. A woman like you, with the mark? I've warned you about them, Marina. They are animals. Lower than animals—base, blood-drinking monsters."

She flicked a glance at Cain, knowing he could hear every word. Marina had grown up with her uncle's fear and loathing of the Breed. Sometimes she wondered if having a niece born with the Breedmate symbol on her had only made his animosity deepen. She had never liked hearing him say awful things about the Breed, but standing there now while Cain listened to such unwarranted denigration made her feel small and ashamed.

"I am fine, Uncle. I'm a grown woman. You raised me to be strong. I can handle myself."

He didn't argue that point, which was a small victory. But he was far from reassured. "Tell me where you are. I will send someone to retrieve you at once."

"I can't tell you that, and it's a long story. Just know that I'm okay." She glanced at Cain, whose steely silver eyes refused to release her. He gestured for her to wrap up the call. "I have to go. I will explain everything when I see you next. For now, just know that I am all right and everything is still on course. I won't let you down."

"No. I don't like this, Marina."

Panic was beginning to override his anger and suspicion. Her uncle was a man who did not tolerate anything less than full control. She could practically see him on the other end of the line, his cheeks turning red with anger for what he'd just learned, his palm most likely skimming over the top of his balding head as he weighed the situation.

"Everything has changed now. The risks are too great. I'm going to call it all off. I want you to come home."

"Give up now, after everything I've just been through? No, Uncle Anatoly. I won't do that. Please, don't ask me to." Marina shook her head, balking at the idea of running home to Russia in a panic. Especially when her meeting with Ernesto Fuentes could be no more than a couple of days away. "If I come home now and something terrible happens to you, I will never forgive myself. You entrusted me to help you, so let me do that. Let me finish this for you. For both of us."

He was silent for a long moment. Then he heaved a short sigh. "You always were a determined girl."

"You didn't raise me to be anything less."

"You have more courage than many of the Vory soldiers I know, Marina. I couldn't have trusted anyone else to do this for me. You were the only one."

His praise warmed her. She heard it from him so infrequently that on those occasions when he did give it, she clutched every word close like a treasure. Did he realize how she pushed herself to excel in everything she undertook simply for the possibility of winning his acknowledgment, of earning his love?

This mission to secure his freedom was no different. No risk was too great if it meant the difference between life and death for the only person who had ever cared for her.

"So, let me finish it, Uncle Anatoly. You say you trust me, so trust me."

Silence stretched, and Cain's stormy gaze edged toward impatience. "It's time, Marina. You need to hang up."

She turned away from him, not ready to sever the connection. "Uncle Anatoly, tell me you won't give up. My future depends on this too."

And there it was, the truth she had not spoken to him until now. She wanted to be free of the fear and violence too. She needed his freedom so she could have hers too.

"Very well." It took him a moment to say the words. "You're right. We have set the wheels in motion and we should not slow them down. I will do what I can to expedite the exchange."

"Thank you, Uncle." She closed her eyes, feeling both relieved and imbued with new resolve. "I will not let you down."

"I know you won't, *moya radost*. Stay safe. Wait for the call."

"Yes, Uncle." She ended the call and pivoted back to look at Cain. "He's worried."

He grunted. "For you, or for himself?"

Marina frowned as he reached out and took the phone from her grasp. It disappeared into his pocket once more. "What are you doing? I need to keep it with me. My uncle's contact may be calling at any time."

"We already went over that. No communications in or out of this Darkhaven without my knowledge. For the duration you're here, you talk to no one unless I'm present."

"You make it sound as if I'm your prisoner."

His broad mouth thinned into a cold smile. "What else would you expect from a base, blood-drinking monster?"

She winced. "I'm sorry you heard that."

"It's the truth." He shrugged, his face rigid and devoid of emotion. "You know what I am, and what I was trained to be. So, you should also know that I'm not someone you should piss off or try to play for a fool."

"I'm not trying to do any of those things. I don't even know what you're talking about."

"Lies, Marina. And half-truths. You've been feeding them to me since the moment you opened your pretty mouth."

She shook her head, feeling cornered. "I've told you everything."

"Like hell you have. I realize your loyalty is with your

uncle, though fuck if I can figure out why."

"Because he's my family. Because I love him like a father, one I never had."

"He's using you, Marina. I've known men like him. I used to work for one in Las Vegas. Nothing truly matters to them except their own skin."

"No, you're wrong."

"Then tell me what you're really using as collateral for dear old Uncle Anatoly's freedom. Because I know damn well it's not a paltry two million dollars." Cain stepped closer, until all of the air seemed to evaporate between them, leaving only the heat of his powerful body and the vibrating pulse of his escalating fury. "You're keeping secrets, Marina, and if you're not careful they could get you killed."

She wanted to come back at him with a sharp denial, but for some reason she found it difficult to lie to him when his thunderous silver eyes were boring into her, his handsome, accusing face barely an inch from her now. She swallowed, hating that she couldn't simply disregard him as an obstacle in the way of her goal.

She couldn't look him in the eye and lie now, but if he thought she was going to cower under his glare and dominating size, he was sorely mistaken.

"I'm not the only one keeping secrets, Cain."

His scowl furrowed deeper on his brow. "What the fuck does that mean?"

She glanced pointedly at the whimsical painting on the wall near the bed. When she swiveled her gaze back to Cain, his expression had darkened to a fury that made her heart skid in her breast. "Lana told me about Abbie. About the car accident and the rift that opened up between you and Knox afterward."

Silent, he reeled back. A hundred emotions played over his face in the matter of an instant. But the one that stuck was rage. And pain. More than she had expected to see.

"You had feelings for her. You loved her."

He uttered a tight, vicious curse. "Is that what Lana thinks? Is that what she fucking told you?"

"No. You did, Cain. Out on the path when I asked you if you lost someone you cared for. Someone your vision failed to save. It was Abbie, wasn't it? You were in love with another man's woman. Did Knox know, Cain? Did she?"

"Enough." Amber light shot into his irises, crackling like fire. "Knox is my brother. Abbie is dead. End of story."

No, she didn't think so at all. Cain had been carrying his anguish—and his guilt—for eight long years. If he wanted to lecture her about secrets and their power to harm someone, all he had to do was look in a mirror.

He stalked away from her, heading toward the door. But then he raked his hand over his ebony hair and swung back around. Moving faster than her eyes could track him, he was suddenly in front of her, a dark force of nature.

Menacing and lethal.

Terrifying in his unearthly rage.

His silver eyes turned as dark as thunder clouds, but lit with flashing sparks of amber light. His pupils had transformed too. Narrowed to slim, catlike slivers that only made the fire in his Breed irises all the more searing.

Good lord, she half expected him to reach out and strangle her. But touching her seemed to be the last thing he intended to do. His hands remained fisted at his sides, the muscles in his thick biceps bulging as he struggled to rein in his fury.

He bore down on her until his face was not even an inch away from hers, his lips peeled back from the enormous, razor-sharp points of his fangs.

"Be careful, Marina. Do not think you have me fooled. If any of your secrets—or your uncle's—end up putting this Darkhaven in danger, there will be no saving you. Breedmate mark or not, if your presence jeopardizes anyone here, there you will have hell to pay. And I'll be the one coming to collect."

CHAPTER 10

Cain stood outside the glass door of the indoor lap pool and watched Marina's lean, strong arms and fluttering legs propel her through the water. It was the first he'd seen of her since their clash in her guest room almost twenty-four hours ago.

He wasn't sure which of them had been more deliberate in avoiding the other, but the break had done him some good. Helped put his head on straight again so he could focus on something other than the woman who had managed to turn his entire world upside down in the course of a single day. Dragging him back to a place he thought he'd never see again. Making him relive the mistakes of his past and the shame he would carry with him as long as he lived.

Abbie's death would stain his hands forever.

He'd be damned if he would make the same mistakes with Marina.

Keeping her alive meant keeping her at arm's length, emotionally and otherwise. Especially otherwise, because whenever he was near her, everything male in him already responded to her as though she belonged to him . . . or would, sooner than later.

"Fuck." He muttered the curse and shook his head, eyes still glued to her tattooed body and the tiny black bikini that had gotten him into this whole unwanted situation in the first place.

Christ, she was beautiful. She swam with determination and power, and a sleek grace that made Cain's blood turn molten in his veins. Arousal flared inside him, coiling tighter and hotter every second he watched her.

It was hard to regret jumping off that hotel balcony to save her when the alternative was the certainty that she would be dead. Yet for what wasn't the first time, he had to tamp down the urge to get in his car and speed away as fast as it could take him.

He had plenty of experience walking away, after all. No one here would be surprised to discover he'd simply packed up and split again, this time for good. He could carry on with his life, such as it was, and never look back.

But where would that leave Marina?

Still determined to help her uncle, no matter the risk. Still marked for death by whomever had tried to take her out from that rooftop in Miami.

He was surprised she hadn't tried to leave the Darkhaven, particularly after the way he'd left things with her last night. But she had little choice other than to stay. So long as he was holding the satellite phone linking her to her uncle's contact, she was as good as shackled to him.

109

Cain scowled at the thought. He knew too well what it felt like to have his freedom—and his humanity—stripped away by someone. He'd spent sixteen years hating the ones who enslaved him and his brothers to the Hunter program. How long would it take before Marina began to regard him as the same kind of monster?

Cain raked his hand over his dark hair on a low growl and backed away from the door. He was about to head back to his quarters, but before he could take the first step, Logan and Razor rounded the corner and saw him standing there. *Damn it.*

"What's up?" Raze asked, even though his slow smirk said he knew full well. "Admiring your captive mermaid? She's been in there for the past hour, swimming laps like she's training to cross the English Channel."

Cain didn't like the surge of possessiveness that washed over him at his brother's remark. Nor did he appreciate the reminder that she was staying with Cain even remotely against her will.

Logan broke the tension. "We're going out for a blood run. You want to ride along?"

Cain shook his head. "No. I'm good."

Raze chuckled. "You sure about that? You don't look so good to me, brother."

His shrewd golden-brown eyes flicked to the *dermaglyphs* that wrapped Cain's arms beneath the sleeves of his black T-shirt. The Breed skin markings pulsed, their changing colors betraying the desire—and the hunger—that had churned to life inside him while he watched Marina in the pool.

As much as he wanted to deny it, Razor was right.

Cain had fed from the blood Host in Miami only last night, but it might as well have been a week ago for the way his thirst was pounding through him right now.

"She's off-limits," he ground out, seeing no reason to pretend in front of the Breed males who had once known him better than anyone. And he supposed the warning was as much for them as it was for himself.

Razor's smile didn't dim in the least. "You keep telling yourself that, brother. Maybe you'll actually believe it."

He cuffed Logan on the shoulder and the two of them headed off without another word. Cain watched them go, waiting until they disappeared around a turn in the corridor before he let out the jagged breath he'd been holding.

He sent a glance toward the pool area, just in time to see Marina climb out of the water. Rivulets sluiced down her nearly naked curves and off the end of her blond ponytail as she padded over to retrieve a fluffy white towel from where it lay folded on a poolside bench. She began drying off, stroking the soft terry cloth over the tangled vine of roses on her arms and legs.

Cain scowled, staring through the glass. He knew he should walk away and leave her in peace. Damn it, he wanted to. Instead, he tamped down the hunger he hadn't been able to hide from his brothers, then he opened the door and strode inside.

Marina swiveled her head in his direction the instant he entered. She looked startled that he was there, but she took her time wrapping the towel around her shoulders as if she refused to let the sight of him provoke her.

"Has there been news?" she asked. "The call I'm waiting for—"

LARA ADRIAN

Cain shook his head as he approached. "Nothing yet."

"Would you tell me if there was?"

He exhaled sharply. "I'm not going to lie to you. You can trust me, Marina."

Her chin came up, burgundy gaze unblinking and ready for battle. "The only thing I trust about you right now is the threat you made against me last night."

He had more than earned the jab—and her doubt. He cursed under his breath. "I was angry and frustrated last night. For some reason, you seem to bring out the worst in me."

"Is that what passes for an apology to you?"

"No. I'm not apologizing for what I said."

She scoffed. "Of course, you aren't."

She folded her arms beneath the dampened towel that draped her and started to walk away from him. Cain blocked her, coming to stand directly in front of her. She stopped short, even though her expression said she would have preferred to barrel through him.

"Why are you here, Cain? Or have you come here to tell me I'm forbidden from using the pool without your supervision too?"

He almost chuckled, astonished by her tenacity. He'd never known anyone willing to challenge him at every turn, let alone a female. Marina might have been raised as a pampered mafia princess, but the woman staring back at him was a warrior to her core.

He was impressed, far more than he should be. "Jesus, you never back down from a fight, do you? You're not a prisoner here, Marina."

"Is that right?" She held out her hand, palm up. "Then I'll be glad to take my phone and be on my way."

"You'll be dead on your own," he pointed out, in case she hadn't grasped that fact. "Your mission for your uncle is probably suicidal as it is. I know that's not going to stop you. I heard your determination when you were talking to him."

She didn't deny it. Her hand slowly fell down to her side. "I would do anything for my uncle."

Cain grunted. "I have no doubt. Does he appreciate just how much you're willing to sacrifice for him?"

"Of course, he does."

"You're sure about that? Because it seems to me that you've got something to prove—even if you have to risk your life to make the point."

Her brow furrowed as he spoke. "Without Uncle Anatoly, I wouldn't be alive. He opened his home to my mother when she was pregnant and alone. After she died, he continued to raise me like his own child. I owe him my life. I owe him everything." She glanced down, her voice softening. "And I want to be free from the Bratva as much as he does."

She said it like a wish she had never spoken out loud before. It was almost a whisper, filled with a vulnerability that took him aback. Cain reached out, lifted her face. "You can have that right now. Safe passage for you to a Darkhaven anywhere in the world. If you want to escape your life in Russia, I can arrange it within the hour."

"But only me."

He nodded, and she stepped back, rejecting everything she'd just heard with a look that conveyed more than any words. "Do you actually think I would consider that? Abandon my uncle, the only family I have, to make a better life for myself? No, Cain. That's not something I would do. Not ever, not for any reason."

She didn't voice the recrimination, but she didn't have to. He could see it in her face. "I had my reasons, Marina. It was better for everyone that I left."

"Better for you, you mean. But without the people who care about you, what else is there?"

He didn't have an answer for that. For the first sixteen years of his life, all he knew was killing and discipline. After escaping Dragos's labs, he'd gotten a taste of family and home with his brothers here at the Darkhaven they built.

And yes, he would have given anything for them—right down to his final breath.

He still would.

Yet, selfishly, he'd turned his back on all of them eight years ago out. He'd been a coward to abandon the people who cared about him the most. Including Knox. Especially him.

He held her defiant stare. "We're not here to rehash my failures or all the ways I've let people down. I won't live a day without blaming myself for Abbie's death and the pain I caused everyone who loved her."

"You think you failed Abbie? How are you to blame for what happened to her?"

This wasn't at all a topic he wanted to discuss, least of all with Marina, but he knew enough about her to realize the only way to steer her away from the subject of his ignoble past was to push straight through it.

"I let myself care for her, and in the end it cost Abbie her life." He saw Marina's gaze flicker with confusion and maybe something even more tender. He scoffed. "She's dead because by letting her into my heart, I failed to protect her. It's a mistake I'll never make again."

Marina seemed surprised by his admission. Hell, he

surprised himself by saying the words out loud. It was the first time he'd uttered them. Too late to take them back now.

She studied him too closely, seeing the cracks he'd always been able to hide behind a shield of cold menace and solitude.

It took a moment before she spoke. "Lana told me what happened. How a tractor trailer lost control in a big storm that night. How could any of that be your fault? You didn't kill Abbie."

He exhaled a bitter chuckle. "Tell that to Knox. He's got every right to hate me."

"Why? Cain, it was an accident."

"One I saw in a vision weeks before it happened."

Her mouth went a bit slack. "You saw Abbie's death? The same way you saw mine?"

"The same way I've seen dozens of deaths. Random people. Strangers. And sometimes I see the last moments of people I know . . . people I care about."

"How awful for you, Cain." She swallowed. "I can't imagine what that must be like for you."

He scoffed. "Do I look like I need sympathy?"

His words were deliberately sharp, and they served their purpose. Marina inched back and pulled her towel a little tighter around her, as though his cruelty chilled her. "Did you tell anyone you saw the accident that was going to happen? Did she know? Does Knox?"

"I didn't tell anyone. Knox found out . . . later."

A bleak understanding filled her gaze. "You mean, after she was gone."

She reached for him then. Her fingers came to rest lightly on his forearm, sending the warmth of her touch all the way into his marrow. Heat licked through him and he drew away from the contact on a low growl. "Fuck this. I've said enough. I don't need to explain anything more."

But true to form, Marina refused to retreat. "What about Abbie? Did she know how you felt . . . about her, I mean?"

"Christ, no." He bit off the reply, irritation flaring hot in his field of vision. "She was in love with Knox and he adored her. I've never claimed to have much honor, but I wouldn't have stooped to that. I would've died before I crossed that line."

"But he knew. Didn't he?" She studied him too closer. "Knox knew how you felt about her."

"I think he probably guessed as much the night of the accident, when he found me cradling her bloody, broken body in the wreckage."

"Oh, my God." Marina's face fell, abject misery in her whispered reply, as if she could feel the depth of his shame.

There was more to the story, but he'd said enough. He'd accomplished what he needed, had extinguished her pity and added more bricks to the wall he was determined to hold in place between them.

Her silence stretched. "Anything else you want to know?" When she said nothing, he tossed her a cold, satisfied smile. "Didn't think so."

He pivoted away and started for the door. He was less than ten paces away from his escape when her voice called out behind him, clear and crisp with challenge.

"It this the way you handle every situation you don't want to face? By walking away from it?"

He stopped. Stood in mute, rigid fury as the sound of her bare feet padded closer. She walked in front of him, the towel abandoned somewhere behind her. All that covered her from his flashing, transformed eyes was the skimpy black bikini that his fingers now itched to tear to shreds.

If Marina felt any measure of the dangerous ire she was stoking in him, she gave no indication at all. Standing toe-to-toe with him, her breast heaving with her outrage, she faced him head on.

"I'm supposed to trust you to protect me when I can't even trust you to finish a conversation with me?"

Color rose in her cheeks as she berated him. At the base of her throat, a vein beat frantically.

Cain licked his lips, preternatural impulse he couldn't control even if he tried. His fangs erupted from his gums, the sharp points digging into the cushion of his tongue.

Marina put her hands on her nearly naked hips. "Nothing to say, Cain?"

"I've got plenty to say." A growled reply, as rough as gravel in his throat. "You won't want to hear it."

"Try me."

"Wrong answer."

"You don't scare me, Cain Hunter." She hiked her chin up as she said it, sending that long ponytail swinging against her bare spine. Cain caught it in his fist. Twisted the damp, golden rope around his clenched fingers. Her head tipped back with the pressure he exerted, making the smooth column of her neck arch under his face.

"You want to know the truth, Marina? I wish I had left you on the curb outside JUSTIS. I wish I never would've seen your damn mark, because now I can't walk away and forget about you. Do I wish I could? Fuck, yes."

She swallowed, eyes locked on his. He should have released her, but instead he pulled her against him and inhaled, dragging the scent of her warm wet skin—and the unique roses-and-spice scent of her blood—into his aching lungs.

"I wish I was the kind of male who could walk away from you. I wish like hell I had more honor, because despite the mark that should be enough to make me keep my distance—despite the fact that you're withholding information that might yet get you killed on my watch— the only thing I can't seem to do where you're concerned is walk the fuck away."

Her breath sawed out of her in shallow pants as he held her ruthlessly against him. Desire coursed like lava through his veins, burning every last thread of his control. She trembled, her soft curves crushed into the hardness of his body. Her lips parted on a wordless gasp.

He stared at her mouth, wishing she would tell him to let her go. Hoping like hell she wouldn't. His mouth curved when she couldn't seem to find any words at all.

"Now, who's unwilling to finish a conversation?"

Before he could think better of it, he bent his head to hers and took her mouth in a slow, deep kiss. There was no gentleness in it. He had none inside him now that Marina's lips were caught under his. He had been craving this kiss from the instant he laid eyes on her.

And she kissed him back with equal fire and desperation.

Arousal lashed him with each stroke and sweep of her tongue against his. On a snarl, he unwound his fist from her hair and smoothed his hand along the sinuous line of her spine. She moaned as he gathered her hips against his, the ridge of his erection grinding into her abdomen, inflaming every cell in his body with the need to claim. To conquer. To fuck.

"Cain," she murmured into his mouth. Another soft moan, then a sharper cry when his fangs grazed the tender flesh of her bottom lip. "Cain."

It took him a second to realize she was stiffening in his arms. She pulled away on a strangled cry, the back of her hand flying to her mouth. Her eyes were wide with uncertainty, wine-dark pools rounded in mounting alarm.

She stared at his fangs, which he knew loomed like daggers behind his parted lips. The heat of his amber-lit eyes bathed her face in an unearthly glow. Her stricken expression cooled him off as effectively as a bucket of ice water.

She was terrified. Of him.

Of what he was.

"I . . . I'm sorry," she murmured, flinching out of his reach. She shook her head. "I'm sorry."

She swung away from him, visibly shaken as she hurried for the door.

"Marina, wait. Fuck."

He started to go after her, then realized it was better if he let her go. Better for both of them.

Keeping his distance was the kindest thing he could do for her. Especially now, when a taste of her kiss had only ignited a deeper hunger. One he wasn't sure he'd be able to resist.

Forcing himself to stand there, he bit off a curse and watched her dash into the corridor outside.

CHAPTER 11

Marina rushed into the corridor, her heart hammering in her breast. *Had she lost her mind?* She squeezed her eyes closed for a moment and all she could see was Cain's face, transformed from human to something otherworldly and lethal. She brought her fingers to her mouth and all she could feel was the graze of his fangs against her tongue.

She had seen the change come over him before, but never like this.

Never when he was holding her in his arms, kissing her with hunger that awakened a similar craving within her. Something that went deeper than physical desire. Something that spoke to a part of her she didn't dare acknowledge.

It shook her, how powerfully she wanted him.

It terrified her.

And if she hadn't broken away when she had, she

knew she wouldn't have found the strength to resist him.

Not when every racing beat of her heart was vibrating with the need for more of Cain's touch, his kiss, his dark, unearthly passion.

Even his bite.

"Oh, God." Marina moaned and picked up her pace.

The strings of her bikini top dangled loose against her spine. She hadn't even noticed Cain had nearly unfastened the feeble knot. She reached behind her, struggling to fix it as she ran. With her head down and her focus distracted, she didn't realize there was a wall in front of her.

An immense wall made of immovable, hard flesh and bone.

Marina crashed into it at full speed.

Or, rather, *him*.

Not Cain. Not any of the Breed males she'd met.

She had seen her fair share of intimidating men over the years. Vory soldiers. Bratva bosses. Not to mention Cain and the three other former Hunters in this Darkhaven who made all of those thugs and crime lords pale in comparison. But this massive Breed male skewering her with an emotionless ice-blue stare threw off a coldness like nothing she'd ever witnessed before.

She stepped back at once, retreating out of arm's reach of him, even though he didn't move at all. Not even a flicker of muscle reaction to her unintentional body slam or her mute backpedal.

Under the crown of his military-cut, short brown hair, his rugged face remained unfazed, unreadable. His bluish-gray eyes traveled over her and her state of undress as if she were inanimate, simply an obstacle blocking his path.

"You must be Knox," she said, feeling ridiculous in her bikini and not a little on edge in front of the male. "I'm Marina."

She didn't bother to hold out her hand. He didn't seem the type for polite introductions, and part of her worried that if she offered him a limb he might only snap it off. His chilling gaze narrowed on her as he drew in a breath through flared nostrils. His lips peeled back from his teeth and the tips of fangs on a snarl. "I can smell my brother on you."

She swallowed. "Cain's, um, just down the hall. We were . . . talking at the pool."

It sounded lame, even to her. Not that Knox seemed to care.

Those unfeeling eyes made another slow perusal of her body again and the flush that was still riding her cheeks from Cain's kiss. When he spoke, his deep voice scraped out of him like a growl.

"I've never been one for sharing, but maybe I should make an exception. I'm sure my brother won't mind." He grunted coldly. "Way I see it, the son of a bitch owes me that much."

Marina inched back another step. As she did, she felt a sudden gust of energy rush past her. It was Cain, moving faster than she could track him. He seemed to materialize out of nowhere, appearing in the space between her and Knox. And he was in a rage unlike she'd ever seen in him before.

Without a word of warning, he shoved Knox. The big vampire shot backward, massive shoulders and spine slamming into the side of the corridor. Concrete crumbled around him, dust and pebbles crumbling from the enormous dent hollowed into the wall from the impact.

Knox grinned, his blue eyes hot with sparks of amber. It was the first sign of any emotion he'd shown and it was pure murder. "Welcome home, brother. About time we finish what you started."

He flew at Cain. Fangs bared, the two big males crashed together in the middle of the corridor, locked in an instant battle for dominance. Knox plowed Cain into the opposite wall, the force of the blow sending jagged cracks in all directions. An instant later, it was Cain who took control. Propelled by sheer preternatural might, he drove his brother like a wrecking ball into the wall a second time, hard enough to make the floor shake beneath Marina's bare feet.

"Stop this," she cried. "Cain, please, stop!"

He swung his head in her direction, eyes ablaze. "Marina, stay back—"

The moment his attention left Knox, the male drove his fist into the side of Cain's face. Bone fractured with a hideous crack. Blood spurted from beneath his left eye.

"Cain!"

She started to run toward him, but his bellowed command stilled her. "Marina, goddamn it. Get the fuck out of here!"

She halted, but her feet refused to obey him. The fight raged on, a terrible impasse of power and fury, neither male willing to give an ounce of quarter. Marina stood there, terrified to stay and witness Cain and his brother trying to kill each other, yet more terrified to leave.

Knox's roar sounded anguished, despite that Cain had yet to land a single blow. The fight was evenly matched, but either one of them could have ended it soon after it started. Neither one seemed willing to deliver that final strike. Yet there was no mercy in their blazing eyes, nor in the thunderous clash of their bodies as their confrontation escalated and they repeatedly slammed each other from one side of the corridor to the other.

At that same moment, Bram rounded the corner of the passageway several yards behind Marina. "Holy hell. Look at you two fucking idiots."

His commanding voice boomed over the violence as he stalked past her and toward Cain and Knox. Lana trailed behind him, her face stricken with worry. She moved slower than her mate, keeping a safe distance from the fray, but also moving gingerly with one hand resting on the large swell of her belly.

Bram glanced back at her. "Baby, take Marina and let me handle this."

Without waiting for her answer, he grabbed Knox by the shoulders and peeled him off Cain. Knox spun around, face twisted with rage. His swing flew wild, connecting with Bram's jaw.

"Enough!" Lana screamed from beside Marina as the altercation showed little sign of ending. "Stop this, all of you. I won't have you fighting in my home!"

She was worked up, breathing too fast. She clutched her rounded abdomen as her knees wobbled. Marina caught her before her legs gave way beneath her.

Lana's distress finally got the attention of all three men. Silence fell over everyone.

When nothing else seemed capable of defusing the situation, the collective concern for Bram's mate erased everything else. Bram was at her side in the next instant. Murmuring quiet, urgent words of comfort, he scooped her up into his arms.

"I'm okay," she said, resting her head against his broad chest. "I just got worked up, and the baby didn't like it."

Bram's face was grim with concern. "I don't like it either. I'm taking you to bed."

He shot a pointed look at Cain and Knox, who both stood in the center of the passageway breathing heavily, concrete dust on their hair and faces, clothing torn. Cain's cheek was hollowed where his brother's fist had shattered the bone, blood running down his face.

"We done here?" Bram demanded.

Knox said nothing as he turned and stalked in the opposite direction of the corridor. After a moment, Bram and Lana went the other way, leaving Marina alone with Cain. She couldn't resist the urge to go to him. He stared at her, his gaze burning bright as coals. His lungs soughed, air rasping past the long points of his fangs.

She reached out to him. "Are you okay?"

He caught her wrist before she had the chance to touch him. His grip was firm and warm, then it was gone.

He stepped past her, walking away without a word.

CHAPTER 12

After burning off some of his leftover aggression with one of the punching bags in the training room, Cain returned to his quarters feeling less like the powder keg he'd been with Knox, but still on edge and unfit for public. The left side of his face was still as sore as hell, but the hour-plus workout and the long shower—a deliberately cold one—afterward had helped.

Still, he wasn't pleased to enter the open door of his room and find Marina seated on the brown leather sofa inside. She glanced from his damp hair and bare chest covered in *glyphs* to the black track shorts which, thankfully, were loose enough to conceal his body's increasing and uncomfortable response to the sight of her. He stepped into the room, scowling at her as she stood up to greet him.

"I asked Lana where to find you."

She wore a sleeveless plum silk dress that skimmed

her curves and ended just above her knees. Even in her black ballet flats, she was statuesque, elegant. Her look was tasteful and refined, yet Cain's cock reacted as though she were standing in front of him as naked as she'd been in her bikini a few hours ago. He glanced away from her without a reply.

"So, these are your quarters? The room you lived in . . . before?"

To maintain his willful avoidance of her, he let his gaze roam over the large living suite. The king-size bed, the comfortable lounge area, the desk and book cases. Not a thing out of place from when he last saw it eight years ago.

He blew out a sharp sigh. "I can't believe they never emptied this room. Hell, I can't believe no one burned all my shit after I left. Everything's been kept exactly how I left it. Who does that?"

"Someone who cares about you. Someone who hopes you'll come back one day."

He shot her a flat look and scoffed. "Yeah, I'm sure Lana and Bram are real happy I'm back now. How was she doing when you saw her?"

"She's fine, resting." Marina moved away from the sofa, edging closer to him. "She says the baby has been temperamental for about a week now. Lana's due next month."

Cain grunted. He didn't want to talk about family or things he was going to miss after his business with Marina was finished and he was free to move on again. "Why did you come looking for me?"

She frowned. "I wanted to see if you were all right after what happened with Knox."

"As you can see, I'm more than all right."

His clipped tone didn't seem to dissuade her. She approached him anyway, her wine-colored gaze tender as it traveled every inch of his face. His shattered cheekbone was already mended, thanks to his accelerated Breed healing capability. The deep cut Knox's fist had opened beneath his eye was closed, leaving only a bruise that would be gone in a matter of hours.

Marina reached up before he realized what she was doing. Her fingertips lit gingerly on the side of his face. "It's remarkable."

"It's genetics." He pulled away from her touch, refusing to let himself indulge in her comfort, or her concern. He still wanted her too much. Accepting even the smallest kindness would be a recipe for disaster. "The only medical care I ever need is fresh red cells taken from an open vein. And fortunately, I paid a blood Host for the use of her vein in Miami two nights ago."

"Paid her? Do you mean a prostitute?"

He shrugged. "More or less. I don't always fuck them, though."

She flinched, a subtle flicker of disapproval flattening the supple line of her mouth. Cain had said it with cold frankness because she needed to be reminded of what he was: Breed. Blood-drinker. The base monster her uncle warned her about.

The one she ran from in terror after he kissed her at the pool.

He wanted to repulse her, make her leave. But Marina only studied him closer. Her scrutiny made him twitchy, anxious with the need to put space between them. Preferably a lot of space, separated by a locked door.

She was undeterred, however. "To hear Lana talk about Bram, I imagined there was a sacredness to that part of their relationship. She talks about her blood bond with him as though it's something holy and precious."

Cain smirked, knowingly cold. "I'm not talking about a blood bond between a Breedmate and her male. Bram and Lana are linked for life. As soon as they took each other's blood, that shackle became unbreakable."

"You make it sound like a curse."

"I wore a collar for the first sixteen years of my life. I've got no interest in another one. I prefer to take what I need from human Hosts."

He could see the disapproval in her eyes. "People you pay to service you?"

"That's right. One and done. No exceptions," he clarified. "I prefer to keep things clean and uncomplicated."

"You mean impersonal."

He shrugged. "Even better."

"Because you're punishing yourself, or because you're still in love with the memory of a woman you would never have?"

"What the hell difference does it make?"

She folded her arms in front of her. "You're right, it doesn't. Either way, you're a coward."

Anger spiked inside him, and not because she was wrong. "Maybe you didn't hear me when I told you that you needed to steer clear of me."

"I heard you," she shot back, color rising into her cheeks as her stubborn chin inched upward.

"Yet here you are. Why?"

"Because you don't scare me, Cain."

"Is that right?" He barked out a harsh laugh.

LARA ADRIAN

"Seemed to me you couldn't run away fast enough after I kissed you tonight."

"Not because I was afraid of you." She frowned and shook her head, but those intoxicating eyes stayed rooted on him, penetrating all of his defenses. Her voice dropped, no longer indignant but softening with an honesty that rocked him. "I was afraid of myself, of how you made me feel. I ran from you because I knew if I let you keep kissing me, I wouldn't want you to stop."

Ah, Christ. It wasn't the answer he was expecting. Nor was it the one he wanted to hear right now. The temptation to drag her back into his arms and pick up where they left off nearly overwhelmed him. It shook him, how fiercely he wanted it.

Wanted her.

"You made the right decision," he muttered, his throat acrid, as dry as cinders. "I never should have let it happen. It's a mistake I won't make again."

He turned away, started to walk toward his closet to fetch a T-shirt. He waited to hear her footsteps retreat behind him. But she wasn't moving.

"That's it? That's all you have to say to me?"

He swung a cold glance at her. "Am I being unclear?"

"No. You're being a bastard. But I see through you, Cain. You're the one who's afraid. Afraid of feeling anything for someone."

"I can feel or I can keep you alive. Your choice, Marina. I can't do both."

Confusion knit her brow and she plunged both hands into the pockets of her dress. "I don't understand."

"My visions," he said, frustrated as he faced her

again. "They're only clear as long as I have no emotional connection to the person in them."

"Tell me about Abbie." It was so like Marina to cut to the heart of the matter. Her frank gaze remained steady on him. "Why do you think you were responsible for what happened to her?"

"Because it's the truth." He considered dropping the gate down on the entire subject, but maybe she should know. Maybe then she'd be the smarter of them both and want nothing more to do with him. He blew out a short sigh. "I used to be able to tap into my ability at will. When Abbie started coming around the Darkhaven to visit Lana, she heard about my gift and kept pressing me to tell her if I could see anything about her. I resisted at first. Every Breed male has his demons to contend with, and this was mine."

"She couldn't respect that about you and let it go?"

He shrugged. "Abbie was a free spirit, and she was persistent. One night she was here with Lana and she'd too much to drink. She asked me again, then started making silly guesses about one ridiculous death scenario after another. Finally, I gave in. I tried to call up my ability, but nothing happened. By then, I was already infatuated with her, so I knew why I couldn't make it work."

"What did you say?"

"I made some lame joke, then left her and Lana to have their fun. The vision hit me as soon as I left the room. It was disjointed, playing through my head in disconnected flashes. Not the sixty-second premonition I might see for a stranger, but murky images in random, rapid fire. I saw the explosion on the highway. I saw twisted, smoking metal. And I saw Abbie's body crushed and broken in the wreckage."

"Oh, my God." Marina closed her eyes on an indrawn breath.

"I couldn't tell her that," he murmured, his horror still as fresh as it was then. So was his regret. "It wasn't clear enough to do anything about it. It's not like I could tell her never to get behind the wheel of a vehicle. I thought it would only scare her to know."

"What did you do?"

"Her death was all I could think about—even after she and Knox became involved. They were in love, and everyone knew he was planning to ask for her blood bond as his mate. I respected that. But I watched over her in secret. Kept an eye on her apartment in Homestead, followed her home from where she worked at the hospital. Finally, one night Knox caught on to me after I came back to the Darkhaven. We fought. He accused me of stalking her, of having some sick obsession for her. In a way, he was right."

"But you didn't tell him what you saw?"

"I should have, then and there. Maybe it would've made a difference. But while Knox and I fought, I saw another glimpse. I hadn't seen one for weeks, no matter how I tried to call up more details. Suddenly, there I was, on scene at the accident, holding Abbie in the middle of the wreckage. She was already gone." He shook his head. "How do you tell a man the woman he plans to take for his mate will end up dead in his brother's arms?"

Marina got very quiet, holding him in a dread-filled stare. "How did that happen?"

"Knox left in a rage. Not long afterward, Lana came looking for him. Abbie had called her on the way home from work. A storm had rushed in. Blinding rain and wind. Abbie's car was stalled on the side of the highway."

Marina's blanched face said she knew where the story was heading. Cain cleared his throat and pushed on.

"I told Lana to try to reach Knox. Then I took off, knowing I could be there in a few minutes. I just wanted to get Abbie off the road and somewhere safe. I got there too late. I saw the flames and black smoke, and I knew. I got out of my car and ran to the crash on foot, praying like hell the vision was wrong."

He saw the whole night replay in his mind's eye now. The unbearable heat of fire and melted steel. The acid stench of burning tires . . . and flesh.

"I pulled her out of it, realizing there was no saving her. Nothing could have saved her, not even Breed blood. I heard a keening, animal roar as I held her. Knox was there. I'd never seen such pain in anyone before. I told him about the visions, that I tried to reach her before it was too late. He took her out of my arms without saying a word. I don't think he was capable of speaking in that moment, not even to voice his hatred of me, or his grief for losing Abbie. He walked away carrying her body and disappeared into the storm."

Marina's silence was almost too much to endure. So was the tender expression of caring on her lovely face. "Cain . . . I'm so very sorry. For all of you."

Her tenderness made him feel trapped, caged in with a flood of emotions he didn't want to feel. Least of all the soft regard he couldn't seem to control when it came to Marina.

He forced a dismissive shrug. "Hey, life sucks. And that's the fucked-up irony of my so-called gift. The only ones I can't help are the people who matter to me. I can see the last seconds of someone's life—and sometimes have a chance to change it—but everything is disconnected and hard to make sense of, when it comes to someone who means something to me."

She scoffed quietly. "Lucky for me, the most you seem capable of feeling toward me is disdain."

He should have let the comment go. Instead, he swore under his breath. "Is that what you think?"

"What the hell difference does it make?" She threw his words back at him, a pained smile tightening her face.

He felt like the biggest asshole as she pivoted and started to leave. Before he could stop himself, he stalked after her and caught hold of her hand. He gently drew her back toward him, feeling how close she was to breaking. He'd finally driven her to the brink of that, and it shamed him.

"Marina, fuck. I'm sorry." She didn't speak, wouldn't turn to look at him now. The hand he held on to was balled into a fist. He moved around in front of her. "You couldn't be more wrong about how I feel toward you."

He uncurled her fingers, intending to lace his through them. But as he unfolded her fist, he realized she was holding something in her palm. A small black device, the kind used for storing data files.

"What's this?"

"My uncle's freedom. This is what it costs." She let out a resigned sigh. "Not the two million dollars in the briefcase. That was only a decoy to distract from the real item I need to deliver."

Although he wasn't surprised to hear her finally admit she'd been lying to him, he was far from pleased to see the data drive in her hand. Nothing good could come from whatever she was about to tell him next. "What's on this, Marina?"

"Boris Karamenko's entire financial portfolio. Bank accounts. Passwords. Everything."

"Holy shit." He could hardly contain his astonishment. Or his dread. Two million in cash was chump change compared to the value of data like that. "Who else knows about the disk?"

"No one." She frowned and shook her head. "At least, that's what Uncle Anatoly and I thought. But Yury seemed to know I was carrying information. When he held the gun on me, he demanded I give him the files."

Cain's blood seethed at the reminder of her bodyguard's attack. "Could Yury have been Karamenko's man? A plant with hidden loyalties to the big boss?"

"I don't know. I wouldn't have thought so. He served my uncle for close to a decade. He was practically family to us." The sting of that deception was still ripe in her voice. "He told me he was never going to allow me to go through with the meeting. He knew about the sniper. He said since the shooter failed, he was going to finish the job."

Cain didn't like thinking about how close to death she'd already come since arriving in the States. Meanwhile, her uncle seemed insulated from the danger. And above his boss's suspicion or his wrath. All of which made Cain's Hunter instincts prickle to attention.

"If Yury and the sniper weren't protecting Karamenko's interests, then whose? If Karamenko or his men have been tipped off that your uncle is making a big move—not to mention using that intel to facilitate it—then it doesn't make sense to me that your uncle is still alive. Karamenko was standing with him like an old friend in that photo from the party the other night in Moscow."

A furrow rankled her forehead. "What are you trying to say?"

"I don't like this. Something's not adding up."

"You would feel better if my uncle was dead?" She blew out a shallow breath. "He's been navigating the world of Bratva for thirty years. He's careful. And he knows to keep his enemies as close as his friends."

Cain grunted, less than convinced. "Is it a friend or an enemy who's agreed to shield him in exchange for the information on that drive?"

"Neither, I suppose. This is a business transaction. The man I'm meeting is a Cuban named Ernesto Fuentes."

"Fuentes. Jesus Christ." Cain's molars clenched at her casual mention of Havana's most notorious crime lord. If enlisting Marina to cross Karamenko wasn't risky enough, Moretskov was also sending her into the orbit of a man reputed to have killed his way to the top of the food chain on the island located some three-hundred miles from Florida's Key West. "Tell me you're joking."

"It's all been negotiated. Fuentes should be calling me with the date and location for the hand-off anytime now."

The fact that she seemed well aware that her contact was the leader of the Cuban mob made him want to punch something all over again. Preferably her uncle, who was either stupidly reckless with his niece's life or willfully negligent. Either way, Anatoly Moretskov deserved a lengthy conversation with Cain's fist.

He took the device out of her hand. "You need to

turn this over to JUSTIS. Let your uncle negotiate with them for his asylum. Not you. And not with a savage motherfucker like Fuentes."

It was a good plan, the only reasonable alternative to letting Marina take this even one step further. But she was shaking her head. "I've already tried to persuade Uncle Anatoly to go to JUSTIS for help. He refused. He said he can't trust law enforcement to protect him. And besides, it's too late to change course. Those files are no good to anyone but Fuentes."

"How so?"

"Because they're locked with a complicated encryption. It takes two keys to open the disk and any tampering or a single incorrect attempt at either key will destroy the data."

"Shit." Cain didn't like the sound of that at all. Not when Marina's life was on the line. "What kind of keys? Who's got them?"

"I have one," she said. "Uncle Anatoly has given the second one to Fuentes. We'll unlock the disk together when I meet with him."

"No. No fucking way." Cain shook his head. "Then you're going to give me your goddamned key and I'll take it to Fuentes in your place."

"I can't do that. I have to be present for it to work."

"What do you mean?"

She swallowed. "I *am* the key."

He had no idea what she was talking about—that is, until she lifted her right arm and turned it over so he was looking at the thorny vine of roses tattooed on her tender, pale skin.

"The code is optical. It's embedded in the ink right here." She ran her fingertips over the top of a pretty blood-red rose on her inner forearm. "No one can access the information without me being there to unlock the first encryption. Fuentes has the second key, a numeric code he'll enter in tandem with mine."

Cain closed his fingers over the device and bit off a low curse. The temptation to crush the piece of plastic and circuitry into dust in his hand was nearly overwhelming. Marina likely sensed the direction of his thoughts, because she reached out and covered his hand with hers.

"You told me I could trust you, Cain. So, that's what I'm doing—trusting you with the truth. But I need to be able to trust you too."

She didn't move her hand from his. Her fingers remained wrapped over his, warm and soft, yet as tenacious as the determined burgundy gaze that also refused to let him go. Cain wanted to pull away. He wanted to rescind the protection he was honor-bound to provide her—protection her imploring gaze demanded of him now.

But he couldn't find the words.

Couldn't muster the will to break their contact, not even when he knew that maintaining his distance might be the only way he could truly keep her safe.

With his free hand he stroked the soft skin of her forearm, running the pad of his thumb over the inked roses and delicate tangle of vines. He couldn't see the code concealed within the design, but he was no longer interested in talking about her uncle or mafia business or the clandestine meeting that brought her into his life in the first place.

The only thing that existed in that moment was the feel of their joined hands and the desire to bring her closer. To never let her go.

Cain cupped her warm nape with his free hand. His other moved to deposit the data drive into the pocket of her dress. Using the power of his mind, he closed the door to his quarters and set the lock.

He was finished thinking about anything but her now. And the need to feel her in his arms.

She didn't resist in the least, melting into him as he bent his head and captured her mouth with his. Her soft moan vibrated against his bare chest, stirring a heated growl from deep within him.

The need that had ignited between them at the pool leaped to life again, burning swifter and hotter than before. His blood pounded in his temples, in his chest, and in the aching length of his surging erection.

He couldn't stop the eruption of his fangs. The sharp points punched out of his gums as he took the kiss deeper, needing to taste her, to claim her. All over his torso and arms, his *dermaglyphs* pulsed to life, the flourishes and sweeping arcs of his Breed skin markings churning with changeable colors as his arousal intensified.

Marina made a quiet sound as her tongue met his, stroking and plunging, teasing and taking.

Cain growled with fevered pleasure, even as their kiss careened toward a hunger he wasn't sure he could control if he wanted to.

It was Marina who broke the kiss. Panting and breathless, her mouth swollen and wet, she drew back from him on a shivery gasp. It didn't sound like fear. It didn't sound even remotely uncertain.

She reached up to his face, her palm resting lightly, tentatively, against his cheek. Her fingers strayed toward his parted lips . . . toward the razor-sharp daggers that filled his mouth. She swallowed, her gaze flicking up to meet his.

"Cain." She spoke his name the way she had on the balcony of her hotel suite in Miami that first night. As it had then, her whisper chased a bolt of need through him. Fire licked along his veins, inflaming every hard inch of him.

The glow of his transformed eyes reflected back at him in her wine-dark irises and fathomless pupils. No hope of gentling the way he looked. He was too far gone. Too hungry for the woman staring at his transformation from man to beast.

He held himself still, refusing to move when he knew if he did it would only be to pull her against him again. And if he did that now, he wasn't going to have the will—or the honor—to let her go.

But Marina didn't back away.

Her fingertips traced his lower lip, grazing the points of his fangs. Then her hand slipped around the back of his neck, the line of each finger searing him with an anticipation that wrenched an unearthly hiss from between his teeth and fangs.

She held his fevered gaze. "You don't scare me, Cain."

Then, as if to prove the point, she drew his head down, her grasp firm at his nape as she crushed her mouth against his.

CHAPTER 13

Marina thought she knew what she was asking for when she pulled Cain down for her kiss. She thought she was prepared for the heat, for the power, of this man. She thought she was ready to feel the dark need he stoked within her, but she was wrong.

Nothing could have prepared her for the erotic intensity of what Cain aroused within her.

Not because he was Breed, although it was impossible to ignore all the ways that he was more than any other man she'd known. More than human. Holding on to him was like wrapping her arms around a storm. Energy poured off his muscled body as he claimed her mouth. His tongue invaded, thrusting past her parted lips and stroking inside her mouth in a carnal rhythm as his big hands palmed and kneaded her breasts over the thin silk of her dress.

Her heart spiked with each startling rasp of his fangs

against her lips and tongue. And in the wake of each dangerous graze, heat licked through her veins, need gathering in a deepening pool in the center of her being.

She wanted more. Her spine arched with the jagged moan that boiled out of her, but she didn't care how obvious her desperation was for him.

"Tell me to stop, Marina." A low command, as coarse as gravel. Yet he continued to kiss her, to caress her. His hands moved around to cup her backside, fingers clenching her ass as he brought her tight against his hardness, leaving no question about where they were heading if she didn't pull away now. "You know what I am. Hunter. Killer. Monster. I don't have it in me to be gentle."

Reaching up, she framed his handsome face in her hands. "I'm not asking you to be."

With her eyes locked on the fiery orbs that stared back at her, she ran her palms over his broad shoulders and the solid muscles of his chest and arms. The elegant *dermaglyphs* that swooped and twisted across nearly every inch of his bared torso responded to her touch like living things, their colors growing richer, more pronounced. She couldn't keep from marveling at them. She couldn't resist lowering her mouth to them and tracing the mesmerizing arcs and swirls with her tongue.

Cain's fingers tangled in her hair, holding her to him as she kissed and explored. His body shuddered as she flicked her tongue over his smooth, hot skin. His pleasure only made her bolder. She licked her way over to the beaded nub of his nipple and suckled it between her teeth while she slid a hand down to cup the massive bulge of his erection over the top of his shorts.

"Ah, fuck." A groan tore from his throat as she

stroked and squeezed him. His pelvis bucked, the hard length of his cock swelling even larger in her grasp. "Marina."

Her name was a growl as the hand clutching her ass swept down to seize the hem of her dress and gather it roughly out of the way. His palm skated like a flame up the length of her bare thigh, back to the rounded curve of her behind. He squeezed firmly, possessively, strong fingers sinking into the cushion of her flesh.

The hand that was twisted in her hair tightened and he tipped her head back to accept his kiss. His mouth took hers, a savagery in the way he claimed her. She melted into his power, swept under by the demand of his kiss and the heat that sizzled through her body everywhere they touched.

His questing hand moved higher under her loose dress. With nimble fingers, he unfastened her bra, then caressed her naked breasts. She moaned at the pleasure of his touch, gasped at the sharp twinge of pain as he pinched her swollen nipple, rolling the sensitive bud between his fingers as his kiss continued to devour her.

Her need was molten now, lust turning her blood into rivers of fire. She groaned when his mouth left hers, then exhaled a ragged sigh when his kiss trailed from below her ear to the curve of her shoulder. The heat of his lips, the careful scrape of his teeth and fangs, opened a craving in her for something she was afraid to let take shape in her thoughts, let alone put into words.

"You taste so good," he rasped, his deep voice thick, hot against her skin. "Feel so good."

The hand caressing her under her dress moved down to the juncture of her thighs. He slipped inside her panties, his long fingers delving into the slick cleft of her sex. "Christ, you're so wet. So fucking hot."

She couldn't contain the desperate whimper that escaped her as he stroked and teased her sensitive flesh. Her body wept for him, desire swamping her in a need that was raw and urgent, and belonged wholly to him.

Maybe this was how every woman felt with Cain. All the nameless, faceless women he seemed to dismiss so casually. Maybe this was his true power—the ability to make a woman burn for him down to her soul, down to a part of her she didn't recognize and was too afraid to acknowledge.

Yet even if it was, Marina didn't care. Not right now. Not when Cain was kissing her, touching her so wickedly.

Sensation arced through her as he toyed with her clit, his thumb and fingers drenched with her juices, his hand flexing and contracting over her mound. She cried out when the pleasure began to build and coil, rushing her toward climax.

"Cain, please," she gasped, but whether she begged for release or some way to prolong the delicious tension he stoked in her, she wasn't sure.

Cool air skated across her behind as he lifted her dress higher. Her panties were gone with a tug of his fingers and a snap of renting satin and lace. Then his hand moved around her, slipping to the back of her thigh. He lifted her leg up around his clothed hip. Holding her against him, he ground into her with the steely ridge of his erection, giving her only a taste of the friction and heat and hardness she was starving for now.

Arousal flooded her, making her bold and wanton, wild with impatience to be rid of their clothing. She moved her hips against his, seeking a deeper connection, relief from the intense ache.

Cain's other hand moved between them and stroked along the exposed seam of her body. "Tell me what you want, Marina."

"You. Oh, God." She shuddered when his fingers cleaved between her folds, drew in a broken sigh when one long digit entered her, plunging deep. Her sheath contracted around him, shameless and needy. He added another finger then, stretching and filling her, yet only making her yearn for more. She rode his hand with abandon, with raw and urgent demand. "Cain, I want . . . Oh, God, I need—"

Her plea broke off on a sharp cry as her orgasm rushed over her. Cain showed her no mercy, just as he'd promised when they began. He continued to fuck her with his fingers, with the heel of his palm rubbing with relentless torment against her clit.

She was still spiraling on wave upon wave of sensation when she felt his touch retreat and fall away. She groaned, knowing her wordless complaint couldn't be mistaken for anything less.

Cain's chuckle vibrated against her. His transformed eyes were ablaze as he drew back to look at her. The points of his fangs flashed with his brief grin. "Don't worry, I'm not finished with you yet."

He kissed her again, then stripped off her dress and bra and shoes. In another moment, she was lifted completely off her feet as he wrapped both her legs around his waist. He carried her to the bed and deposited her on the king-size mattress.

His gaze riveted on her, Cain shoved down his shorts and stood before her like a god. Naked. Immense. Unearthly masculine and fully aroused.

Marina reached for him, greedy to feel the heft and strength of him in her hands. But he allowed her only a few strokes of his heavy shaft. On a feral growl, his hands settled on her shoulders, pushing her onto her back. She waited for him to cover her with his body, practically whimpering with the need to feel him inside her.

But there was no mercy in his molten eyes. Lord, not even close.

Spreading her legs wide, he sank down between her thighs. His dark head lowered, then he claimed her sex the same way he'd dominated their kiss. Hot. Ruthless. A scorching siege of her body and senses that incinerated all of her control.

She had none with him now.

He owned this wanton part of her, and God help her, but he knew it.

She was lost to him, and she couldn't even hope to pretend she would ever be the same.

CHAPTER 14

He told her he couldn't be gentle, and damn it, he'd meant it.

He had never known himself to have much honor, but he had issued the warning in the hopes that Marina would have the clearer head. Hell, he'd hoped to scare her off with the truth and spare himself the torment of wanting her the way he did.

Of craving her like the beast he truly was, down to his marrow.

The man who could never be worthy of a woman like Marina.

And a Breedmate besides, for fuck's sake.

That fact alone should have given him the strength to turn her away.

Now, nothing could save her. The first orgasm she'd surrendered to him as he stroked her with his fingers had damned them both. If he had any decency in him, that understanding would shame him. Instead, all he felt was a dark satisfaction. And a singular need to make sure no other man—Breed or human—could ever show her the kind of pleasure she was sharing with him tonight.

She was on the verge of another orgasm, her slick, tender flesh scorching his lips and tongue as he feasted on her sex. Cain suckled her clit, drawing the taut pearl deep into his mouth. She writhed against his face, uninhibited and wild. Greedy for more.

He couldn't get enough, either. As much as he wanted—needed—to be inside her, he couldn't drag himself away from the honeyed sweetness of her sex.

Or the strong, steady hammer of her pulse.

He could hear the blood rushing through her arteries and veins, could smell its unique roses-and-spice fragrance all too close to his mouth and the sharp fangs he struggled to keep in check. Saliva surged in his mouth, a Pavlovian response from the preternatural side of his nature. He growled in denial of the urge that swamped him.

No. *Fuck no.*

That part of her would never be his.

Only her pleasure.

"Come for me," he demanded, glancing up at her while he intensified his fevered assault. "I want to taste it this time. Give it to me, Marina."

She quivered and shook on his tongue, then shattered with a strangled cry of release. Cain had been on a thread-bare leash; watching her break apart for him snapped the last bit of his control. Gripping his aching cock, he came up on his feet and guided himself into place at the mouth of her body.

He was beyond the ability to take things slow. Her

sheath was drenched and soft and inviting. He buried himself inside her on a ragged groan, seating his shaft to its root.

"Ah, Christ," he uttered, moving within the tight fist of her channel. "Ah, fuck . . . you feel too good, baby."

Need racked him, ragged and raw, unstoppable. He couldn't drive hard enough. Couldn't get deep enough. He'd spent so many years chasing empty, anonymous pleasures with women of no consequence to him that he wasn't prepared for the depth of craving he had for this woman.

For Marina.

He had never known hunger like this.

Savage with it, he pressed her bent legs higher and rocked into her with an even greater ferocity. She clung to him, panting and flushed with rising passion, tilting her hips to meet every fevered thrust.

"Harder," she urged him, dragging his head down for a hungry kiss. "Don't stop."

He couldn't if his damned life depended on it. Maybe not even if hers did too.

Her fingernails dug into his shoulders as her tremulous aftershocks combusted into another swift and powerful climax.

He was right behind her. His release ripped through him, scalding hot and furious. He roared as it slammed into him, his hips pumping restlessly while the tiny muscles of her channel clenched around his cock like a vise.

The force of his orgasm staggered him . . . but it barely slowed him down.

He was still hard, still on fire for more of his beautiful Marina.

The glow from his transformed eyes bathed her pale skin in a heated amber light as he gazed down at her nakedness. He had hoped a taste of her would be enough to sate him. God knew, he ought to be. But tasting her, being inside her, had only increased his appetite for more.

He flexed his hips, pushing deep with a hiss of pleasure. When he withdrew, it was on a shudder of pure torment. "Christ, what have you done to me? I could fuck you all night. I've never wanted anyone like this."

She smiled at the praise, but glanced away, almost as if she didn't believe him. As if she didn't trust him to tell her the truth, perhaps especially while their bodies were still bathed in sweat and intimately joined.

After all the callous things he said to her tonight— not to mention what he'd told her about his feelings for Abbie—he shouldn't be surprised to see her doubt.

But he meant it.

He caught her chin on the edge of his fingers and drew her gaze back to him. "No one, Marina. Not like this."

He lowered her legs and spread her out beneath him, telling himself he owed it to her to find some tenderness. He'd given her the animal side of him, the savage otherworlder. Now he wanted to show her he could be a man too.

He kissed her again and searched for an unrushed tempo, even if he thought it was going to kill him. And Marina wasn't helping. She fit him too perfectly, and every small ripple of her body against his shaft sent a jolt of fire licking through his bloodstream.

He uttered a low curse, knowing he was fighting a losing battle.

"What do you think you're doing?" Her accented voice held an edge of demand, but there was a playful glimmer in her deep burgundy eyes. "I'm not finished with you yet."

She didn't give him a chance to respond or react. Slapping her palms against his glyph-covered chest, she pushed him onto his back and rolled atop him, straddling his hips.

Her body still held him nestled deep inside her. She sank down on him and rolled her pelvis to take even more, her sheath devouring every hard inch.

And then she began to move.

Cain snarled with the intensity of his pleasure as she rode him hard and fast and deep. A wave of possessiveness swamped him as he watched her take what she wanted of him. She was extraordinary, and not only because she was the first woman—the only woman—who challenged him on every level. She made him crave something he'd never thought he could have.

A partner.

An equal.

A future where he wasn't alone.

Fuck. He was in real trouble here. With Marina, he had a terrible feeling that he would never know any limits to all the things he craved with her.

And as they both chased the crest of another staggering release, he couldn't find the decency to regret it.

CHAPTER 15

S he woke to cold sheets and an empty bed.
Not that she was surprised to find Cain gone, but dammit, she was disappointed.

And embarrassed.

She hadn't intended to fall asleep in his quarters. She hadn't come here last night with the intention of getting naked with him, either, but that had happened.

God, had it ever. Her body hurt in countless delicious ways. Her senses had been obliterated, overwhelmed with pleasure and a gnawing, insatiable need that still smoldered deep in her marrow. Somewhere around her sixth orgasm, she had finally surrendered to a blissful exhaustion and drifted into a sound and heavy sleep.

Clearly, she had overstayed her welcome.

She didn't want to guess how long it took for Cain to extricate himself from his own bed and make his escape. A couple of hours? A few minutes?

"Shit." She sat up and took quick stock of her situation. Her hair was a mess, her muscles loose and achy. She needed a long, hot shower and a toothbrush, both of which would require her to slink out of Cain's quarters and back to her guest suite. Hopefully without being seen by anyone else in the Darkhaven.

On a groan, she slipped off the bed to hastily collect her scattered clothing. Memories of Cain undressing her made the act of putting them on again a torment all of its own. She couldn't purge the feel of his strong hands on her bare skin, or his wicked mouth. She couldn't deny how much she wanted to feel him inside her again.

Even worse, she couldn't pretend there wasn't a part of her that wanted to believe he'd meant the pretty, solemn things he'd said to her when their bodies were tangled together.

But they were just words. And sex was just sex, especially when Cain had made it clear he had no interest in anything more.

One and done. No exceptions. She couldn't say he hadn't warned her. Nor had she stepped into his arms with any false expectations. So why did she feel so stung as she fixed her dress and stuffed her shredded panties into the spare pocket?

To her relief, the flash drive was still inside the other pocket where he'd returned it. She had taken a big step, trusting him with the information she was carrying for her uncle. He hadn't been happy about it, but he wouldn't betray her. She believed that without question, even he had gone to the effort of taking the satellite phone with him when he left his quarters. The bastard.

Marina wanted to hold on to her resentment for his

strong-arm tactics and arrogant assumption of control. But from the beginning, she'd seen that Cain was accustomed to taking charge. He was a natural leader, a protector, even if he had been born and raised to be a killer.

In her gut she knew she could count on him. Her life, and the secret that would buy a safe future for her and Uncle Anatoly, couldn't be in safer hands than Cain's.

After the way he made her feel last night, she realized now that the biggest risk she could take would be in trusting him with her heart.

Marina slipped on her ballet flats then crept to the door and peered out. No one there. The corridor was quiet and vacant. Thank God. She ducked out and walked as briskly as she could without breaking into a run.

Unfortunately, from this area of the Darkhaven she had to pass the kitchen on the way to her guest room. The aroma of breakfast foods and coffee drifted out to the passageway as she attempted to avert her gaze and steal past unnoticed by whomever was inside.

"Hey." Cain's deep voice reached out to her like a caress. It stilled her feet and forced her to turn her head toward him, even though he was the last person she wanted to see at the moment. "Where are you going in such a hurry?"

"I slept longer than I intended." She gestured vaguely over her shoulder, hoping she didn't look as uncomfortable as she felt. "I need a shower. And fresh clothes."

Panties would be a good place to start, because standing in front of Cain with nothing on beneath her dress but her bra made her acutely aware of her own nakedness.

And that only made her acutely aware of how gorgeous he looked, obviously recently showered and leaning against the kitchen counter barefoot in a pair of faded jeans and a black T-shirt. His thick ebony hair curled damply at his forehead and around his ears as he chopped some pale green melon and put it in a small bowl on a tray laden with other wonderful things to eat.

Warily, she stepped inside the kitchen. "What's all of this?"

"Breakfast." His silver gaze locked on her, sending her stomach into a little flutter that had nothing to do with hunger. At least, not for anything on the tray. "I was just about to bring this to you. If you want it."

She didn't know what surprised her the most: The fact that he hadn't actually abandoned her to his bed after getting what he wanted from her, or that he would have come back to her bearing a veritable feast.

Her stomach rumbled in appreciation as she stared at the bowl of cut melon, purple grapes, and bright red strawberries. A small plate held two pieces of buttered wheat toast and a fluffy biscuit. On a larger plate was a serving of scrambled eggs and several strips of bacon.

"You did this for me?"

He shrugged an affirmative. "Have a seat."

She slid onto one of the stools tucked under the tall counter and popped a strawberry into her mouth, reveling in the fresh burst of sweetness that ran over her tongue. She couldn't bite back her happy moan, or the coil of arousal that unfurled within her as she watched Cain turn away to fetch a cup and saucer from the cabinet.

With unabashed interest, she followed his fine ass in those faded jeans as he walked away from her. Muscles bunched and flexed across his broad back as he reached into the cupboard, and on his strong arms his *dermaglyphs* danced like otherworldly works of art.

He filled the flowered porcelain teacup with coffee and came around the counter with it. In his big hands, the dainty cup and saucer looked like it belonged to a doll's set.

He glanced at her, his black brows furrowed. "I hope you like flavored coffee. This hazelnut shit was all I could find and I didn't want to wake Lana to ask if she had anything else stashed somewhere in the kitchen."

"It's perfect." Marina actually preferred tea with plenty of milk and honey over any kind of coffee, but she wasn't about to tell him that. "Thank you, Cain."

She could hardly contain her smile, or the flood of warmth that opened up in her breast. Apart from saving her life on two separate occasions and giving her some of the best orgasms she would likely ever have, this was the first real kindness he'd shown her.

He placed one hand on her shoulder as he leaned around her and set the cup down. Electricity shot into her veins as his palm settled on her. She couldn't move, could hardly draw a breath under the sudden flush of heat that washed over her, through her, gathering in the smoldering pool at her core. She should be sated after the hours they'd spent together in his bed, but all it took for her to be ready for him all over again was one simple touch.

His touch lingered, then began a slow descent along her bare arm, his fingers tracing the tattooed vine that connected the inked roses. He stroked the spot where the optical key for the data drive was concealed on her skin. "Thank you for trusting me with the truth, Marina."

She pivoted to face him, drawn toward him like a moth to a flame. His handsome face seemed too rigid, too sober. Unreadable in its stillness.

She reached up to cup his rigid jaw. "I needed to tell you. I needed to trust someone. And I do, Cain. I trust you."

A rumble vibrated against her fingers as he looked at her. In the depths of that stormy gray stare, amber sparks gleamed to life. He closed his eyes on a heavy sigh and turned his face into her palm. He pressed a kiss there, the flick of his tongue against her skin as powerfully erotic as even his most sinful caress.

All the doubts she woke up with a short time ago were chased away by the heat of what still blazed full of life between them. If anything, making love with him had only added fuel to a fire neither of them seemed able to contain.

"Cain," she murmured, spearing her free hand into his silky dark hair. "Last night was—"

"A mistake." He said the words with such certainty she drew her hands away from him. He slowly shook his head, his sensual mouth curved in a grim line. "It was a mistake taking you into my bed, Marina. But I'll be damned if I can tell you I'm sorry about it."

He caged her between his body and the counter, his hands braced on either side of her as he leaned down and kissed her. His tongue dipped into her mouth and he smiled against her lips. "Delectable. I never realized how fucking good strawberries tasted."

He kissed her again, deeper this time. Marina

moaned, wrapping her arms around his shoulders as he pulled her to the edge of the stool, wedging his hips between her knees.

"This is a very dangerous idea," he rasped thickly as she wrapped her legs around the backs of his thighs and brought him closer. The tips of his fangs flashed behind his upper lip. "If I loosen my grip on the edge of this countertop, my hands are going to be up your skirt before you know it. And don't think I've forgotten you're not wearing any panties under there."

She laughed and bit her lip, daring him with wriggle against his growing erection. "Breakfast is highly overrated, anyway."

"I wouldn't know." He grinned, fire leaping in his eyes. "But I'm willing to put that to a test. Let's take some of those strawberries back to my quarters and—"

"Bram, I told you I smelled toast and coffee . . . *Oh, God*." Lana sucked in a startled breath. "We are so sorry to interrupt."

Marina winced, wishing the hardwood floor would open up and swallow her. Cain's reaction to the unexpected intrusion was far smoother. He stepped back from the V of her spread legs, his strong hands guiding her knees together as he pivoted in front of her, using his body to shield her from any embarrassing exposure to his friends.

Bram cleared his throat. "We'll come back later."

"We are so incredibly sorry to barge in like this," Lana said again. "It's just that I woke up with this craving for buttered toast and jam, and when I smelled it from the corridor—"

"It's all right," Marina said. Composed now, she peered around Cain and offered the mated couple a smile. "Really, it's fine. Please, come in. Cain and I were just talking."

He grunted, but didn't contradict her. The massive bulge in his jeans would probably do that without any additional help.

Lana's curious gaze bounced between them as she entered the kitchen under Bram's sheltering arm. Only a naive fool would miss the current of heat that charged the air in the room, and the petite Breedmate's slight smile told Marina there were few things that escaped her notice.

"Are you sure you don't mind?"

"Not at all," Marina insisted. She slid the tray down the counter toward Lana. "Take whatever you like. I'm happy to share it with you."

Lana hardly hesitated. She picked up a triangle of toast and nibbled on the edge, glancing at Cain. "You made breakfast."

Not a question, and he didn't answer, either. Moving with predatory stealth to the other side of the counter, no doubt to give his body time to cool, he frowned pensively at his friends. "How are you feeling today, Lana?"

She gave him a dismissive wave of one hand while she munched another bite of the toast. "I'm fine. It was nothing. The baby is just a little restless, that's all."

Bram seemed less nonchalant about it. "This pregnancy hasn't been without a few . . . concerns."

"How so?" Cain asked, gravity in his tone.

"Lana's body is so tiny, and trying to carry one of my sons hasn't been easy for her." He stroked her long dark hair with reverence, love in the tender gaze that held hers. And a pain borne of loss. "I've told her I can be happy without children, but my beautiful mate is stubborn. Fearless to a fault."

"The other time was different. The problems started happening so early." She smiled sadly, but with a determination Marina could relate to. "We're almost there now, my love. You'll see."

"I pray you're right." He pressed a kiss to her forehead. "You are my heart, Lana. I can live without children, but not without you."

Cain's face drained of some color. "You lost a baby?"

"Three years ago," Bram said, drawing Lana close. "I almost lost far more than that."

"Damn. I'm sorry. I didn't know."

Bram nodded, speaking without condemnation. "You were gone, brother, so how could you know?"

"I hope everything works out this time," Marina offered. She hadn't missed how quiet Cain had gone, and she could practically feel his regret in the silence. "Your child will certainly have a wonderful, loving home. And I doubt better parents exist."

Lana smiled and placed her hand atop Marina's. "Thank you. I hope you'll be able to meet our son after he arrives."

"I'd like that too."

Until that moment, she hadn't paused to consider what her future might look like after she completed her mission for her uncle. For so long, a safe future and freedom from the Bratva's yoke had been a formless, changeable dream. Now, she didn't know what to hope for, or where that dream might take shape.

Two nights ago, the only absolute she'd had was the certainty that whatever her future looked like, it wouldn't include Cain. Now, she was finding it difficult to imagine the moment when she would need to say goodbye to him.

Sitting at the counter with him and talking with Lana and Bram over breakfast felt like the most natural thing in the world. In the strangest sense, it felt as if she had come home.

But not to any home she'd ever known.

A home she hadn't even realized existed.

More voices carried from the corridor as Logan and Razor entered the kitchen. Marina smiled at Logan, who had made her feel welcome from the moment she first arrived. The massive, dark-skinned Breed male shot her a wink, a broad smile breaking over his handsome features as he glanced from her to Cain. "Someone called a family meeting and didn't tell us?"

Razor seemed equally amused to find them there, but the only indication he gave was the slight quirk of his lips and an upward flick of one tawny brow. He dropped onto the stool on the other side of Marina, his loose blondish-brown hair like a mane around his ruggedly attractive face. "This looks cozy. We interrupting?"

Cain grunted. "Yes."

"Not at all," Marina and Lana replied at the same time. Marina smiled at her friend, who had moved on from the toast and was now digging into the fruit and berries.

"How was the hunting last night?" Bram asked the two males in a wry tone.

"Plentiful." With a smirk, Logan leaned against the end of the long counter. "Bachelorette party sailed in around midnight. Nothing like a dozen drunk babes in tiaras and miniskirts to liven up an otherwise dull night."

161

"Speak for yourself," Razor interjected. "By my count, you'd charmed your way around the carotids of the whole party, including the bride-to-be, before I finally dragged your ass out of there. Save some for a brother once in a while, why don't you?"

Logan barked a laugh. "Fuck that. You weren't even trying last night. Lately, you've been making it damn easy for me to outpace you."

Cain's low chuckle drew Marina's gaze along with Razor's. "Maybe Raze's tastes are shifting away from the tropics and toward more rugged terrain. I hear the mountains are full of good game."

Razor flipped him off, the two males exchanging a cryptic look. He swiveled his head toward Bram. "Knox joined us in town. Showed up about an hour before we were cutting out. He was in a hell of a mood."

"Not like that's a newsflash or anything," Logan said. "But Raze is right. Dude wasn't even trying to act civilized. I swear, he was hot to kill something."

"Or someone," Razor added.

Cain crossed his arms. "I gave him his chance to do that last night."

"No shit?" Razor narrowed his gaze on him. "You run into him here at the Darkhaven?"

Cain nodded. "Yeah, ran into his fist. We also did some minor demo work on the corridor walls down near the pool. You know how rowdy family reunions can get."

He was playing it off lightly, but Marina couldn't find any humor in the memory of Cain and his brother nearly tearing each other apart. The fact that she had been the spark that ignited their confrontation only made it harder to bear. Her heart ached for the friendship the brothers had lost.

Cain cared about the other male, even if he wouldn't admit it. That much she knew. But she worried that Knox's festering animosity and pain were eventually going to cost him even more than he'd already lost.

Bram cleared his throat, his stare fixed on Cain. "You two knuckleheads are going to fix those damn walls, by the way. And I mean you're going to do it together."

Razor snorted. "That ought to be interesting."

Cain's impassive expression told Marina the odds of getting him anywhere near Knox were slim to none. But he remained silent.

"Where is Knox?" Lana asked, her fork pausing on her third bite of scrambled eggs. "Did he come back to the Darkhaven with both of you last night?"

Logan shook his head. "No. I saw him take a blood Host into a corner booth at the bar, but next time I looked for him, the woman was chatting up someone else and Knox was gone."

Bram stroked Lana's arm. "He'll come around, love. He always does."

"Right." Cain grunted, a sober look in his eyes. "Until the day he doesn't."

A muffled chime sounded from beside Marina. Razor checked his phone and slid it back into the pocket of his jeans without comment or reaction. "I'm out of here. Gotta check on something."

Cain studied him, a vague but wry tilt to his mouth. "Give her my best."

Swiveling off the stool, Razor bared his fangs in a parody of a smile. "You're an asshole, you know that?"

"Yeah," Cain said, smirking. "But tell me you haven't

missed me."

The other male chuckled. "You be sure to let me know when the renovation party starts. I wouldn't want to miss watching Knox kick your ass in person. Hell, I might even help him."

As he headed out of the kitchen, Logan made his excuses to leave, too, and fell in behind him.

Once they had gone, Lana pushed the breakfast tray away from her on a sigh, her hands resting on her belly. "That's it for me. I think I'm ready for a nap now."

Bram kissed the top of her head. "You just woke up."

"Yes, I did," she said, glancing up pointedly at her mate's questioning gaze. "But now I'm saying it's time for us to leave Marina and Cain to enjoy a little privacy— and whatever else they were enjoying before we all intruded on their morning."

Marina never blushed, but when her eyes met Cain's a rush of heat filled her cheeks. She didn't have to guess if he was thinking about how good they felt together, or how quickly they could get naked and into the nearest bed. The glimmer of fiery amber in his gaze told her he was just as eager as she was.

Still, Marina didn't want to be rude. "Lana, Bram." Her voice sounded raspy and a little out of breath. "Please, you don't have to leave."

"I know, but we will." Lana squeezed her hand. "I'm sorry I gobbled so much of your breakfast. Who knew Cain had kitchen skills?" She shot him a teasing smile. "It's really good having you home."

He didn't respond, and Lana didn't wait for him to say anything. Looping her arm through Bram's, the couple said their goodbyes and walked out.

"Sorry about all of that," Cain murmured once they were alone again.

"You don't have to apologize. They're wonderful. Even Razor."

He smirked. "Now, you're pushing it."

"I'm serious. Your family is great, Cain."

She didn't miss the shuttered look that dimmed his gaze in the instant before he glanced away from her. "I've been away too long. Everything is different now. I can't believe Lana and Bram lost a baby. Now, they're struggling to carry another. Meanwhile, Knox is self-destructing in front of everyone's eyes. And Razor is hung up on a female he's stalking from several thousand miles away—"

"What? He is?"

Cain cut his hand through the air as if he hadn't intended to say that much. "Logan's the only one of us who seems to have his shit together, which is ironic as hell considering he was the most fucked-up of anyone when we broke away from the program."

"What are you trying say?"

"I don't know these people anymore. They don't know me, either. We were part of one another's lives for a short time several years ago. That's all."

"I think that's what you want to believe. But it's not the truth." He picked up the plate of cold eggs and took it to the sink as if the conversation was over. Marina slid off the stool and walked up next to him. "Growing up, I had everything I could possibly want. My uncle took me in when I had no one else. He gave me an amazing home, a rich and full existence with every luxury money could buy."

"I'm glad you didn't want for anything." Cain turned

a hard glance at her. "I don't have much respect for your uncle's choices, except for that. Because you deserve all those things, Marina."

She slowly shook her head and reached up to cradle his taut jaw. "I never had anything close to what I see here. The kinship, the bond, the love. All my life I've longed for ties like that. The kind of ties you have here, just waiting for you to grab hold of, yet you can't seem to cut away from them fast enough."

"It's easier to be alone."

He said it so firmly, she knew his mind was already made up. He pulled out of her loose grasp and she had to work to bite back the anger that crept up her throat.

"You're not going to be here when Lana and Bram have their baby, are you? You and Knox aren't going to patch up anything—least of all the rift between you. You're going to walk away again."

"And if I do? Why the fuck does it matter to you?"

"Because I care. I care about you, Cain."

"Don't." He exhaled a tight curse. "Jesus Christ, I'm the last person you should say that to."

"Why shouldn't I say it?" She scoffed softly. "Because you're afraid it's true? Or because my saying it forces you to acknowledge there's something happening between us? Something deeper than just a one-time fuck that you can dismiss and leave behind you like everything else that should matter to you?"

She wanted to stay and argue her point, if only to make him admit she wasn't the only one taking part in the wreck they were making in an already fragile relationship. But there was an ache building in her breast as she stared up at his bleak expression.

Her heart had formed a fissure where Cain was

concerned, and she was terrified to realize just how inadequate the word "care" came to describing how she felt about him.

She took a step back, needing the distance now.

Cain uttered a wordless sound of frustration as he reached for her nape and held her in place. "Your life is the only thing that matters to me. Not because you have a Breedmate mark on your ankle, Marina. But because I can no longer imagine the world without you in it. I refuse to live in that world."

His grasp remained firm at the back of her neck, his thumb stroking over the pulse point that kicked in a frantic tempo below her ear. Every fiber of her being arced toward him, her breath hanging on every tender, urgent word that left his lips.

"My first and only priority is keeping you alive, making sure you get that safe future away from men like Karamenko and any other Bratva thug with the capacity to hurt you. I *will* make it happen for you, Marina. You will be safe. And I will take out anyone who stands in the way of that goal. Anyone. Including your uncle, if I have to."

She shrank back at that, cold horror jolting her. "No, Cain—"

He gave a harsh shake of his head. "That's what my caring about you means. Nothing else matters but your next breath. If you're not ready for that, then you never should've let me touch you."

With that, he hauled her into the hard planes of his body, then slowly lowered his head and covered her mouth with his. Although he spoke of no mercy, of all the brutal things he vowed to do in order to protect her and pave a path toward her safe future, the kiss he gave her now was shocking for its gentleness.

She melted against him, giving herself over to the soft unfurling of her defenses. She had none with him, not anymore. If the gale-force power with which he'd overtaken her body and senses last night hadn't shown her that truth, this tender assault left no doubt.

She melted against him, into him . . . lost to him completely.

A low vibration pulsed at her belly. At first, she was so swamped by desire and emotion, she didn't understand what the insistent, electronic buzzing could be. Not until Cain hissed under his breath and broke their kiss.

The satellite phone. It pulsed again with the incoming call.

Her meeting with Uncle Anatoly's contact was finally going to happen.

Cain dug the phone out of his jeans pocket and met her with a grim stare. "Are you sure you're ready to do this?"

She nodded, even though her thoughts were scattered and desire-soaked, every nerve ending lit up from the revelation of Cain's kiss. "I'm ready. Give it to me."

He held the phone from her for a moment, his expression grave. "I'm going with you, Marina. Whenever and wherever this meeting with Fuentes takes place."

"He won't like it. He won't be expecting me to show up with a Breed bodyguard."

"Without me, there is no meeting."

The flash of amber fire that crackled in his transformed eyes left no room for argument. Marina took the phone from him and put it to her ear.

"Hello, Mr. Fuentes. Yes. My uncle Anatoly told me I should expect your call."

CHAPTER 16

The meeting with Ernesto Fuentes was set for nine o'clock that evening at a waterfront park on Key Largo.

Cain had to give Marina credit for how smoothly she had handled the conversation with the notorious Cuban mob boss. Leveraging all the advantage she had as the courier of the high-value intel she had to trade with Fuentes, and putting into play every ounce of the cool confidence Cain had witnessed in her from the moment he first laid eyes on her, she had not only secured a meeting time well after sundown, but had also insisted on a public, open-air location.

All without tipping her hand to Fuentes that she would be arriving at the rendezvous with the lethally skilled Breed male who was currently guarding her body.

That is, when Cain wasn't busy doing other things to that same incredible body.

Those other things were foremost on his mind in the hours after Fuentes's call. Marina had gone to her guest room for a shower and a fresh change of clothes, while Cain had returned to his quarters to gather a few attack and contingency plans, as well as the various weaponry he might need on hand should things go sideways with Anatoly Moretskov's criminal ally.

And all of his Hunter instincts were still prickling with the knowledge that the target Marina had acquired back at the hotel had yet to make another move. Yury's apparent sniper comrade had been a bur in the back of Cain's conscience since he and Marina left Miami.

Sooner or later, that bastard was going to lock his sights on her again. When he did, Cain would be ready. And if her attacker didn't come out of the shadows on his own, Cain would turn the crosshairs on him instead and hunt the shooter down. He wasn't going to rest until he'd annihilated every potential threat to Marina's life.

Because he'd meant every word he'd said to her in the kitchen earlier today. She mattered to him. In spite of all his determination to keep her at a distance—hell, in spite of the often cruel way he treated her and spoke to her, all in an effort to keep a wall firmly in place between them—he cared for Marina.

He wanted her.

Right now, with only a few hours before they would need to depart for the meeting with Fuentes, he just wanted to see her.

"Hi," she said, opening her guest room door to him after the first knock. She took his hand and pulled him inside, closing the door behind him. "I need your help."

Although it was obvious she'd been showered for some time, she wore a white bathrobe tied with a sash at her waist. Her pretty face was enhanced with its usual minimum of makeup, just some mascara that made her wine-colored eyes look impossibly deep and wide, and dusky rose gloss slicked on her pillowy lips.

Instead of leaving her long blond hair loose around her shoulders, she had gathered it into a sleek ponytail that rode high on the back of her head, giving her the appearance of an innocent girl-next-door who could probably also kick someone's ass if she needed to. It also bared the graceful length of her neck, and for a dangerous instant, there was nothing Cain wanted more than to feel that smooth skin give under the sharp points of his fangs.

Fuck.

He stood there with a hard-on rising fast against the zipper of his jeans and his gums prickling with the pressure of his lengthening canines.

"What can I help with?" He had several excellent ideas, all of which began with peeling her out of that robe as quickly as possible.

"I've changed my clothes four times and I still can't decide what I should wear tonight."

Not exactly what he had in mind, but he could work with it. For now.

Marina left him standing near the bed as she disappeared into the large walk-in closet. She came out holding two hangers in her hands, each with a different outfit on it. "What do you think? Wrap dress, or skirt and blouse?"

Both were classic and understated, equally solid choices that would command respect from anyone who saw her in them. Cain stared at the dove-gray wrap dress, picturing how lovingly it would hug her curves. A growl curled up from his chest, his cock straining now.

"The skirt and blouse," he muttered thickly. "Save the dress for me."

"All right." She smiled, a sparkle of invitation dancing in her eyes. Laying the outfit he chose on the edge of the bed, she returned the dress to the closet, then came back out and began to unfasten the knotted sash at her waist.

Cain reached for the end of the tie and reeled her in close. "Allow me."

He opened the robe and pushed it off her shoulders to pool at her feet. He'd hoped to find her naked underneath, but the sight of her in nothing but a lacy bra and matching panties was even more enticing. He cupped her breasts, coaxing the nipples to attention as he stroked his thumbs over the top of the delicate lace that covered them.

"You look good enough to eat," he whispered, leaning in for a kiss.

She sighed as he caressed her, dropping her head back on a moan when he scooped one perfect globe into his hand then bent forward to suck its tight little peak into his mouth.

"Even sweeter than strawberries," he murmured, flicking his tongue over her soft skin.

The scent of her Breedmate blood rushing so close to the surface in the delicate web of veins under his mouth and fingertips nearly undid him. His fangs ached for her, agony that was echoed in the raging throb of his cock.

Her hand pressed against his erection and he groaned with need. "I've been waiting for you all day, Cain. I want you inside me."

Ah, Christ. He couldn't even pretend he had the patience to take his time.

He slid her panties off her hips, then reached into the wet, silken heat between her thighs. "Fuck, you're drenched. So ready for me."

"Yes. Oh, God, yes."

She shuddered as he stroked her velvety folds and the tight bundle of nerves nestled above them. When he penetrated her with his finger, her moan and the greedy clench of her tiny muscles around him was more than he could bear.

He brought her to the bed and she lay back on the mattress, watching him with rapt attention as he stripped off her bra and panties then made quick work of his own clothing. She was so beautiful, spread before him like a feast. He sank down between her open thighs, unable to resist running his tongue over the glistening folds of her sex. She squirmed against his face, her hips bucking as he cleaved deep into her core and lapped hungrily at her juices. She shattered on a strangled scream, his name spilling through her parted lips like a prayer.

"I can't stop wanting you," he rasped, his cock on the verge of exploding now.

He needed blood to sustain him, but he had never known a craving like the one he had for this female. For the taste of her desire.

Possessiveness swamped him, too intense to be contained.

He tore his mouth away from her on a snarl and pushed her legs wide as he rose between them. He pushed inside her on a grunt and a hard thrust that sent him deep into the hot, wet fist of her body. She clutched his shoulders, wrapping her thighs around him with her ankles locked above his ass as he pounded into her at a ferocity and tempo he couldn't control if he tried.

His release bore down on him like a hurricane. When it hit, he threw his head back and roared her name as the bolt of pleasure ripped through the center of him, scalding and unstoppable. Marina's climax broke over her at the same time. She bowed beneath him on a breathless shout, the sudden arch of her spine seating him impossibly deeper inside her.

Cain rolled to his side and brought her with him, still sheathed in her heat and moving slowly now, easing them both back to Earth. For long moments, the only sounds in the room were the mingled rush of their breathing and the thundering hammer of their heartbeats.

When he opened his eyes, he found Marina staring at him. The tenderness in her eyes—the open affection—made it hard for him to find his voice. "Looking at me like that is going to get you nothing but trouble."

She smiled and dropped a kiss on his chin. "Is that a promise or a threat?"

"Both." He pressed his palms against the curve of her backside, pulling her into his slow, deep thrust. "Fuck, you feel good wrapped around my cock."

"You feel incredible inside me, Cain." She made a pleasured sound that only ratcheted up his arousal. "There's nowhere else I'd rather be than right here."

He groaned. "Now that we're both in need of another shower, eventually, I'll have to let you out of bed."

"Eventually," she murmured, brushing her fingers into his hair as she moved her hips into his. "But not yet."

He grunted in agreement. "No. Not yet."

Smoothing his hand onto the underside of her thigh, he bent her knee and lifted her leg higher, giving him access to plunge even deeper into the hot, wet haven of her body. He kept his strokes slow and measured, savoring the unrushed pace.

He'd have time to chase the roar of another hard release for both of them. Right now, he was more interested in holding her against him for a while.

With her leg draped over his side, he grazed his fingers along the tattooed vine and delicate flowers that snaked up the length of her gorgeous limb. "These roses were the reason I stopped to look at you on my balcony that night in Miami."

She smiled, a note of surprise in her burgundy gaze. "They were?"

He nodded. "The unusual tattoos, and the fact that the woman they belonged to was just about the sexiest thing I'd ever seen." He traced the petals of one blood-red bloom on her thigh, then followed the thorny vine to the next flower on her hip. "Why roses?"

"They've always been my favorite flower. They were my mom's favorite too."

"So, they're a tribute to her?"

"I suppose they are. They remind me of her. But the first one I got, the one on my ankle, was done at Uncle Anatoly's suggestion."

"The rose that conceals your Breedmate mark?" Cain frowned. "He wanted you to do that? Why?"

"He said he felt I would be better off if no one knew I had the mark. He forbade me to acknowledge that part of who I was. He believed I would be happier living as an ordinary person."

"Ordinary?" Cain scoffed as he stroked her cheek and rocked his hips against her. "That's something you could never be, with or without your mark."

"Well, he worried for me, so I did what he asked. After the first tattoo, I started adding a new one every year. I'm not even sure why anymore. I felt some need to mark time, as though I were waiting for something." Her eyes softened on Cain's. "Or waiting for someone."

He shouldn't feel the punch of satisfaction at those tender words. If Marina was waiting for anyone, she sure as hell deserved a better man than him. But that didn't stop him from cradling her lovely face in his hands and kissing her as though he never wanted to let her go.

When he finally released her, Marina moaned. Her desire-drenched eyes made everything male in him spike with dark, hot need.

"Maybe your uncle had a point, trying to keep you sheltered in his world. It's hard for me to disapprove if he only wanted to prevent you from running into a bastard like me."

She shook her head. "If not for you, I wouldn't be alive."

"Christ, don't remind me." He stilled, his blood ran cold just to think about it. Especially when she was far from safe, even now.

As long as she was carrying that data drive for her uncle she would have a target on her back. And for as long as Cain allowed Yury's sniper comrade to continue breathing.

As much as he was enjoying having her naked in his arms, the Hunter in him was itching to be let loose to do what he did best.

He caressed her shoulder and resumed moving at an easy pace inside her heat. "If your uncle really wanted to keep you safe, he should've let you grow up in a Darkhaven. Better that than raising you among the Bratva."

"Perhaps. But I was his sister's only child. As much as he disapproved of her choices, he only treated me with kindness. Except for one time . . . and that was completely my fault."

Cain grunted. "When you were grounded for trying to use your ability to get a bratty Breed kid in trouble at the symphony?"

She looked up at him in surprise. "I didn't think you were paying attention to any of my rambling that night."

He stroked the tip of her nose. "I've listened to every word you've said."

"Is that right?" At his sober nod, she gave him a cryptic little smile. "I was in a lot of trouble with him that day, but the incident I'm talking about happened a few years later. That was the first—and only—time I used my ability on Uncle Anatoly."

"Ah. I don't imagine that went over well."

"No." Her voice turned quiet, regretful.

"What happened?" He caressed her shoulder, waiting for her to explain.

"As a teen, I fell in love with horses. I rode every chance I could get, and eventually I began competing. I did that for several years, and actually got quite good."

Cain recalled Razor mentioning some of Marina's equestrian awards that first night he dug into her background for him. Sensing the darker turn in their conversation, he withdrew from her and gathered her into the shelter of his arms. "Tell me what happened with your uncle."

She sighed. "There was a horse I wanted desperately. He was a proven champion already, and ridiculously expensive. Uncle Anatoly rarely refused me anything I wanted, but this time he said no. I was upset, and very spoiled. So, when we were visiting the farm where the horse was stabled, I bent my uncle's will and compelled him to buy it for me."

Cain frowned. "He didn't know what you had done?"

"Not for a while. I don't know when he started to realize I had done more than talk him into it. We had the horse for about a week, and then one day I came home from class and Uncle Anatoly was waiting. He pulled me aside and told me he knew what I'd done. That I had betrayed his trust. I'd never seen him so furious. He forbade me to ever use my ability again. I promised him I wouldn't. I felt awful for disappointing him."

"You were a kid," Cain pointed out. "And he was asking you to reject something that's as much a part of you as breathing."

"But he was right. I had betrayed his trust. And no one does that to Anatoly Moretskov without paying a price."

"What kind of price?" Cain's jaw clenched. God help him, if she said her uncle lashed out at her physically, he might still decide to kill the son of a bitch. "Did he hurt you?"

"If you're asking if he struck me, the answer is no." She took a breath, then let it out on a shaky exhalation. "He's never raised his hand to me."

"Then what, Marina?"

"When he was finished talking to me, he brought me

out to the stables where the veterinarian was waiting. Uncle Anatoly told me he couldn't let me keep the horse after what I'd done. I thought he meant he was giving him away." She paused a moment, then pushed on. "He ordered the veterinarian to euthanize my horse. He made me stay there the whole time, until it was done."

"Jesus Christ." Outrage poured through him. "What kind of fucking monster—"

"No. It was my fault." She closed her eyes and slowly shook her head. "I don't blame him. I blame myself. Manipulating him with my ability was wrong. His punishment hurt, but it was a long time ago. I've shed my tears."

"And you forgave him?"

"That took some time," she admitted quietly, pain still shadowing her beautiful face.

"Come here." Cain shifted so he could hold her closer.

Lowering her leg, he pulled her against him until there was no space between them on the bed. Nothing but skin on skin everywhere their bodies touched.

"I'm sorry you went through that. All of it. Including your uncle's inability to accept who you truly are. You're a Breedmate, Marina. You will never be ordinary." He caressed her cheek, fumbling for the words he wanted to tell her. Promises he had no right to make. "If I were a better man, I would do everything I could to make you see that. If I were a better man, I'd . . . *fuck*."

He shook his head on a curse, realizing only now how fast he was falling for her. How deeply she affected him after only a handful of time together. He cared about this woman with an intensity unlike anything he'd ever known. It staggered him, humbled him.

And he couldn't deny that those feelings also filled him with dread.

All these years, he'd been so careful not to let down his guard. No emotional attachments. No complications. No fear of failing someone when it mattered most, because no one had been permitted to mean anything to him.

It had been easy until Marina.

And yet nothing was easier than holding her naked in his arms.

Her fingers tangled at his nape, her eyes tender on him, but smoldering. "Do you know what I wish?"

"Tell me."

A sexy little smile played at the edges of her mouth. "I wish I could make my ability work on you. I'd use it to make you stay inside me for the rest of the day."

He didn't even try to curb the low, approving growl that leaked out of him in reply. "Baby, I don't need any convincing to go along with that plan."

"You don't?"

His cock surged against her belly, beyond ready for duty. "What do you think?"

She laughed softly, but her humor melted into a throaty sigh as he entered her. They moved together in silence, settling into an easy, but building rhythm. Cain rocked into her with deep, hungry strokes, addicted to her pleasure.

She gasped his name and tilted her hips to meet his thrusts, color blooming across her throat and the pretty tops of her breasts as she climbed toward release. He would never tire of seeing her shatter for him, each shudder and sigh like a drug to his senses. "That's it, baby. God, you're so fucking beautiful when you come."

He slowed his tempo only to prolong her orgasm, yet nowhere close to showing her any mercy. She wanted him inside her for the rest of the day and he was more than willing to oblige.

"Oh, God, Cain. You feel so good. I wish we could stay like this forever."

Selfish bastard that he was, he wanted that too. For now, he contented himself with watching her break apart in his embrace. His name boiled out of her, the sexiest sound he knew.

His own release coiled tight and hot, a knot of burning pressure at the base of his spine.

The tether on his control was thin, but he held on. With closed eyes and molars ground together, he powered through the deep shudder that gripped his shaft as Marina clung to him and rode the wave of her orgasm.

When he lifted his lids in that next moment, her lovely face was floating in front of him, blond hair undulating loosely around her head. Her mouth was slack, eyes open but unseeing. Dark water surrounded her, dragging her down.

What the fuck?

He jolted. The sudden stab of confusion—and terror—speared straight into his heart.

He blinked several times, unsure what he just saw.

But yet, he knew. It had lasted only a second, but it was enough to chill him to his marrow.

"Jesus Christ."

No sooner had that bracing glimpse vanished from his mind's eye than another one, even worse, flew at him. Like a spliced section of video without a beginning or end, he now saw himself leaning over Marina's unmoving body. Blood trickled from her blue lips and onto her colorless chin. Cain's head filled with the sound of his own voice, bellowing in grief.

As awful as they were, he tried to call the premonitions back, glean more detail to help him make sense of what he saw. But they were gone.

Seeing Marina die once in that swimming pool in Miami had been bad enough. Then, he had been able to act on it, to thwart the trajectory of the event on the spot. These broken snippets, a mosaic of brief, murky seconds, gave no clue as to how or when or where they might occur.

He only knew with cold certainty that they would.

He went utterly still, barely capable of drawing breath into his lungs.

"Cain, what is it? Are you all right?" Marina's concern pulled him back to the here and now. She was staring at him, her hands gentle on his face. "What's wrong?"

He shook his head and rolled off her. "Nothing. Fuck. I'm sorry."

"What happened?" Her tone turned hesitant. "Cain, did I do something wrong?"

"No." The denial burst out of him with more vehemence than he intended. He cursed and sat up, swiveling to the edge of the bed and placing his feet on the floor. "You didn't do anything wrong."

"Did I say something that—"

"No." He raked a hand over his head, then stood up. "You didn't do anything wrong."

"I don't believe you." Her voice quieted, so uncertain it was breaking his heart. "Cain, you're scaring me."

He couldn't look at her. He was scaring her with his

shell-shocked reaction, but he was fucking terrified of the vision that had just flashed in front of him.

And he couldn't put it into words.

He shot a glance at her over his hunched shoulder. "I should go. We meet with Fuentes in a couple of hours. I have things I should do."

Silence stretched behind him. "Okay."

He grabbed his jeans off the floor and shoved his legs into them. He didn't bother with his black T-shirt, just snatched it in his fist.

Marina sat on the edge of the bed, naked, her arms crossed in front of her as if she were looking at a stranger now. He hated that he had done that to her. Hated that nothing he told her now would bring her any comfort.

He walked over to her and placed a brief kiss to the top of her head. "I'm sorry."

Without waiting for her reply or the questions that were sure to follow, he walked out of the room.

CHAPTER 17

"I don't like that this meeting is taking place on his boat."

It was the first he had spoken to her since they'd left the Darkhaven that evening. He glanced at her, his face solemn. "Are you sure you're ready to do this?"

Seated next to Cain in his Aston Martin at the Key Largo waterfront park, Marina nodded.

"It all comes down to this, right? Give Fuentes the power to ruin Boris Karamenko while adding more fortune to his coffers, and then my uncle's safe future is guaranteed."

"And yours," Cain said, his deep voice sober. "Most importantly, yours."

She wasn't sure if he sounded so earnest because he truly cared, or because he was suddenly eager to send her on her way to a new life somewhere else. Somewhere far away from him. He had been acting distant since he'd left her guest room that afternoon, had managed to avoid her completely until just a few minutes before they had to leave.

The way he'd bolted out of her bed had left her more than confused. It was hard to believe him when he insisted she had done nothing wrong—said nothing wrong—yet he'd abruptly stopped making love to her and couldn't get away fast enough.

Perhaps not coincidentally, his odd behavior had happened immediately after she'd blurted that she wanted to stay in his arms forever.

Cain wasn't a man who scared easily, if at all, but evidently the suggestion that she might want a future that included him was too much for the lethal Hunter to handle. At least she had learned that lesson now, before she allowed herself to fall any deeper in love with him.

"Here's the briefcase," Cain said, reaching into the backseat for the aluminum case of money and the data disk. "Remember what I said. Stay close to me and be ready to abort on my call. If Fuentes gives me any cause to doubt him, I'm taking him out."

Marina nodded, knowing there was no arguing that point with him. Taking the briefcase, she looked out at the moonlit docks and boat slips. A dozen assorted sailboats and cabin cruisers were tied up and bobbing in the dark water. At the far end of the docks a dark mega-yacht loomed like a sleek shadow, its windows illuminated with warm yellow light.

"Here come two of Fuentes's men now," Cain said. He grunted, sounding pleased. "Humans. That's a point in our favor."

Marina watched the pair of bulky guards who were stepping down from the yacht and onto the wooden planks of the dock. Dressed in dark suits that looked vastly out of place among the rest of the boaters who came and went from their vessels in beachwear and flip-flops, the two guards approached the end of the dock where Marina had been instructed to wait once she arrived.

"Okay, let's get this over with," she said, unfastening her seat belt. Briefcase in one hand, she pivoted to reach for the door handle. Cain's hand came to rest on her shoulder, making her pause. Confused, she swiveled to face him. "What is it? Have I forgotten something?"

"Yes. This." He leaned across the car's cabin and caught her mouth in a sensual, if fleeting, kiss. His gaze was sober, even grim, but amber sparks smoldered in the depths of his stormy silver eyes. He stroked her cheek, seeming to struggle finding words. "Stay safe, Marina. Do what I say. Promise me."

She nodded. "I promise."

His intense stare stayed locked on her for another long moment before he released her. He climbed out of the vehicle, and went around to her side as she opened the passenger door and stepped onto the parking lot. Cain's palm settled at the small of her back, his heat and strength reassuring as they approached the pair of dangerous looking men.

Marina walked ahead, shoulders squared and chin held high. She knew how to act in front of men like these. Years under the watch of her uncle's Vory soldiers had equipped her with a confidence she drew on now, as she strode up to Fuentes's guards and gave them each a cool nod.

"Miss Moretskova," the larger of the two said by way of greeting. "Señor Fuentes is waiting for you. We'll escort you to his vessel."

"Thank you." She took a step, but stopped short when the second man parked the flat of his palm against Cain's chest. She glanced at the guard in charge. "Is there a problem?"

"Señor Fuentes said nothing about expecting anyone else to be accompanying you."

The man still holding Cain back sneered. "Especially not one of his kind."

Marina swallowed past the knot of dread climbing up her throat. Cain's silence and lack of reaction only meant he was twice as deadly. The last thing she wanted was for this meeting to end even before it began. "I am Anatoly Moretskov's niece. I do not go anywhere without my personal security detail. I'm sure Mr. Fuentes will understand. If he doesn't, please let him know my uncle and I will be happy to take our business elsewhere."

The men exchanged a look, then the first guard touched the communication device in his ear and murmured to someone on the other end. He glanced to his comrade, then tightly shook his head.

"As you wish," he told Marina. "Señor Fuentes says your man is welcome. But we've been instructed to hold on to his weapons until after your business is concluded."

When Marina looked at Cain, he gave a vague shrug. His face remained impassive, devoid of expression as the second guard patted him down and removed a semiautomatic pistol from the back waistband of his dark jeans. A couple of nasty looking blades were confiscated, too, one from a sheath under his arm, the other taken from where it was strapped to his left ankle.

Only when the weapons were taken did Cain allow

the slightest smile to ride the edge of his broad mouth. Marina had seen firsthand that he was no less lethal armed solely with his bare hands. She only hoped Fuentes or his men wouldn't be foolish enough to test him.

She arched a brow at the two guards. "Satisfied?"

The bigger one indicated that she follow him. "This way, please."

Ernesto Fuentes was seated aboard his yacht on a cushioned velvet sofa inside a lavish salon. Warm, polished wood and opulent millwork paneled the walls. Brass fixtures gleamed beneath the sparkle of crystal chandeliers that swayed and tinkled with the soft rocking of the vessel on the water.

As wide as he was tall, the Cuban mafia boss didn't bother to stand up as Marina and Cain were escorted inside. His thinning hair was dyed inky black and slicked to his round skull with an enormous amount of pomade. When his dark gaze lit on Marina, an oily smile spread beneath the pencil thin line of his dark moustache.

"My good friend Anatoly neglected to mention how lovely you are. Please, come in." His smile frozen, he patted the small space beside him on the sofa. "Have a seat, my dear."

At her side, Cain's stoic silence belied the menace pouring off him. Before she could even consider taking the first step toward the man, Cain reached for one of the club chairs opposite Fuentes and pulled it out for her instead. She lowered into it without comment, setting the briefcase on her lap.

"A drink, perhaps?" Fuentes offered, disapproval in the flat look he gave Cain before focusing once more on Marina.

"No, thank you." She curved her mouth in what she hoped was a pleasant smile. "If you don't mind, Mr. Fuentes, I would prefer to get straight to business."

He chuckled. "A pretty girl with a head for commerce. My favorite kind."

At the comment, Cain's entire body radiated barely restrained menace. Marina pretended not to notice the change in the air, or the avid way Fuentes studied her as she placed the briefcase on the cocktail table between them and popped the locks. She took out the money, stacking the bundles of U.S. currency on the table in front of him.

"Two million dollars," she announced. "With compliments of my uncle."

He gave a short grunt. "And the disk?"

She reached into the case and unfastened the false wall containing the hidden compartment. As she took out the flash drive, Fuentes eagerly held out his hand. Marina glanced at him without relinquishing the prize. "Do you have your key?"

"Of course." He grinned and tapped his temple. "I've memorized it to keep it safe. And I trust you've brought yours as well?"

"I have." She held out her tattooed arm.

Fuentes's eyes widened with understanding. He wagged his finger, nodding in amusement. "Anatoly is a clever one. My old friend never fails to make sure his interests are well protected."

"He takes his freedom very seriously," Marina replied. "And he cannot be too careful considering what's on this drive."

"Yes. You are so right my dear."

The cryptic smile that flashed across the Cuban's

face sent a twinge of doubt through her bloodstream. He snapped his fingers to one of the two bodyguards posted in the salon and the man brought over a laptop and opened it for his boss.

Fuentes's gaze turned serious and dark as he waited for her to give him the disk.

Marina hesitated, suddenly unsure. Unsure of Fuentes. Unsure of the deal she was about to make. At the moment, she was suddenly unsure of everything. Even her faith in her uncle.

Cain glanced at her, his face tense with a similar foreboding. He clamped his hand around her arm, pulling her to her feet. "We're out of here."

"What the fuck?" Fuentes snapped. His two bodyguards reached for their weapons. "You're not going anywhere yet. Give me the disk, girl."

A faint thump sounded from somewhere above their heads. It sounded like a body hitting the roof of the salon.

"Shit." Cain pulled Marina to his side, hissing a sharp curse. "We've got company."

Someone shouted in Spanish. Then gunfire erupted from outside on the yacht.

"What's going on?" Fuentes shouted. "You think you can double-cross me?"

His two men held their guns on her and Cain, but panic filled their faces as the chaos and shooting continued outside the salon.

"It's not us," Cain snarled. He looked at Marina, his face grave. "He's here."

She didn't have to ask who he meant. His chilling seriousness sent an icy realization flowing into her veins. The assassin who had failed to kill her in Miami had caught up to her again.

Cain pushed her behind him. "Stay down, baby. He's not getting to you without going through me first."

At the same moment, the salon window behind Fuentes exploded. Marina hit the floor, covering her head as glass shards rained down and a massive figure in full black tactical attire swung into the room on a hail of automatic gunfire.

~ ~ ~

Flying glass, splintering wood, and a blinding spray of AK-47 rounds turned the yacht's ostentatious salon into a battlefield in a matter of seconds.

Fuentes's two guards were mowed down like bowling pins, both men dropping in dead heaps. Their boss was bleeding from a nasty wound to the side of his neck. He screamed like a terrified animal as he scrambled off the sofa to the floor.

Cain barely noticed the Cuban casualties. With everything unfolding in an instant, the only thing that mattered to him was Marina. She was hunkered down behind the cocktail table where he put her, arms folded over her head to shield herself from the falling debris as the sniper dropped to his feet inside the room.

Jesus, the man was huge.

No, not a man. A Breed male, built like a tank with a squared head and hawk nose. Beneath the black skull cap pulled low on his brow, his eyes crackled hot with amber.

With weapon raised at Cain, the male started to squeeze off another stream of bullets. Cain took a hit in the shoulder, but it was a lucky shot won at close range.

His Breed genetics powered him forward. He plowed into the shooter's torso, knocking the rifle's barrel up toward the ceiling.

Cain kicked out the male's ankle, dropping him to the floor. They wrestled for the AK, a stream of wild rounds tearing up the paneled walls and shattering the large chandelier overhead. When Cain smashed his elbow into the vampire's throat, the bastard howled and finally lost his hold on the weapon. Cain grabbed it, jammed the barrel under the bastard's chin and pulled the trigger.

Empty.

Fuck.

Strong hands came up, clamping around the weapon still in Cain's hands. On a roar, he flipped Cain off him and rose to his feet. The male was still choking and sputtering from the damage inflicted on his larynx, but it wasn't slowing him down. If anything, rage only spurred the assassin on.

He leaped at Cain, going for a stranglehold. Cain didn't give him the chance. He threw him off, sending the big body crashing into a sturdy wooden desk. The piece splintered under the force of the impact. Cain was on him in a flash, poised to drive his boot heel through the vampire's rib cage. But the male flew at him even faster. They went airborne, bouncing each other off the walls and trading punishing blows that would have already stopped a less disciplined opponent.

This Breed male had training and experience that went beyond the militaristic style of his clothing and weapons. He was professional, a born and raised killer. Cain ought to know.

"You're a Hunter," he snarled, his forearm braced

beneath the assassin's jaw. "Who sent you after her?"

Instead of answering, the bastard head-butted him. Cain snarled and shook off the pain, blood dripping into his eyes.

"She's a Breedmate, you asshole."

"You think I give a fuck?" The Hunter bared his fangs. "Hundreds of lives at stake. All because of this bitch and her uncle. She's not worth even one of them."

Cain scowled. "What are you talking about?"

On a roar, the assassin shifted in his grasp. Hot agony slashed across Cain's abdomen. Marina screamed as the knife tore him open. He staggered back. The Hunter came after him, the blade hacking and slicing through the air.

Cain caught the male's fist and wrenched it hard, snapping the limb. He jammed it higher, inflicting maximum anguish. The Hunter bellowed, but Cain showed no mercy.

"Who do you work for?" he demanded. "Not Karamenko. Tell me, damn you!"

"Doesn't matter who. And I won't be the last. Not as long as she has that file." The big male groaned sharply and broke loose, chest heaving. His eyes were on fire with murder, his fangs like daggers in his open, panting mouth. "The bitch has to die, brother."

Cain shook his head, feeling no kinship for the killer who would harm his woman. "You want her, you gotta get through me first."

"Your call."

They crashed together again, an almost even match of strength and savagery. Cain had to work damn hard to take the bastard down. But his rage had gone from volcanic to deadly cold and focused. With the big male pinned and struggling beneath him, Cain reached for one of the bodyguards' dropped pistols.

With utter calm, he emptied it point-blank into the Hunter's skull.

"Cain!" Marina was hunkered down near Fuentes, her hand on his arm. She scrambled to her feet and rushed over to Cain as he rose off the dead assassin. "Oh, my God, Cain. You're bleeding everywhere."

He set her away from him, still vibrating with violence and too on the edge to accept her comfort. "I'm fine. Ah Christ, you're bleeding too."

"No." She shook her head. "I'm okay. The blood isn't mine." She gestured to Fuentes's slumped corpse. "He's dead."

He ran his hand over her hair. "I don't care about him."

She swallowed, glancing down at the unmoving body of the assassin. When her gaze came back to Cain, her eyes swam with fear and uncertainty. "The things he said . . . about me. What did he mean?"

"I don't know."

"He said lives were at stake, Cain. Hundreds. Whose lives?"

Cain shook his head, hearing the confusion in her voice. And the edge of a reluctant, but deepening dread. He had his suspicions about her uncle before. After tonight, those suspicions had hardened into a cold certainty. Anatoly Moretskov had used Marina. He'd deceived her. Sent her out knowing she would have a target on her back.

Cain wanted to kill the bastard for each one of those offenses.

For now, the only thing he wanted more was to take

Marina away from the carnage that surrounded them.

He just wanted to take her home.

"Come on, sweetheart." He pressed a kiss to the top of her head. "Get the flash drive. This place is going to swarming with JUSTIS any minute now. Let's get out of here."

CHAPTER 18

B ram and Lana met them as soon as they walked into the Darkhaven.

"Oh, my God," Lana gasped, all the color draining from her face.

"It looks worse than it is," Cain muttered, although even that was probably less than reassuring. He had more bruises than he could count, and probably a couple of broken bones. His torso wound had finally stopped bleeding, but his shirt was soaked and hanging off him like a shredded rag.

Marina didn't look much better. Blood-splattered from Fuentes's injuries and coated in a layer of dust and debris, she walked in alongside Cain with sallow cheeks and eyes glazed with a kind of battle fatigue that made him want to gather her in his arms and not let go for the rest of the night.

Or maybe for the rest of his life.

"What the hell happened?" Bram asked, concern furrowing his brow.

Cain had filled him and the others in about the meeting with Fuentes, and the possibility that it wasn't going to end well. But returning home reeking of gun smoke and death had not been part of the plan.

Razor and Logan came into the room now too.

"So much for diplomatic relations with Cuba," Raze said around a smirk.

Logan's dark eyes ran over Cain with a decided lack of surprise. "Local news and internet's losing their shit over a war zone situation on Key Largo tonight. I'm guessing that's no coincidence."

Cain gave them a rundown of what took place on Fuentes's yacht. As he relayed the attack by the other Hunter and the cryptic comments about the data on Moretskov's disk, he couldn't keep from glancing at Marina. She had gone quiet, retreating into herself.

For a woman he knew to be so self-assured and determined, her withdrawal now told him how truly terrified she was—not of the attack or their hard-won escape from it, but of the questions tonight's meeting had raised. About her uncle. About the disk. About the secrets that still needed to be uncovered.

"You say the sniper was one of us?"

Knox's deep voice came from behind Cain. He leaned against the doorjamb, not quite part of the group, yet not fully on the outside, either.

Cain nodded. "He was a Hunter, but no one I knew from the program."

Bram fisted his hands at his hips. "We're scattered all over the world now. No telling how many of us escaped or where they are now."

Razor inclined his head in agreement. "And no telling when we might run up against a brother who needs killing."

Cain couldn't take any satisfaction in what happened tonight. He'd killed the fellow Hunter because he posed a threat to Marina. He would never regret that. But the act left a hollow in Cain's chest. In some fucked up way, taking his unknown brother's life felt as empty as ending a life on a battlefield.

Fitting, since the Hunter had shown up dressed for war.

"Marina," Bram said. "You believe the Hunter who attacked tonight knew your bodyguard, Yury?"

"Yes," she answered woodenly. "In Miami, Yury let on that he knew the sniper. They were working together to stop me from delivering the disk to Fuentes."

Knox stepped into the room now. "Was the Hunter a Russian?"

Cain shook his head. "No. American. I'm sure JUSTIS will ID him. A fleet of squad cars were screaming down the highway as Marina and I were heading back here."

"News reports didn't mention any Breed among the dead," Logan said.

"You sure about that?"

Razor backed up Logan's statement. "Just Fuentes and his entire yacht crew. It's all over the TV and internet. We're talking major international incident."

"No way. He's dead. I made sure of it." Cain glanced at Marina, who nodded in confirmation. "It's not like he was going to get up and walk out of there. That is, unless someone else removed his body from the scene."

Knox grunted. "Can you think of any reason JUSTIS

199

would want to keep a dead Hunter off the record?"

"Only one," Cain said, and Knox's shrewd gaze said he was on the same page. "He was working for them."

"Working for JUSTIS?" Marina recoiled as if she'd been physically struck. "Then what about Yury? He'd been part of my uncle's security detail for some ten years."

The pieces were starting to fit together. Cain's instincts prickled with an answer he hoped was incorrect, at least for Marina's sake. Because if he was right, her entire world was about to blow up in her face.

"We need to know what's in that file."

She swallowed, staring up at him. "You're right. I need the truth. We all need to know the truth."

"Yes," Cain agreed. "But as you said, the file is locked and encrypted. We can't hack it without destroying the contents. Without knowing Fuentes's key, our hands are tied."

"I know." Some of the strength returned to her voice now. "I know we needed his key to open it. That's why I took it from him."

"What?"

"Before he died, I used my ability on him. I bent his will, made him tell me the code my uncle gave him."

Holy hell. Cain exhaled a short sigh, marveling at the resourcefulness—the smart and steady courage—of this woman.

His woman.

He kissed her in front of everyone in the room, holding her beautiful face in his bloodstained hands. "You're fucking amazing. Do you know that?"

The ghost of a smile played across her pale lips.

"You've got the disk and both keys?" Raze asked. At

her nod, he grinned. "Then what are we waiting for? Let's crack the son of a bitch open and see what's inside."

Everyone moved to Razor's quarters. He had every computer and electronic device imaginable, and it took him all of a minute to be ready for Marina's instructions with the data drive.

"The program will prompt you for the keys once you plug in the device," she told him. "The encryption is going to look for a tandem key. Use the camera to scan this tattoo. At the same time, you'll need to enter this numeric code."

She recited a ten-digit number and Raze scribbled it down. "Got it. Let's go."

Cain stood back, watching in anticipation as the program accepted the pair of keys and a folder of data files opened on one of the large monitors mounted on the wall.

"The file names are coded," Razor said. "We'll have to open them up individually to see what they contain."

He clicked a random file and the screen filled with a dossier of a JUSTIS agent working undercover in a terror cell in Morocco. Photos. Name. Cover story. Field reports.

No one said a word as Raze moved on to the next file.

Another JUSTIS agent, this one embedded in a Romanian trafficking ring.

A third detailed a JUSTIS agent with a dozen different identities, all of them spelled out in the dossier.

Raze opened another, and then another. More than a few files identified agents working inside Cuba, some embedded in Ernesto Fuentes's inner circle.

There were easily hundreds of confidential dossiers contained on the disk. They all contained the same kind of personal information and assignment data as the rest. The kind of information that could get a JUSTIS operative killed.

The kind of information, if it fell into the wrong hands, that would be worth even more than Boris Karamenko's bank accounts and passwords.

"Holy shit," Bram hissed. "Every one of these files is someone's life."

Razor opened one more and as a photo came up of a menacing Breed male with a block head and raptor's nose, Cain's blood went cold. "Fuck, that's him. The Hunter I killed tonight. He'd been working with JUSTIS for eleven years."

Standing just behind him, Marina made a strangled noise. Cain glanced back and found her staring at the monitor as if her heart were being torn out of her chest.

"These are good people, Cain. Hundreds of them . . . just like that man said tonight." She held his gaze bleakly. "This has nothing to do with neutralizing Boris Karamenko. If Uncle Anatoly is trying to buy his freedom, he's doing it on these people's lives. Why would he do that? How could he do it?"

Cain pressed his lips together, unsure what to say to make her feel better. Everything she said was true. He knew how badly she must be hurting to see it all unravel before her now.

Raze kept opening files, until the faces and documents began to blur in front of Cain's eyes. He was livid for Moretskov's deception. Not only because it jeopardized people who had committed their lives to good and dangerous work, but because of the pain that deception was inflicting on Marina.

"Enough," Cain murmured, placing his hand on Raze's shoulder. "We've seen enough."

He turned to look at Marina, but she was gone.

CHAPTER 19

Marina stood in the shower of her guest room, her head bowed under the spray, hands braced against the tiles in front of her as the hot water poured over her naked body. She felt wrung out, standing in a shell-shocked daze as a river of blood and grime swirled into the drain at her feet.

The ordeal on Fuentes's yacht had left her shaken, but it was the opening of the data files that had rocked her to her core. All those names and faces. All those men and women risking their lives in dangerous, covert operations for law enforcement. And her uncle had intended to sell them out to the highest bidder.

She wanted to deny it. She wanted to rationalize some excuse for how confidential JUSTIS data could have ended up on the disk instead of what he'd claimed it held. She wanted to believe it was some kind of mistake.

But it was true.

Uncle Anatoly had lied to her. He had made her complicit in a heartless, heinous crime. He had been using her, just as Cain suggested. She had been nothing but a pawn and a patsy, and her fool's errand might have gotten her killed any number of ways.

If that file of JUSTIS agent dossiers had actually fallen into the hands of someone like Ernesto Fuentes, she would also be a murderer.

A fresh wave of guilt and outrage swamped her. She wasn't sure if she was holding back the tears that burned her eyes, or if the torrent of steaming water simply washed them away. She moved farther under and turned the lever to the highest, hottest setting.

It wouldn't be enough. She didn't think she would ever feel totally clean again.

Warm hands reached around her, drawing her gently out from the downpour.

"Hey." Cain turned her around in his embrace, smoothing her wet, plastered hair out of her face.

He was still dressed. Water soaked his torn and bloodied T-shirt and dark jeans he'd had on when they met with Fuentes. He gathered her to him and held her for a long while, saying nothing.

When Marina finally found her voice, it came out choked and rusty. "He was right, Cain. That Hunter, all of the things he said tonight. He was right. My life isn't worth any of those others."

Cain's lips pressed against the top of her head. "Not true. Your life is worth everything."

She drew back, lifting her gaze to his. "He was only trying to do what was right, and we killed him."

"No, love. I killed him. Not you." Cain's eyes were

tender on her. "And right or wrong, no matter what reason, I would do it all over again if it meant keeping you alive."

As miserable as she felt toward herself, she couldn't help nestling into his touch when he reached out to stroke the side of her face. "I just keep thinking about Yury and the fact that he must have been working with JUSTIS too. No wonder he looked at me with such contempt that night in Miami. He actually believed I was willing to jeopardize the lives of all those people in order to help my uncle? Never. I never would've done that. I would have found a way to stop him."

Nodding, Cain rubbed his thumb over her cheek. "Your uncle knew that too. That's exactly why he didn't tell you the truth about the intel you were carrying."

"I just feel so foolish. I'm angry at myself for trusting him."

"Don't be angry at yourself for that. He deserves all the blame."

"I've been trying to come up with explanations that don't make him a monster, but I can't think of a single one. Nothing he can say will excuse this, but there's a part of me that needs to understand. I want him to tell me why. I want to force him to look me in the eye and explain how he could use me like this."

Cain's expression turned grim. "No, sweetheart. You're not going to do any such thing. His reasons don't matter. Not now. All that matters is we stopped him. And you're here, safe in my arms."

His kiss was gentle and chaste against her lips, and regardless of the tumult of distress that had been churning inside her the past few hours, her body responded to the feel of his mouth on hers. Would there ever be an instance when she didn't desire him? When she didn't yearn for his touch, or the heat of his smoldering gaze?

She stepped in close again, starved for his comfort as much as she craved the feel of him against her. He traced the lines of the roses inked onto her arm.

"We need to turn the intel over to JUSTIS, Marina." He seemed to be choosing his words carefully, sensitive to what they might cost her. "We need to turn him over to them as well. Let law enforcement do what must be done."

Even knowing he was right, this hurt. In spite of her outrage, she wanted to believe there was some good in her uncle. Otherwise, her entire life had been a lie. And then what did that leave her with?

"He's all I've ever had, Cain. My only family." She swallowed the raw ache in the back of her throat. "I only had my mom for three short years. Years I hardly remember. Uncle Anatoly was the only person who ever cared about me."

"You have someone else now too."

He cupped her face, his strong hands impossibly tender. He brushed his lips over hers, teasing the seam of her mouth with his tongue. She let him in, sighing as some of the distress and anguish fell away, melted off her by the heat of his kiss.

She moved her hands over his shoulders, needing to feel his skin against hers. "You're overdressed for the shower."

His smile was dark and wicked with agreement. Together they peeled away his ragged T-shirt and drenched jeans, careful of the torso wound that had ceased bleeding yet still looked serious and painful.

LARA ADRIAN

Marina dropped his clothes in a wet heap on the built-in bench inside the spacious glass enclosure, then reached for the soap.

"Does this hurt?" she asked, sliding her lathered hands over his bruised chest.

He gave a faint shake of his head, his eyes simmering as he watched her move on to his biceps and down the length of his arms. His *dermaglyphs* began to fill with deep colors, changing from a shade darker than his golden skin tone to variegated shades of indigo, wine, and gold.

"I love watching your *glyphs* come alive like this," she said, following their pattern with her fingertips and marveling at how the elaborate arcs and flourishes responded to her lightest touch. She moved more gingerly over his abdomen, wincing at the memory of how the Hunter had slashed him open. "I was so scared tonight, Cain. I hate that you're suffering because of me."

"Suffering?" His fingers speared into her hair and wrapped warmly around her nape. "The only suffering I'm feeling is the need to be inside you."

His erection had been hard against her from the moment he held her against him. Now that he was naked, it jutted long and thick between their soapy bodies, a column of heat and power that called to the wildness in her that belonged solely to this man. This magnificent Breed male who held her heart in his hands.

She reached down and stroked his length, a spiral of hot need coiling through her as his cock kicked in her grasp, surging even larger. He dropped his head back on a groan while she caressed and squeezed him, her fingers dancing over his balls before sliding up the underside of his steely shaft to the broad, velvet-soft crown.

208

Pooling heat gathered in her core, stirring a hunger she couldn't resist. She sank into a crouch before him, still stroking him as she admired the masculine power and beauty of his body. His hand tangled in her hair, then tightened into a fist when she ran her tongue from base to tip. When she closed her mouth over the head of his cock, he hissed a tight curse.

"Ah, fuck. Your mouth is like a furnace." He moaned, hips bucking against her as she savored him. "So fucking good, baby."

She could have sucked and licked him all night, but it didn't take long before he urged her up to her feet. He took her mouth in a savage kiss, his tongue plumbing deep, fangs rasping against her lips.

His touch roamed her body, one hand ultimately sliding between her legs. She gasped as he delved inside her, his thumb teasing her clit while his fingers stroked her.

"I've never felt anything so soft. I have to be in you now, Marina."

Already on the verge of climax, all she could do was whimper as his touch slipped away. He turned her around in front of him, guiding her hands to the tiled wall. His muscled body seared her everywhere it pressed against her as his cock slid inside her, one slow, delicious inch at a time. She shuddered with the pleasure of it, moaning in bliss as he stretched her, filled her, consumed her.

His low growl vibrated into her veins, into her marrow. "I didn't come in here looking to get off, but holy hell, Marina." He rocked against her, long and unrushed, each thrust sending her higher and higher toward release. "I need to feel you come. I need to know you need this as much as I do."

"Yes," she gasped, her orgasm roaring up on her. "Oh, God, Cain . . . yes."

As soon as she cried out, he pulled her hips back and powered into her with new urgency. When he came, it was on a roar and a thrust that drove him so deep she didn't know where he ended and she began.

Even then, he didn't stop moving. Not for a long while, until the water had run cold, her arms aching, thighs quivering against his.

He turned off the shower and carefully helped her straighten. He kissed her sweetly, hungrily, his pupils narrowed slits in the fiery blaze of his transformed eyes.

"That was amazing." He kissed the tip of her nose. "You're amazing."

"So are y—" She touched his torso and her hand came away bloody. "Oh, shit. Cain, your wound is torn open."

He grunted, sounding totally unconcerned. "I'll heal. It'll just take a little time."

She knew the severe laceration would have been enough to send a mortal man to the hospital, if not the morgue. Cain's Breed genetics gave him an accelerated healing ability, but even still, he had to be in pain. He needed something more than just a little time.

"You need blood."

A brief frown furrowed his brow. "Not for a few days. I'm fine."

Her heart ached for the injury he'd taken while protecting her. She wanted to help, but she also wanted to give him comfort. She wanted to give him all he could ever need.

"You can take mine."

He moved back as if she'd just grown horns. "No. Jesus Christ. No, Marina. You don't know what you're offering."

"Yes, I do." She couldn't believe she was saying it. Not because she had any doubts, but because she didn't think she could ever want anything more than this. A blood bond. With him. "You need blood, Cain. If you want mine—"

"No." He stepped out of the shower, almost faster than she could track him. Even that didn't seem far enough for him. He grabbed a towel and slung it around his hips. When he glanced at her now, his eyes were still blazing, but also lit with something that looked a lot like fear. "One taste is forever. There's no taking it back."

She couldn't pretend she wasn't stung. Worse than stung, bereft. "Oh, that's right. And that's the last thing you want, a shackle you can never break."

He cursed under his breath. "That's not what I meant, not with you."

"No?" She sounded bitter, but she couldn't help it. She had lost so much tonight, but none of it hurt like the thought of losing him. If she'd ever truly had him. "I suppose I should have gotten a clue when you bolted out of my bed earlier tonight, after I mentioned the word forever."

"What?" His scowl deepened. "That's not why I left. You have it all wrong, Marina."

She pulled on her robe and followed him into the living area of the guest room. His long strides carried him toward the closed door. "If I'm wrong, then why are you leaving right now? Why does the idea that I care for you—that I—" She bit back the confession that leaped to her tongue, the terrible truth that she had fallen in love with him. "Why does the fact that I want to be with you make you so eager to walk away?"

He stopped cold. It took him a moment before he pivoted to look at her. "I'm hurting you. I never wanted that, Marina. Coming here like this, right now, was a mistake. And I'm . . . sorry."

"A mistake." Some of the air squeezed out of the room. "What are you talking about?"

He let out a breath, his face rife with torment. "I saw another vision today, while I was inside you. I saw you in murky water. You had stopped breathing, Marina. You had drowned. And I was there too. I tried to save you, but . . ."

"That's why you acted so strangely." She swallowed. "What exactly did you see? Where were we? How did it happen? When?"

"I don't know any of those answers. All I saw was a glimpse. Only a couple of seconds, no more. Not enough to make any sense of it. Not enough to do anything to change what I saw . . . except try to stay away from you." He scoffed. "Obviously, I'm doing a damn fine job of that so far."

Marina walked toward him. "Cain, it doesn't matter what you saw. If my fate's decided, neither one of us can change it. Your vision doesn't scare me."

"It should. Christ, it sure as fuck scares me."

"So, you're just going to walk away? It's that easy for you?"

He shook his head. "No, it's not easy. Staying away from you will be the hardest thing I'll ever do. But I'll do it, if it means preventing what I saw from coming true."

Understanding settled on her, but it brought little relief. He was leaving her because he hadn't been able to save Abbie.

"I'm not her, Cain."

"I know that." His reply was sober, as grim as his gaze. "You're not her, and I never wanted you to be. I never wanted Abbie the way I want you, Marina. I never loved her like this . . . not like you. Christ, not even close. There's never been anyone the way I feel about you. There never will be."

She wanted to take comfort in those choked words. With all of her heart, she wanted to believe he meant them.

Yet he stepped out of the room, saying nothing more as he closing the door behind him and left her standing there alone.

CHAPTER 20

Standing in the private bathroom of his quarters, Cain fastened a bandage around his midsection to stanch the fresh bleeding. In the mirror in front of him, his reflection stared back like a mask of anger and loathing. All of it self-directed and well-deserved.

He'd walked out on Marina like a fucking coward just now.

Lots of noble talk about doing what was best for her—sacrifices he was committed to making in hopes of altering the fate he'd seen in his latest vision—when deep down it was his own pain he wanted to avoid.

The pain of losing the woman who had not only broken down all his strongest defenses, but had ensured no other would ever be able to take her place in his heart.

She had nearly wrecked him with her tenderness tonight. He had gone to see her out of concern for her well-being, and instead she had been the one to take care of him. She'd been through hell tonight. A gauntlet that would have leveled even the most stalwart of his kind. Instead, she'd offered him her body, her sweetness . . . and her love.

She had offered him her blood.

Her eternal bond.

Holy hell.

Cain stared at the haggard face in the mirror. Glowing irises. Sliver-thin pupils. Fangs filling his mouth, their points razor-sharp and pulsing with the need to feed.

His wounds were serious, but they would fade. Mainlining a human carotid would fast-track his healing. If he was lucky, it might also take the edge off the savage thirst he had for Marina. Since she'd entered his life, everything Breed and male in him seemed caught in a gravitational field that pulled him inexorably toward her.

If he stayed in the Darkhaven any longer, especially while his body needed nourishment and veins were still vibrating with want of everything Marina had offered him, he didn't trust his honor to hold.

He got dressed and swung past Razor's room, where the low murmur of his brothers' conversation filtered out to the corridor. Lana had gone, but Bram and Logan were crowded around Raze at the monitors where another collection of JUSTIS covert operative files were open on the display. Knox stood apart from the other Hunters, one thick shoulder leaned against the wall.

The male's flat gaze met him as he entered the room. On a scale of contemptuous to homicidal, Knox's guarded stare pushed the needle somewhere near the middle. Their wary truce of the past few hours was nowhere near affirmed, but it was a start.

Cain gave his brother a slight nod of acknowledgment as he entered the room. Knox didn't return it.

"You look like shit." The male gave him a disapproving once-over, his nostrils flaring. "And you smell like roadkill."

Bram glanced his way. "Your wounds worse than you let on?"

Cain shook his head. "I'm fine. Just got a little careless and tore myself open again."

Razor pivoted away from the keyboard, a knowing smirk on his face. "I have a feeling it was worth it."

Hell, yeah. As much as he wanted to bust his brother's balls for the remark, Cain's voice dried up as his thoughts snagged on the image of Marina bent forward in the shower as he buried himself in her heat. And then there was the equally erotic memory of her crouched in front of him, her soapy hands caressing him while her wicked mouth took him deep into her throat.

He got hard just recalling it, even as regret for how he'd left things with her weighed him down.

"How's she doing?" Bram asked.

"Better than most, considering her whole world just blew up in her face tonight." The pain in her voice over her uncle's betrayal would haunt him for as long as he lived. And there was still work to be done—a price to be paid—by Anatoly Moretskov for that betrayal. "I told her we need to bring JUSTIS in on all of this, including her uncle."

Logan met his gaze. "How'd she take it?"

"She knows that's what has to be done, but she's hurting over it. Her uncle has been her sole family for most of her life. It's not going to be easy for her to start over."

Bram nodded, contemplative. "Well, we can help her do that. You know Lana won't let her feel like a stranger. She's already talking about Marina as if she's been here forever."

"Thank you for everything you've done." Cain reached for his brother's hand and clasped it briefly. "I mean that, man."

He couldn't deny the gratitude he had for Bram and his mate, particularly for how generously they had welcomed him back into the Darkhaven and made Marina feel comfortable and accepted too. Razor and Logan had picked up with him right where they'd left off eight years ago, almost as if no time had passed at all.

As for Knox, the rift Cain had caused between them would take time to heal, but he could feel some of the rawness of that old wound fading already.

A shame he wouldn't be staying at the Darkhaven much longer.

He'd meant what he said with Marina. He wasn't going to jeopardize her future by staying in it. The danger her uncle had put her in was over now. JUSTIS could take care of Anatoly Moretskov however they deemed fit.

Marina would have a home here at the Darkhaven for as long as she wanted with good people who cared about her.

Bram studied him as if he knew the direction of Cain's thoughts. The shrewd male never missed a thing, and he didn't now, either.

"Why am I getting the feeling you're coming in here after laying a goodbye speech on that female?"

Razor frowned at Cain. "Nah. He can't be that

stupid. Anyone with eyes in his head can see our man's in love with her."

He wasn't going to pretend his brother was wrong. Not on either count.

"I've spent the better part of my life chasing every itch that needed scratching. I even had myself convinced I was enjoying it." He shrugged. "I've been solitary by choice, keeping my life simple, no complications. Then she came along and showed me how empty my existence has been."

Logan let out a low whistle. "Damn, you really do have it bad for this girl."

Bram nodded. "And it's not a one-way street, either. Seeing you two together leaves no doubt about that."

"Nope," Razor said. "So, why are you here wasting time with us instead of sealing the deal with Marina?"

"Because he's scared." Knox's deep voice cut through all of the levity and well-meaning advice. "Hell, you're fucking terrified of something."

Cain met the penetrating stare of his brother and one-time closest friend. There were few people would dare accuse him of letting fear rule his actions. Knox was one. Another was the beautiful blonde he would do anything to protect. "You're right. I'm scared, Knox. Because I know if I stay with Marina any longer, it'll be to watch her die."

"You're talking about a vision?"

"Yeah. And the only way I can be sure that the horror of what I saw never happens is to let her go."

"That's some damn heroic thinking, brother. Some fine fucking sense of honor you got there." Knox's reply was clipped, and not a little cutting. "Too bad you had none when it came to Abbie."

The jab delivered with marksman skill, Knox stalked out of the room without saying another word.

Cain stood there in the silence that fell over the room, knowing he deserved all of the rancor his brother threw at him. It didn't make him feel any less of an asshole.

Nor did his spike of anger do anything to curb the blood thirst still running hot through his veins for a woman he was never going to have.

"I'm heading out for a while," he announced in a growl.

If he stayed cooped up in the Darkhaven any longer, he was either going to end up at Knox's throat . . . or Marina's.

CHAPTER 21

Cain wasn't in his quarters.

After getting dressed and pacing her guest room in a fog of conflicting, draining emotions, Marina had finally decided she'd had enough. Enough hurting. Enough waiting for him to come back and tell her he was wrong, that he couldn't simply walk away and live his life without her.

That he wanted a future with her, no matter how soon it might end or in what manner.

She kept hoping he would change his mind, barge into her guest room and ask her to be his forever. Because she already was his. She would be whether he accepted that truth or not.

But he didn't come back.

Not for several long minutes. Not for an hour and counting.

So, she was taking this fight to him instead.

Except he wasn't there. She stood in the quiet of his empty living area of his quarters, her breaking heart pounding out of her chest, girded for battle. One she couldn't deliver.

No sign of him anywhere at all.

"Dammit."

She spun around to leave the room and found the open doorway filled with the immense bulk and palpable power of a Hunter. Just not the one she wanted to see.

She felt awkward, caught chasing after Cain like a lovesick fool. "Do you know where he is, Knox?"

"Nope." Blue eyes the shade of a dark thunderhead gave away no emotion at all as he stared at her. "I do know he left the Darkhaven a while ago. Razor and Logan went with him."

He left. The fact that he had gone with his two carousing brothers wasn't the kind of news she wanted to hear, especially coupled with the fact that Cain was injured and needed blood to help him heal.

Any blood but hers.

She tried not to think about what he might be doing—or with whom. She tried to pretend she didn't remember how casually he had talked about slaking his thirsts on nameless, faceless females. Would it be that easy for him to return to that way of life?

As much as she wanted him, she didn't know if she could live with the idea that he would turn so quickly and easily to another woman for sustenance . . . or anything else.

"How are you holding up?" Knox's question took her aback.

"Fine," she said, an automatic response.

She didn't imagine he actually cared. But he was still

standing there, soberly watching her when it would have been the most natural thing in the world for him leave her to her misery.

"Actually, I'm not fine." She shook her head and glanced down at her feet, hating how broken she sounded. "I'm in love with your brother."

A low, contemplative sound rumbled in his chest. "Well, there's no accounting for taste."

She glanced up, astonished to hear the wry note in his voice. She couldn't laugh, but humor from a male like Knox made it seem as though maybe the whole world wasn't crumbling around her. Maybe there was a little hope to be had.

"I've only known him for a few days, Knox. Now, I can't imagine what my life would look like without him in it. How is it possible to fall so deeply for someone so fast? It just doesn't happen."

"It does," he said quietly. "It's rare, but it happens. The hell of it is, sometimes it slips right through our fingers. If Cain's smart, he'll hold you close for as long as he can."

Knox stepped away from the open doorway, about to head back into the corridor.

"He didn't betray you with Abbie."

Her words halted the big male, but he didn't turn around. Marina pushed on, wanting him to know the truth because it seemed that both of the stubborn, hard-headed brothers needed a little help to bridge the divide that had separated them for too long.

"He cared for her, Knox, but as soon as he realized you and she had something special between you, Cain stepped back. He kept watch over her only in the hopes of thwarting the vision he saw, to try to protect her. He didn't want to see either of you in pain."

Knox absorbed the information in silence, without turning around to face her. When he finally spoke, his voice scraped out of his throat. "He should have said something. He should have told me what he saw."

"He knows that," Marina said. "It's a regret he's lived with ever since. But he wasn't betraying you or trying to undermine what you had with Abbie. You need to know that."

He nodded once, standing there for a moment. Then he continued on his way.

Marina let out her breath. She didn't know if she had done the right thing, trying to patch up the rift between the brothers. Cain might be furious to learn she had inserted herself into their private business, but it was a chance she was willing to take. She only wished she knew how to convince him that what they shared was worth keeping together.

Hard to do when she wasn't even certain where he'd gone.

And she had too much pride to sit and wait for him to return.

She started across the room, but her feet slowed when she spied the satellite phone resting on the table beside Cain's bed. The message light was blinking.

She walked over and picked up the device. The log showed three recent missed calls. All in the past half hour.

All from her uncle.

She sat on the edge of the bed holding the phone in numbed state of inertia. As much as she wanted to make Uncle Anatoly explain what he'd done, in her heart she knew there was nothing he could say to make this right.

He was a monster, and she hoped she never had to see him again as long as she lived.

Marina flinched when the phone began to ring in her hand. She didn't want to answer, didn't want to hear his voice or give him the opportunity to tell her more lies. But her finger hovered over the screen as the chime continued to bleat with his call. On an inhaled curse, she took the call.

"Hello, Uncle."

"Marina? Oh, thank God!" The current of panic in his voice sounded authentic. "Are you all right? Where are you? Why haven't you answered my calls, *moya radost?*"

My joy. The endearment that used to make her feel safe and cared for now grated over her senses like the lie it was.

"Say something, Marina. I've been hearing news that Ernesto Fuentes has been assassinated in America. What the hell is going on?"

"It's true," she said. "Fuentes is dead. He was killed a few hours ago on his yacht."

Anatoly swore in stunned, vivid Russian. "How is that possible? Who would do this?"

"He was shot by a JUSTIS sniper. The same one who attempted to kill me in Miami."

Silence fell over the line for a long moment. "JUSTIS. Is that what the news is reporting over there?"

"No, Uncle. I saw it with my own eyes tonight. Fuentes and all of his men were killed moments after I arrived to meet with him and deliver the disk for you."

"You . . . what? You were there when it happened?" He practically sputtered the words. "You're making no sense, my darling. How is it you sound so calm? Were you injured? Tell me where you are and I will send for you immediately—"

"That won't be necessary."

"Not necessary? Marina, what are you talking about?"

Anatoly Moretskov was no fool, and as he spoke, Marina sensed the moment when he began to understand that his niece was no fool, either. He took a breath. Then another.

A strange hesitation crept into his voice. "Do you still have the disk, *moya radost*?"

"Yes, Uncle. I have it."

"Good . . . good. That's very good news, Marina." Another inhalation hissed over the line. "You will come home at once. Bring the disk."

He was dangerous now. She knew him too well to think otherwise. But she was dangerous too. He'd made her so.

"That's not going to happen," she replied. "That data belongs to JUSTIS. I'm turning it over to them."

A cold silence held for an instant. Her uncle's voice was pure ice. "I have copies, Marina. I can sell those files to someone else even before this call is over. Do you really want that on your conscience?"

God, he didn't even pretend to be confused about what was on the flash drive or the real cost of it in terms of good people's lives. Nausea rose inside her, but her outrage kept it at bay.

"You lied to me. You used me." Even though his reasons no longer mattered, she had to ask. "Why?"

"Because I knew you were the only one I could trust to carry this through." It was the same thing he'd told her initially, only now his deception had manipulated her trust into a weapon. One he'd turned on her. "Fuentes and I had it all worked out. I give him lucrative JUSTIS data to use—or cash in on—as he saw fit. In turn, he would arrange to take out Boris Karamenko, clearing the way for me to assume control of Karamenko's fortune and his seat at the head of the table."

Marina struggled to find her voice. "You were never going to leave the Bratva."

"And you were never going to stop trying to persuade me to," he answered tonelessly. "Sooner or later, you might even try using that damnable gift of yours to bend me to your way of thinking. I couldn't have that, Marina."

She sat back, the coldest realization finally settling on her. "You knew the risks involved in me carrying that data. You had to know if anyone in JUSTIS was tipped off to your plan, your courier was as good as dead. You sent me on a likely suicide mission."

Cain had been right to suspect him. He had been right to call her uncle a coward, one who claimed to love his niece yet patted her on the head and sent her out with a target on her back.

She had been so blinded by her devotion to him, by the need to prove to him that she was worthy of his love, that she never so much as considered doubting him. She would have defended him to her last breath. All the while, she was nothing but a pawn to him.

A knot of anguish lodged in her throat. She swallowed past it, refusing to give him the satisfaction of hearing her break. "Trust no one. That's what you told me before I left Russia. That's what you told me nearly all my life while you pretended to care for me. The only one I couldn't trust was you."

He released a sigh filled with mounting impatience. "Come home, Marina. Bring the data disk. It is not a request."

"Fuck you, Uncle." She scoffed. "Fuck you and your orders. I've already told you what I intend to do with those files."

"No, Marina. You won't do any such thing. Because if you don't return to Russia with that flash drive, I will unleash hell on that nest of vampires you've apparently gotten so friendly with." He chuckled, no doubt sensing her dread. "Do you really think I would let the disk and two million dollars out of my hands without ensuring I could trace its whereabouts at all times?"

All of the blood drained from her head. Cold panic filled her veins. "You stay away from here. Do you understand? If you order your Vory soldiers anywhere near this place, I promise you, Cain will send them back to you in pieces."

He let out a low chuckle, full of amusement. "Who said anything about my men? I've got resources at my disposal that you can't imagine. So, please. Come home, Marina. Bring me the fucking disk. If I don't see you in Saint Petersburg within twenty-four hours, all it will take is one call for me to arrange for a pack of Breed mercenaries to swarm that Darkhaven and annihilate everyone in it—including the pregnant bitch. And then you'll come home . . . after you've watched your friends die."

CHAPTER 22

"Pink hair in the strapless dress keeps giving you the come-hither."

Cain followed Razor's chin tilt to the corner of the bar in the Key Largo dive where they'd been sitting for about the last hour. The young human woman chewed on the end of a red cocktail straw, her gaze colliding with his across the room.

"Shit." He scowled with complete disinterest. "She doesn't even look eighteen years old."

"She's twenty-four," Logan said. "Her name's Lacy and she's a real sweetheart. She's blood Hosted for me a time or two. You wanna meet her?"

Cain grunted. "How many women in this state do you know on a first name basis?"

Raze smirked. "Better question is how many doesn't he know? Can't take him anywhere."

"What can I say?" Logan's grin lit up his dark face.

"I've got a magnetic personality. Don't ask me to apologize."

"I don't want to meet Lacy." Cain leaned back in his seat at the table. "I'll leave her for you two to bicker over."

Razor flicked a narrowed glance at him. "Did you come here to find a carotid to tap, or are you going to sulk all fucking night?"

"In the time we've been here, you've scared away three gorgeous ladies," Logan pointed out. "I don't know, Raze. I'm thinking he's got an appetite for something specific. Something a little more . . . cosmopolitan."

"I believe the word you're looking for is Moscovian," Razor suggested around a chuckle.

Cain shook his head. Marina was from Saint Petersburg, but he wasn't about to give them any help. "Did you two tag along to be my wingmen or my babysitters? You know what, fuck this. It was a bad idea. My wounds are healing up as we speak, so there's nothing here I need. Least of all, the two of you on my dick all night about what you think I need."

"We know damn well what you need," Raze muttered. "And so do you. It's waiting for you back home at the Darkhaven."

"We're not rehashing this again." Cain pushed his chair out. "What I should do is head out now. Make this whole fucked-up situation easier on everyone."

"Make it easier on you, maybe." Raze stared at him. "I think you're afraid if you see Marina again, even for a minute, you aren't going to have the balls to leave her behind."

"You think it'll be easier if I stick around?" Cain

shook his head, struggling to reject the idea. "If I stay, my choices boil down to watching her die one day, or watching her find some other male who'll never be good enough for her, either."

Razor glanced down, cursing under his breath. But Logan was nodding in agreement now. Cain looked to his brother, surprised, yet grateful for the support.

"You're right, man. Both of those scenarios are going to be torture."

"Damn straight," Cain said.

"You should go."

"The fuck, Logan?" Raze scowled, incredulous. "That's some kind of bullshit. Don't listen to him, Cain."

But Logan kept talking, his expression about as solemn as it had ever been. "You won't have to worry about Marina. We'll keep her safe. Maybe in time she'll be happy again too. Shit, in time, she might even forget all about your sorry ass. I'll be glad to help her with that."

"Like hell you will." Rage ignited, launching Cain out of his seat. He grabbed his brother by the collar, fangs erupting out of his gums. "Anyone touches her, and I'll fucking kill the son of a bitch. Including you."

The Hunter chuckled, leaning back with his hands up. "Now, try to tell me you can survive a single day without her in your life."

Razor barked out a laugh. Cain let go of Logan, sending a warning glare at all of the human heads now turned in their direction. He glowered at his brother. "You're an asshole."

"Yeah, I am." Logan grinned, unrepentant. "Now, go prove to Marina that you aren't."

Cain stood there for a moment, his heart pounding like a jackhammer. Fear tore at him. The fear of losing the woman he loved to a vision he couldn't control and didn't know how to prevent.

But the greater fear was living another second of his life without her.

He couldn't do it.

Selfish bastard that he was, he needed her in his life—for however long fate would allow him to keep her there.

He stepped away from the table, a smile spreading over his face as he looked at the two Hunters who knew him better than he knew himself. His brothers. His family. The best friends he could ever have.

"I gotta go."

Razor smirked. "Yep."

Cain stalked out of the bar, then started running. He could reach the Darkhaven just as fast on foot and he had no patience to wait on his brothers.

If he had any kind of future ahead of him, it would be with Marina . . . as his mate.

He only hoped she was still willing to have him.

~ ~ ~

Cain didn't slow until he was inside the Darkhaven. Even then, his boots ate up the distance through the corridor until he reached the open door of Marina's guest room. The rose-and-spices scent of her wrapped his senses, an instant balm that never failed to soothe him . . . and entice.

"Marina."

She stood at the side of the bed, her back to him as he took the first tentative step inside. Her spine stiffened when he said her name. Her blond head came up, but didn't turn.

Cain approached her and realized what she was doing.

Packing her suitcase with a silent, steady resolve.

He walked up beside her. A cold hollow gusted behind his sternum when he saw all of her neatly folded clothing laid out on the mattress. "What's going on?"

"I cannot stay here. It's time for me to leave."

She picked up the dove-gray wrap dress and started to place it in the case. The curve-hugging dress he hadn't yet had the pleasure of seeing her in, or out of. He took it out of her hands and laid it back on the bed with the rest of her things still to be packed.

"What do you mean you're leaving?" When she seemed determined not to look at him, he closed the lid of the case then gently grasped her shoulders, turning her to face him. "Marina, leave to go where? This is your home now . . . if you want it to be."

"No, it's not." Pain shone in her burgundy eyes, despite the steel of her spine. "I need to go back where I belong."

"You belong here."

She shook her head, her expression doleful. "I'm going back to Russia, Cain."

Moving out of his loose hold, she resumed packing. The coldness in his chest ripped wider, deeper. Now, it began to fill with a different kind of fear. "You can't go back there now. It's too dangerous."

She slanted a brittle smile at him. "Only if I go near water, right? I'll be fine. It's no longer your obligation to keep me safe. Not that it ever was."

Jesus Christ. She was serious. She really was doing this.

He had fucked up. Irreparably, based on the lack of hesitation in her voice or her actions. He had pushed her away because he was too afraid to bring her closer—into his life, into his blood as his bonded mate.

"I've been an ass, Marina. I said a lot of things I didn't mean—"

"Stop, Cain. Please." Her voice sounded choked. "This has nothing to do with you . . . or with us."

"Then why won't you look at me?" He caught her chin on the edge of his fingers and drew her face back to him. "I hurt you tonight, and I'm sorry."

She blinked, but it didn't seem to stanch the sudden welling in her eyes. "Please, don't make this harder for me. I have to go. There's a flight leaving Miami in a couple of hours and —"

"I take it back, Marina. Every stupid fucking word." He stroked her cheek, hating how real it felt that he was losing her. Maybe already had. "I want to take it all back. Except the part about being in love with you."

Those tears she couldn't squelch spilled over now, running in streaks down her lovely face. "It's too late for that, Cain. I have to be in Russia tomorrow."

As she said it, he noticed the satellite phone peeking out from under some of her clothing. The pain and fear taking up residence in his chest was now joined by a bleak realization.

"You spoke to your uncle."

She reached up to swipe at the wetness on her cheeks. "I went to look for you in your quarters a while ago, but you were out with Logan and Razor. The phone was lying next to your bed. My uncle . . . *Anatoly*," she amended quietly, as if she needed to put the space between the man who raised her and the one revealed to her tonight. "Anatoly had been calling repeatedly after hearing about what happened to Fuentes. He called again while I had the phone in my hand."

"Ah, fuck." Cain reached up and raked both hands over his head. "You shouldn't have answered, Marina. What did the bastard say to you?"

She shook her head. "He denied none of it. He never intended to leave the Bratva. He planned to trade the list of JUSTIS covert operatives in exchange for Fuentes arranging to have Karamenko killed. Then Anatoly would have Karamenko's billions and control of his organization. He chose me as his courier not only because he trusted me, but because it didn't matter to him if I got killed along the way."

Fury seethed into Cain's marrow, even though this only confirmed most of his suspicions about Moretskov. "That son of a bitch. He's a dead man."

He practically shook with the depth of his rage. Yet Marina, who'd been the one to hear Moretskov's confession firsthand seemed oddly subdued. She seemed strangely, woodenly, resigned. But he knew her too well. He saw behind the mask of her courageous calm.

"He threatened you." Dread clawed at him as he studied her now. "Jesus Christ. Tell me what he said."

"It doesn't matter what he said. I'm doing what he wants. He's ordered me to bring him the data drive."

"Bring it to him?" Cain erupted with a curse. "That disk is going straight to JUSTIS. And you're not going anywhere near Russia. If I have to chain you inside this Darkhaven to keep you here, I'll fucking do it, Marina."

"He's got copies, Cain. Giving the disk to JUSTIS won't save any of those people."

Right now, he didn't give a damn about a single one

of the hundreds of law enforcement lives hanging in the balance. The only life that mattered to him belonged to the woman looking at him as if this entire conversation were still going to end with goodbye.

"You're not taking the disk to him, Marina. You can't save any of those people by going back to Russia. If he told you that you could, it's just another of his lies."

"I know I can't save them," she murmured. "But maybe I can save you and everyone else in this Darkhaven."

"What are you saying?"

"If I'm not in Saint Petersburg to hand over the disk to him tomorrow, he told me he will send a pack of assassins here to kill all of you. Breed mercenaries, Cain. He said he would make me watch everyone die. And when it was over, he would bring me back to Russia anyway."

Cain went coldly, lethally still.

Even though he was confident he and his Hunter brothers could handle any threat, he was loathe to imagine what an attack like that might look like. The risk of casualties—even losses—was high.

Too high.

And then there was Lana and the baby to consider.

He would die to defend this Darkhaven and the people in it, but Marina was his heart. She was his soul and everything good he ever dreamed of having in this life. He wasn't about to let her sacrifice herself for him or anyone else.

"You're not leaving me, Marina. Not to go back to Russia or anywhere else."

"I have to." Anguish twisted her expression. "I don't have a choice."

"Then neither do I." He stepped in close and wrapped his arms around her. "I'm going with you."

CHAPTER 23

Saint Petersburg had been her home for nearly all of her life, but as Marina exited a rented Mercedes with Cain the next evening, the beautiful Russian city felt like an alien land.

They stood outside the busy restaurant where Anatoly Moretskov had agreed to meet them—a compromise he hadn't been pleased about, but had grudgingly accepted. That he had been willing to concede to any of her terms only told her how serious he was about seeing her in person again. The thought of having to look him in the eye knowing all that she did now put a chill in her veins. It joined with the fury that had settled there and might never abate.

Still, as the valet whisked their car around to the lot, Marina's heart raced, her feet leaden beneath her. With damp palms she brushed the creases from her black skirt and blouse.

"You okay?" Cain asked, his touch a comforting warmth at the small of her back.

She nodded. "I will be, once this is over."

He pressed a kiss to her temple. "He can't hurt you. Not anymore. I'll see to that."

His growled promise was one he'd made on the flight out of Miami as well. Marina knew it was all but guaranteed a lethal vow. The only reason Cain had agreed to let her go through with the meeting was to bring him within arm's reach of Anatoly. Access that would otherwise be next to impossible to arrange, even for a skilled Hunter like Cain.

He made no secret of the fact that he preferred to see Moretskov dead—and he'd brought enough weapons to make it happen—but it was JUSTIS that deserved to hand down her uncle's punishment. As for Cain, executing a man in full view of the public was hardly his habit, but Marina didn't doubt that all it would take was a threatening word or action toward her for the measured and cool Breed male at her side to erupt into pure, deadly menace.

She let go of a shuddery sigh and felt for the flash drive in the pocket of her skirt. "All right, I'm as ready as I can be. Let's get this over with."

Cain opened the restaurant door and she strode in, pausing until he was at her side. There was no need for the hostess to show them to their seats; Marina spied her uncle immediately at one of the tables situated near the back of the crowded dining room.

Squatty and going soft around the middle, Anatoly Moretskov seemed diminished in many ways now that she knew his true character. Her step faltered only for a moment when her gaze connected with his. Dark eyes held her with an unmasked contempt—one that sharpened as he glanced at Cain.

At both of her uncle's sides stood a pair of Vory soldiers in dark suits. Their tattooed hands were clasped in front of them in an at-ease stance, but the men were far from relaxed. It would take only seconds for them to reach for the weapons they carried beneath their jackets.

But not even four heavily armed men would pose much of a threat to Cain. She reassured herself with that certainty—and Cain's calm strength at her side—as she made her way through the restaurant toward her uncle's table.

He rose from his chair like a gentleman, offering her a thin smile. "*Moya radost*, stunning as always."

Wincing at the awful endearment and oily compliment that came with it, she said nothing in return. She halted a foot from the table, taking Cain's pause as her cue.

In the hours since she'd last spoken to Anatoly, her regard for the man as her uncle had coalesced into a dull, almost phantom ache, the sort of sensation that might linger after the removal of a diseased limb from her body. Her connection to him was severed. What she saw before her now was a stranger, the ambitious Bratva boss he'd always aspired to be.

"Don't be rude, Marina. Have a seat."

"We'll stand," Cain growled. "We aren't going to be here long."

When Marina remained unmoving, Anatoly's narrowed gaze flicked away from her to Cain. A sneer stretched his mouth. "My headstrong niece has spent twenty-five years balking at my authority, yet she obeys you like a pet dog." He grunted and eased back down into his chair. "She always was a willful girl in need of a strong hand, so I suppose I should be impressed. It only took you a few days to put a yoke on her, Hunter. I do wonder, though. Did you have to beat her or fuck her into submission?"

Cain's body vibrated with the low rumble of his fury. Marina brushed her fingers against his, a subtle signal that she was okay, that Anatoly's words didn't hurt her. He didn't have that power anymore. And she wasn't the least bit embarrassed to be standing next to Cain as his lover.

"Your crudeness doesn't mean anything to me," she said, shrugging. "What else should I expect from a man who values nothing but himself?"

He chuckled, smoothing a hand over his balding head. "Unfortunately, it seems you've inherited your poor taste in bed partners from my sister. But you are still my blood, and I can be forgiving. So, if you're done slutting around with this subhuman, you may come home, Marina. In fact, I insist."

She scoffed. "I hate that I have even a drop of your blood in me. I'm not your niece anymore. I was never anything to you. I know that now. I've seen through you, finally."

"What you were, and are, Marina, is a constant reminder of Ekaterina's mistake. You, with your blond hair and odd-colored eyes. You look nothing like a Moretskov. I was always aware that you were *other*." He leaned back, considering her now. "And I did care in the beginning, when you had no one else. But then you used your abominable gift on me. You *dared* to manipulate me, and at that moment I knew you were dangerous."

No. She shook her head, rejecting the twinge of guilt

that still pricked her over that incident. She had been wrong to do it, but she was not going to allow him to excuse anything he'd done now by blaming a single, impulsive action of a teenage girl.

"If you felt I was so dangerous, then why not kill me that day? You were angry enough."

"Yes, I was. But you were so upset, begging me to forgive you. It was obvious that you loved me, even after I had that animal put down. It was your remorse that saved you, Marina. Your desire to earn back my trust." He blinked at her, his expression lacking any feeling whatsoever. "I knew eventually that depth of devotion could be useful to me. I just didn't know how, until I obtained the information on that disk."

Her stomach roiled at the admission. She glanced at Cain. He stood unmoving, the hardness in his features intensifying as he absorbed everything Anatoly said. Dark energy pulsed off his body. If not for her gentling stroke of his hand, Marina knew he would already be in motion, leaping onto her uncle and tearing him to pieces.

Which would only unleash the foursome of Vory killers armed and waiting for the order to attack.

Anatoly leaned forward, placing his forearms on the edge of the table. "Show me the data drive, Marina."

She reached in her pocket and took out the device. Holding it in her fingers, she made no move to hand it to him. His deep brown eyes locked on to the disk with satisfaction, even relief.

"Good girl." He rose then, sliding his chair back with a scrape. "Now, come with me. Let's go home so you can help me open it, and we can talk some more in private."

"She's not going anywhere with you, asshole." Cain

snarled the statement, moving himself protectively in front of her. "If you have copies, you don't need Marina to help you open this one."

"He doesn't have copies." How had she not seen that until now? The truth astonished her, although she should have guessed as much. "He lied to me. Again."

Anatoly chuckled as if she'd just told the richest joke. "What can I say? My niece has always been a clever girl. Moretskov genes are hard to water down."

Cain reached behind him to move her farther back from Anatoly's table. Her uncle seemed unfazed by the Breed male standing menacingly in front of him.

"Time to go now, *moya radost*. The bloodsucker can stay behind."

"Like hell, I will," Cain muttered. "You think four Vory will be enough to keep me from ripping your head off?"

"No," Anatoly said. "No, I don't expect they would be."

At that same moment, from all directions inside the restaurant, men stood up with semiautomatic weapons in their hands—every one of them trained on Marina. Men who until that instant had been ostensibly enjoying their dinners with dates or wives, even a few tables containing groups of chattering children. All a ruse. All a twisted game orchestrated by the monster who was her uncle.

Shocked, she gaped in horror as the remaining diners all got up from the tables and silently left the restaurant.

"Cain," she whispered, unable to count the number of pistols aimed at her head from every corner of the dining room. Easily more than a dozen, possibly twenty or more.

Then, even worse, peeling away from the shadows of a darkened hallway came two hulking males with arms the size of tree trunks and eyes glowing with amber.

Breed males.

Anatoly laughed. "Tell me, Hunter. Do you think you can move fast enough to keep a hundred rounds from blowing Marina's pretty skull to pieces? More to the point, do you think you can do it before these two vampires tear you in half?"

Cain's stillness communicated his concern . . . and his doubt.

Marina had never been so terrified. Not only for herself, but for the sheer outnumbering of Anatoly's personal army against Cain.

The gunmen closed in gradually, tightening their ranks on her.

"Come now, Marina," Anatoly said. "Move slowly toward me. Your Breed friend here doesn't want to see your brain splattered all over this room. As for me, all I need is that tattoo on your arm. You can either come along willingly, or defy me and I'll use your corpse."

CHAPTER 24

Complete and brutal annihilation.
    That's what the killer in Cain wanted more than anything else—to give his rage its head and unleash holy hell on the room full of Bratva soldiers and the pair of mercenary Breed males taking orders from Anatoly Moretskov.

But he couldn't risk it.

Not when Marina's worried gaze held on him and her uncle's four Vory guards moved in to take her away.

"Stay alive," he whispered to her, leaning close and breathing in her sweet scent. "That's all you have to do, love. Stay alive. Leave the rest to me."

She nodded, but he could see the doubt in her burgundy eyes. Two of Moretskov's men grabbed her wrists while another bound her hands in front of her.

And all the while, those two dozen semiauto guns stayed trained on her from all sides.

Cain told himself this wasn't the way he was going to lose her. It couldn't be.

In the back of his mind he took cold comfort in the vision that had been haunting him for the past days. A bullet wasn't going to be her end. As horrific as the vision of her drowning death was, he clung to it now as he watched Moretskov take her away from him at gunpoint.

Fury ran like black acid in his veins the instant she was gone from his sight.

The muffled sound of vehicle doors closing outside the rear of the restaurant reached his heightened hearing like gunshots. It took all the self-control he had not to follow her now.

Twenty-plus Bratva men could fill him full of rounds and he could probably still make it long enough to rescue Marina from Moretskov's hands. He could move faster than any human. He could be gone in mere seconds and none of the gunmen would stand any hope of catching up to him.

But the two Breed males were the larger threat—to his chances and to Marina's ultimate safety. To get to her, he needed to take them out first.

Cain bared his fangs at the pair. "Well, what are you waiting for?"

The bigger of the two smirked. "For the limo to leave."

Yeah, fuck that. Cain had a dagger concealed in his hand. He'd retrieved it from under his loose shirt during the instant Moretskov's thugs took hold of Marina. Now, he leaped on the smirking Breed male who stood closest to him, plunging the blade into the vampire's chest as bullets began to fly from all around them.

He and the male crashed into a server's station on their way to the floor. Deafening gunfire and splintering tables, chairs, and dishware created an instant explosion of chaos in the room. Cain ignored it all, focused on the thing he was born and raised to do.

Coldly, swiftly, he dragged the blade across the Breed male's throat, all but severing the head from the vampire's body.

Meanwhile, the second male attacked. He jumped Cain from behind, trapping his skull between massive, powerful hands.

Cain roared as the pressure in his temples turned his vision gray. He reached back with the dagger, stabbing his assailant in the eye. The male let go of him on an anguished howl.

But Cain wasn't finished with him yet. He flipped around in a blur of movement, grabbing the bulky body and holding it in front of him as a shield while Moretskov's gunmen closed in with weapons blazing.

More than a few hit the Breed male's head, enough to prove lethal.

Cain heaved the limp corpse at the swarming human shooters.

Then he flashed out the back door of the restaurant and took off at the full velocity of his Breed genetics to save the woman he loved.

He only prayed fate would be on his side.

~ ~ ~

Marina sat silently in the backseat of the chauffeured black limousine that had been her ride to countless dinners and social events over the years. Tonight she crowded against the soft leather seat and window, her bound hands in her lap and her gaze fixed on the pistol her uncle held on her from his seat across from her.

She knew why her hands were tied. All she needed was the opportunity to touch Anatoly for a few moments. Then she could bend his will and make him release her. But he was out of reach, and if the tight bindings didn't thwart her, the gun he brandished certainly would.

He had taken the flash drive out of her pocket before they got in the car. His fingers caressed it idly as he stared at her in the dark of the limo while his driver sped along the fast moving stretch of multi-lane Ivanovskaya Street, heading east through the city.

"How could you do it?" Marina shook her head, glancing at the device. "Those are real people you're exposing, hundreds of innocent lives on that disk."

"Innocent?" He scoffed. "JUSTIS has been sniffing around me for years. Their agents infiltrating the Bratva and other organizations like an infestation. I'm glad to help root the traitors out."

"It's you who's the criminal," she reminded him. "You and your friends like Ernesto Fuentes and Boris Karamenko. All of you are in the wrong, not the other way around."

"Please." His face twisted with anger. "Spare me your self-righteousness, girl. Bratva money paid for your pampered lifestyle—and my sister's. It paid for her musical education in America, which she squandered by spreading her legs for anyone who said a pretty word to her. You were a product of that flaw of hers."

At the cutting disregard, Marina glanced out the window at the buildings and storefronts they passed in a blur of lights and speeding cars. "You speak as if you hated her."

He chuckled. "Hate is a strong word. I didn't feel that deeply for Ekaterina. She was a silly, idealistic girl. And she was only too happy to spend Bratva money on fancy holidays and expensive clothes—all while condemning me for how I earned it. I should have dumped her on the street instead of giving the ungrateful bitch a home she didn't deserve. I suppose I finally reached my limit with her after she took up with that activist professor from Moscow."

Marina knew the basic details of her mother's final few months of life. She had read the news reports about the accidental deaths of both her mom and her boyfriend while the pair was on a boating holiday in Spain. Drugs and alcohol had played a factor according to the coroner . . . but now she wondered.

"What do you mean you reached your limit?" Her blood chilled. "What did you do?"

But she knew. God, she was beginning to see the true depths of her uncle's evil now.

"You killed her." Marina's voice rose with the force of her pain and outrage. "You took my mother from me, you bastard."

And in Anatoly Moretskov's utter lack of reaction, she knew another truth.

She was as good as dead too.

He couldn't let her live knowing what he'd done. All he needed her for was the key to open the disk. Then he was going to kill her as easily as he'd killed her mother.

Marina turned her head to gauge their location—and how slim the odds were for her escape from the speeding vehicle. There was only one chance to break out and hope to survive the leap.

Up ahead, before they would reach the Volodarsky Bridge that spanned the Neva River, was a wide green space. If she could tumble out and onto the soft grass, she might make it.

Heart pounding in her ears, she bided her time as they approached. The gloom inside the limousine concealed her movements as she inched her fingers toward the door handle. All she had to do was wait another few seconds . . . almost there.

Sucking in a breath, she hit the unlock button. The click seemed as loud as a gunshot.

"What the—" Anatoly's gaze snapped to her scrambling fingers as she hurried to grasp the door's release. He shouted to the driver in Russian, demanding he speed up. "Marina, damn you!"

The vehicle lurched forward, tossing her against the seat. The green space lay behind them now, the driver flooring the accelerator as they approached the bridge.

She had no choice now. She had to get out of the car, no matter what.

With her bound hands, she swung them forward, knocking her uncle's weapon off its aim on her. His arm flew up and back in the struggle.

Three shots fired wildly, sharp pops that sparked in the darkness.

One shattered the passenger window. Another tore into the ceiling of the limo.

The third hit the driver in the back of the head.

Blood and brain matter exploded against the windshield. He slumped forward. The car careened onto the bridge and out of control.

Marina screamed, still struggling for purchase on the

door handle. She couldn't get it open. And even if she did, the tumble onto the pavement was all but certain to kill her.

"Oh, my God!"

In terror, she watched the bridge guardrail loom closer and closer in front of them as the limo veered across the lanes.

It slammed into the low barrier . . . and crashed right through.

The impact shattered the cracked windshield. The sound of groaning, twisting metal seemed to go on endlessly. And so did the slow-motion plunge toward the dark, rippling water of the river far below.

Water gushed in through the broken glass and crumpled seams of the doors and hood. It was frigid cold, so dark it was black. Marina scrambled to open her door as the front of the car tipped forward and began to sink.

"Marina!" Her uncle clawed at her from the other side of the backseat as the water rose up to his face. He grabbed the hem of her skirt, dragging her away from the door. "Marina, help me!"

He was going to pull her down if she didn't get free. But her tied hands were of little use to her. The door wouldn't open against the pressure of the water outside the vehicle. Finally, she found the button for the window instead. The glass slid down, bringing in a massive wave of dark, briny water.

It hit her face, pushing into her nose and mouth. She choked, fighting against the incoming force of the river.

She *couldn't* drown.

She couldn't let Cain's vision come true.

She wanted to live.

Please, God. Let me live.

She tried to swim out the open window, but her uncle's grasp held her back as he tried to use her body as a ladder for his own escape. Marina kicked at him, her face completely submerged now.

She screamed Cain's name in her head as the vehicle descended under the waves.

CHAPTER 25

Allowing Marina anywhere near Russia was a mistake he'd regretted the instant they stepped off the plane.

But the even bigger regret—the one that had Cain's heart caught in a vise as he raced on foot through the middle of Saint Petersburg—was the fact that he'd allowed her to leave the Everglades Darkhaven without first offering her his blood bond. He should have fucking demanded it.

If he had, that blood connection to each other would have led him to her like a beacon. He would have felt her location with a thrumming in his own veins.

Instead, he chased through the streets as good as blind, trying to guess where she was.

He knew Moretskov's estate lay east of the city. Before leaving the States, he and Raze had gone over the mansion's location and the property schematics in case

Cain needed the information. But knowing where Moretskov was likely taking her didn't tell Cain where she was now. And he didn't want her spending another minute in the bastard's hands.

Cain paused at the corner of a wide, six-lane boulevard, searching for any sign of the black limousine. The busy city pulsed all around him, crowding his senses. The din of ceaseless nighttime traffic on the street in front of him. The blare of car horns and the intermittent, marrow-shaking thump of music playing over vehicle sound systems. Restaurant smells competing with the belch of exhaust . . . and something else.

Water.

A large body of water, rushing somewhere in the distance. Probably only a couple of blocks from where he stood. Dread sank cold talons into his chest when he recalled the wide river that cut a snaking path through part of Saint Petersburg.

And now he heard the scream of sirens on the approach.

Emergency vehicles.

No. It can't be for her . . .

Cain bolted into a run, nothing but a blur of movement as he dodged vehicles and flew over the pavement, following the freshwater smell of the Neva River. Brake lights glowed up ahead. All three lanes of traffic onto the bridge were stopped, no cars coming from the other direction either. Cain's nostrils filled with the stench of scorched rubber, pulverized concrete, and twisted steel.

Ah, fuck.

He tried to tell himself that none of this meant Marina was in danger, but his blood knew. Every fiber in his body seized with the jolting certainty that he was about to lose the woman he loved. That it might already be too late.

He raced to the middle of the bridge and saw the limousine-size hole in the guard rail. The smashed barrier hung loose over the twenty-foot drop to the fast-rushing current of dark water below.

"Marina! Oh, God, no!"

He didn't hesitate, not even to fill his lungs. He dove off the bridge, plunging into the cold black waves.

Some thirty feet deep in the murky water, the limo rested head-down on the river bottom. Cain swam toward it, cutting through the clouds of blood that rose up from inside the vehicle.

Not hers.

The copper tang belonged to a human, not a Breedmate. But that gave him little relief as he reached the submerged car.

Marina was inside, trapped in the backseat compartment. She wasn't moving.

Cain roared his anguish. Reaching in through the open window, he grabbed for her but she floated too far away. He grabbed onto the door and ripped it loose, tossing it to the river bottom.

Marina hung suspended in the water of the backseat, her blond hair floating all around her. Her eyes were open, but they couldn't see him. Her mouth was slack, lips parted.

Just as he'd seen in his vision.

No. Goddamn it, no.

He caught her arm and pulled her toward the window opening. There was a sudden drag on her body—added weight from inside the vehicle.

Moretskov held on to Marina's ankle like a life line as Cain began to pull her out. Her uncle's wild-eyed face stared at Cain through the turbid, dark water. He screamed for help, expelling precious air in his panic.

No fucking way, Cain thought, his gaze burning red with fury.

Holding on to Marina, he kicked his boot heel into the center of Moretskov's desperate face.

Blood gushed from the man's broken nose and shattered teeth, fouling the water. The blow made him lose his hold on her. In slow-motion, he flew farther into the vehicle, limply unconscious.

Let the river have the sadistic bastard. It wasn't going to take Marina.

Cain swam to the surface with her under his arm. He brought her to the nearest embankment, lifting her lifeless body onto dry ground.

"Marina, can you hear me?"

Laying her on her back, Cain turned her head to the side to help the water drain from her nose and mouth. He tried resuscitation, but she didn't respond.

Her face was bloodless, her lips a disturbing shade of blue.

"Marina, please wake up. Come on, baby."

On the bridge some distance behind them, first responders scrambled to action. Lights and sirens pierced the night. Divers in wetsuits descended into the bracing water. He shouted to the crew for help, but the rushing river and the general chaos on the bridge drowned him out.

"Marina, please. Don't leave me." He smoothed her wet hair off her cheeks and forehead. "I love you, Marina. I can't let you go. Not ever."

Desperate, he brought his wrist up to his mouth and bit into his veins. Blood dripped from the twin punctures, splashing down onto her lips and chin.

"Drink, sweetheart," he urged her. "Take just a drop."

He knew he couldn't bring her back to life. That's not how the blood bond worked. But if there was anything left inside her, any spark of hope, his blood might give her the strength her body needed to repair itself. One taste of his blood might be able to pull her through.

"Please," he begged, no pride left at all.

This woman was his heart, his future . . . his everything. He refused to lose her.

But she didn't take the blood that fell onto her parted lips.

She really was gone.

Cain sat back, shock stabbing him as the reality of his vision pressed down on him. Her lifeless body submerged in dark water. His blood staining her lips, useless to save her.

All of those disjointed, brief flashes he had seen that night in her bed had come true. Just as he feared they would. He'd failed her.

"No!" He threw his head back on an agonized roar.

No. He wasn't giving up. The vision had played out, but that didn't mean it was the end. He refused to let it be the end.

With pain racking him, he gathered Marina's limp body against him and stood up, scooping her into his arms. As fast as his Breed genetics would allow, he carried her to the bridge where paramedics raced to him, speaking in frantic Russian.

"Do something, please," he urged them. "Please, help me save her."

They took her out of his arms and wrapped her in a blanket, then immediately went to work.

Cain had never felt so helpless, or so humbled. He'd never felt this depth of fear. It leveled him.

He sank to his knees on the asphalt and prayed—the only thing left for him to do.

CHAPTER 26

Marina came awake with a start.

She sucked in a breath, expecting to feel the pain and shock of cold, heavy water entering her lungs, but instead all she felt was air. Weightless, wonderful air.

"Thank God." Cain's deep voice was strangled and rusty next to her. "Marina. I'm right here, love."

Her eyelids felt glued together. She lifted them slowly, smiling as his handsome face came into focus. "Cain."

At least, she thought that's what she said. The croak that came out of her mouth tasted like gravel and sounded like it too.

"You don't have to talk," he said, gazing at her tenderly.

Monitoring wires and IV lines ran from the back of her hand, which was caught between the warmth and strength of both his palms. The beeps and soft hisses that had been the soundtrack to her many hazy, disturbing dreams made sense now.

"Hospital?"

He nodded, his expression grave. "Saint Petersburg. You've been in a coma for the past two days, but you're going to be all right. You're alive, Marina." His voice caught for a moment. "Ah, Christ . . . I lost you, but you came back to me."

Memories buffeted her like fast-forward frames of a movie. Cain and her entering the restaurant. Her uncle's gunmen coming out from all directions. Being taken away while Cain was left to contend with all those Bratva killers and the pair of Breed males. All the awful things Anatoly Moretskov admitted to in the limousine. And then, the harrowing crash into the river.

The cold, dark water she couldn't escape.

"I drowned." As impossible as it seemed, she knew it was true. "Just like in your vision, Cain. I died."

"Yes." Black brows creased over sober silver eyes. "For two minutes and thirty-four seconds, you were dead. Paramedics brought you back. I tried to, but . . ."

He shook his head and glanced down at their clasped hands. When he swallowed, she heard his throat work. That quiet hitch in his breath told her so much.

This formidable Breed male—this Hunter who could take on an army and still emerge on top—had almost been broken by the thought of losing her.

"You came for me," she whispered, overwhelmed by emotion. Relief. Gratitude. And love. So much love. "You did save me, Cain."

"No." He shook his head again, more emphatically now. "No, Marina. I failed you. There was nothing I could do."

She reached up with her free hand, stroking his jet-black hair. "You saved me that first night in Miami. And you've saved me every night since, Cain. I don't even remember what it was like without you in my life. I don't want to know what that would be like."

"Marina." Her name was a low, rumbling growl as he moved closer and carefully pressed his lips to hers. His gaze held hers, searching and tender. Filled with such depth of emotion, it staggered her. Shattered her. "I love you. You are my heart, Marina. Mine won't beat without you. I knew that even before I pulled you out of the river. But afterward, when nothing I did could bring you back, part of me died too."

She caressed his face, wishing they were home instead of in Russia. When she thought of home now, she pictured the sprawling corridors and tall, timber-beamed ceilings of a Darkhaven in the Everglades. If she closed her eyes she could hear Lana's laughter and Bram's good-natured humor. She heard Logan and Razor bantering like best friends, like brothers. She even pictured Knox, with his searing thunderhead gaze and broody aloofness.

But most of all, she pictured Cain.

She pictured herself naked and nestled against him as they made love.

And she pictured the kind of bond that Bram and Lana shared. A true bond, unbreakable, eternal. Sealed in blood.

She didn't know if Cain was ready for that.

She couldn't help noticing the contusions and lacerations that had yet to heal on his arms. His *dermaglyphs* were darker than she'd ever seen them, nearly the same color of his numerous lingering bruises.

She touched one of the beautiful skin markings that tracked under the short sleeve of his black T-shirt.

"I will need to feed soon," he murmured.

His frank statement was an unwelcome reminder of the uncertain way things had been left between them before they departed for Russia. The last time Cain needed to feed, he denied her to seek out another Host. His rejection stung, even now. Even after all of the lovely things he'd just said to her, it hurt to recall how easily he had been able to turn to someone else for what his body needed.

Her uncle's deception, and the phone call that demanded she return to Saint Petersburg, had put her hurt and everything else on hold. Now, it was time to face it.

The man she loved was Breed. She accepted that. More than accepted, she embraced everything he was.

So, as much as it pained her, she couldn't condemn him for any part of his nature.

She nodded. "You don't have to stay with me. I'll understand if you need to leave for a while to find a blood Host."

Even if the idea of him taking a stranger's vein made her feel like dying all over again, she would try to understand.

Cain studied her, a solemnity in his steady gaze. "I'm not going anywhere. There hasn't been anyone since I met you. Not to Host me. Not for anything."

"But the other night I offered you my blood. Instead, you left with Razor and Logan . . ."

"Yes, I did." His expression hardened. "I'm sorry for the stupid things I said and did. I was a jackass for refusing you. And I was an idiot for even thinking I could walk away, even to protect you. But I didn't drink from anyone that night. I didn't look at anyone else. I came back for you."

"You did?"

He nodded, running his fingers over her brow, then down along her cheek. "I don't want a blood Host, Marina. Not ever again. I'd rather have a blood bond. If you're agreeable to that."

Elation flooded her. She managed a wobbly dip of her chin as her joy overflowed, bubbling out of her on a teary sigh. "Yes, I'm agreeable to that, Cain."

He chuckled as she sat up in the bed and wrapped her arms around his neck. She didn't care about the wires and electronic leads that complained with her sudden movement and the spike in her heart rate.

Outside the windows of her hospital room, a couple of nurses walked over to peek inside. Marina barely noticed. None of her lingering physical ailments bothered her, either.

All of the weakness and discomfort she'd felt upon waking evaporated within the comfort of Cain's embrace.

"Take me out of here," she murmured against the warm curve of his neck and shoulder. "I don't want to wait another second to start the rest of our lives together."

"Neither do I, love." He shivered as she pressed her lips against the strong pulse beating so near her mouth. She nipped him playfully, overcome by an urge she couldn't resist. A pleasured groan rumbled deep in his chest. "Baby, you're killing me. As much as I want you right now, we are not going to initiate our blood bond on a hospital bed."

She laughed. "Why not?"

"Because I want it to be special." He drew her away from him, but only to kiss her. When their lips separated, she saw the sharp points of his fangs gleaming in his mouth. He exhaled a quiet curse, his touch reverent as he caressed her face. "When I take you as my mate, Marina, I want it to be perfect for you. I'm going to make certain it is, because you deserve nothing less."

She smiled, overcome with love for him . . . and a stirring hunger for all the things his heated amber gaze promised.

"I love you," she whispered, moving deeper into his arms. "Please, don't ever let me go."

He held her close. "Baby, not a chance."

Marina could have stayed in the comfort of his embrace forever, but outside her room a group of big men approached the closed door. Dark suits, grave faces. And at the front of them was someone even more dangerous than Anatoly Moretskov.

"Cain." She backed out of his arms, fear leaching into her veins. "Oh, my God. It's Boris Karamenko."

The Bratva boss opened the door without knocking. None of the hospital staff stopped him or even delayed him with a question. Karamenko had that effect on everyone who knew his name, and his savage reputation. Like the swaggering bull he was, he entered the room along with the four grim thugs accompanying him.

"It's all right," Cain said, giving her hand a reassuring squeeze as he rose to his feet.

But it wasn't all right. It couldn't be all right if one of the most treacherous heads of the Russian mafia was coming after them now.

"She is awake." Karamenko's growly Russian accent

clipped the words into a toneless observation. He moved next to her bed and stared down at her, scowling. "You've had everyone very worried these past two days."

She gaped at him, unable to hide her shock. "W-what?"

He swung that dark glower on Cain. "You haven't told her yet?"

"There, ah, hasn't been time to cover everything." Cain actually looked a little sheepish. But when he glanced at her, his silver eyes were filled with solemnity. "We had more important things to talk about first."

Marina sat up straighter, confusion and disbelief swirling through her as Cain took a seat on the edge of the narrow bed. "What's going on?"

"After the paramedics revived you and brought you to the hospital, I had a visit from a couple of JUSTIS men . . . and Mr. Karamenko." He took her hand, stroking her fingers as he held her stunned gaze. "Marina, JUSTIS knew what your uncle was up to. They knew he had obtained covert operative intelligence, and they knew he was looking to sell it. They also knew you were carrying it for him when you arrived in the States."

Karamenko nodded. "What we didn't know was that he intended to use it as payment for having me assassinated. We didn't realize that until we spoke with your man here and he explained what Anatoly confessed to you."

"Wait a minute," Marina said, uncertain if she was hearing correctly or if the trauma her body had endured was playing tricks on her mind. She stared up at Karamenko. "You're saying we as if you're—"

"Working with JUSTIS." The Bratva boss nodded

his large head. A smile spread over his jowly face. "I am a career JUSTIS agent, Marina. I've been providing intelligence and assisting in arrests and sting operations from the very beginning."

"But you're one of the most feared members of the Bratva," she pointed out. "Forgive me for saying it, but you're a cold-blooded killer. Your reputation for violence and treachery—"

"Has been carefully crafted and supported with the cooperation of my JUSTIS colleagues," he finished for her. "My rise through the syndicate was crucial in helping law enforcement take out the real killers and criminals. Unfortunately, that number included your uncle. We were tightening the noose around Anatoly when rumors reached us that he had somehow gotten his hands on highly sensitive intelligence. A couple of months ago, we began applying some subtle pressure, just to see if we could flush out the data. He got anxious."

Marina nodded. "That's around the time that he came to me and told me he wanted out of the Bratva. He said he was afraid and had someone willing to give him asylum for a price. He knew I would do anything to help him."

"JUSTIS knew that too," Karamenko said. "Your devotion to him was well understood in our organization. That's why, when he sent you to Miami as his courier, we were certain you knew exactly what you were carrying for him."

"But I didn't know. He lied to me. He said the disk contained bank information and passwords worth billions. Your bank accounts," she admitted, ashamed that she had been willing to rationalize her part at any time in her uncle's scheme. "I thought you were a criminal. I thought it would be a good thing if you were removed from power—especially if it would also buy freedom for my uncle and me."

Karamenko shrugged. "You are a loyal niece. He's not the first to use a family bond to further his own criminal goals."

"I never would have agreed to help him if I had known what that flash drive actually contained."

"We know that," he said, glancing at Cain. "We know that now, at any rate. But we had to be sure. We had a man deeply embedded in your uncle's security detail for the past decade. He was tasked with locating the data and taking any measures to ensure it didn't reach its destination."

"Yury," she said, her guilt still raw over his death. "He was only trying to do the right thing. Both he and the sniper who tried to shoot me at the hotel. Now, they're both dead because of me."

Cain brought her hand up to his lips and tenderly kissed it. "You didn't know Anatoly had put you in the crosshairs. You had no idea what was actually on that disk. There's no reason for you to feel guilty about any of this."

Karamenko nodded. "He's right. And because you lived, that stolen intelligence has been contained. There are over a hundred covert operatives who owe their lives to you. And to Cain."

"The disk," she blurted. "I don't have it anymore. Anatoly took it from me before the limousine crashed into the river."

"Yes," Karamenko said. "We found it still clutched in his dead fist when divers pulled his corpse out of the water. We have a team searching his premises now to look for the possibility of other copies."

Marina shook her head. "There are none. He only had the data on that one device."

"Then that's good news, indeed." Karamenko gave her a rare smile. "JUSTIS owes you a debt, Marina. It would not be wise for you to remain in Russia now. So, we're prepared to offer you asylum anywhere else you might wish to go."

As he spoke, two more men in dark suits came into the room. She instantly recognized the salt-and-pepper whiskers of the older JUSTIS officer and his ginger-haired Breed partner.

"Officers Powell and Jonas from our Miami office wanted to thank you in person." Karamenko stepped aside to make room for the pair at her bedside.

Officer Powell spoke first, the older man reaching out to rest his hand against her shoulder. "How are you doing, Ms. Moretskova?"

"I'm okay." She took a breath and let it out on a sigh when her gaze met Cain's gentle regard. "I'm better than okay now. And please, call me Marina."

"All right, Marina." The JUSTIS man smiled. "We cannot understate what you and Cain have done for us. For all of us in law enforcement around the world."

"That's right," added Jonas. The Breed officer who had been so suspicious of her in her hotel suite, even combative, now looked at her with gratitude shining in his eyes. "I'm sorry we pushed you the way we did that night in Miami. We had to push in order to see if you would be willing to bend or give anything away about the disk and where you were supposed to deliver it."

"I understand. I'm sorry for my part in all of this. I'm

only glad to know the information can't hurt anyone now."

Karamenko cleared his throat. "We'll make arrangements with the hospital for your release. You'll have the full protection of JUSTIS once you're ready to leave. And, of course, your security will be provided for on a permanent basis once you're settled in at your new location."

Cain's grasp on her hand flexed almost imperceptibly. He watched her with sober intensity, and she knew him well enough to understand that he was remaining quiet to let her consider all of these new options.

But she didn't need to think about anything. Her mind—and her heart—were already decided.

"No," she said. She held Cain's gaze and slowly, but firmly, shook her head. "Thank you, but no. There's nothing JUSTIS needs to do for me. I've already accepted a better offer from someone else."

A grin broke over Cain's handsome face. He leaned down and kissed her. Not a small one. Not some sweet peck on the lips, but a kiss that promised so much more.

Karamenko and his colleagues began to file out of the room, leaving them to their joy.

But then Cain drew away from her mouth, a grin tugging at his lips.

"Actually, there is something JUSTIS can do for us," he told the departing men. "Any chance we could get a lift back to Miami?"

CHAPTER 27

*H*ome.

Cain hadn't expected the word to pack such a punch. But after the fifteen-hour flight from Saint Petersburg, followed by two hours in the car from Miami to the Darkhaven nestled in the center of the Everglades, he couldn't think of anything more welcome—nor more restorative—than the place he was now.

Home.

It wasn't only a place to him anymore. It was a feeling—one that overwhelmed him every time he looked into Marina's burgundy eyes.

He hated letting her leave his arms even for a moment as they entered the Darkhaven and were greeted by Lana and Bram. Raze and Logan jogged into the living room a few minutes later, everyone talking at once and asking a hundred questions.

Amid the excitement, Knox's absence couldn't be

ignored.

Bram shook his head when Cain asked where he was. "Not sure this time. I found him repairing the corridor wall on his own a couple of days ago. When I went to talk to him that night, he was gone."

Cain couldn't deny his disappointment, or his concern. "He'll be back, though. Right? He always comes back eventually."

"Maybe." But Bram's grim face said more than he was letting on. He blew out a low curse. "He cleared out his quarters."

"Shit." A constriction took up space behind Cain's sternum at the news. He had hoped he and Knox might find some way back to the friendship—and the trust— they once had. But now his brother had taken that chance with him. And given the male's volatile nature, Cain dreaded the kind of trouble Knox might find wherever he'd gone.

Seeing his concern, Marina came back to him, wrapping her arms around his waist and nestling close. "He'll be all right," she said, more certain than anyone else seemed. "Knox just needs time alone to figure things out. But he'll come back again."

Cain kissed the top of her head. "I hope you're right, love."

Lana leaned against Bram, her hands settled atop the swell of her belly. "You two must need some time alone as well."

She was more than right. The questions and explanations could wait.

There was so much to tell, and no easy place to start.

Besides, Cain had Marina in his arms again and he was in no rush to let her go.

They made their excuses and slipped away to his quarters. Once they were closed inside, Cain turned the shower on in the other room and came back to carefully undress each other.

Feeling Marina's warm, naked body against him was a balm he needed more than anything else in this world.

She was alive.

She was home.

And she was his.

Cain stood under the steamy water, holding her close. Her touch was tender on his contusions, loving as she caressed all the unmarred places on his body.

He couldn't keep his arousal from stirring as she stroked him. Nor did she seem to want him to. Her wet fingers traveled down his abdomen to the jutting length of his erection. She traced the underside of his shaft, rising up on her toes to kiss the sensitive hollow at the base of his throat.

He growled as her tongue darted out to lick at his throbbing pulse. "You're not playing fair."

"Who says I'm playing?"

He chuckled, but inside he was on fire. His desire had twined with his joy to be holding her and with the relief of knowing that she was safe—truly safe—for the first time since he'd first laid eyes on her.

And he wanted her.

He wanted her kiss, her touch, the hot, wet haven of her sex.

He wanted her blood too.

His fangs surged against his tongue as she licked a teasing path along his chest and drove him to the brink of utter madness with her touch on his cock. The memory of nearly losing her was still fresh in his mind, her return to the living only a few days past, yet she moved against him full of passion and life.

"Marina . . . holy hell."

She drew him in like a siren, and he had no will to resist her. Not now. Not after everything they'd been through.

His need for her was only secondary to his love for her.

And right now, he wanted all of her.

"Take it," she whispered. She gathered her long hair over her shoulder. The smooth column of her neck drew his gaze like a beacon. Delicate purple veins pulsed beneath the velvety cream of her skin. "I don't want to wait another minute. I love you, Cain. I need you. All of you."

"You're mine." His growled reply sounded inhuman, otherworldly, even to his own ears.

He took her beautiful face gently in his hands and kissed her. Her eyes wrecked him, so full of love for him. So full of hunger for the bond they were about to share. With trembling fingers, he smoothed his hand along her neck, guiding her head to the side and baring her throat for his bite.

His thirst for her was fierce, a fever raging in his blood. But it was also reverent. She was so precious to him, a gift he would spend the rest of his long life striving to deserve.

On a low sigh, he placed his mouth over her carotid . . . then carefully sank his fangs into the soft flesh of her neck. She gasped as the sharp points pierced her. Her hands came up around his shoulders as he dragged her deeper into his embrace and took the first, incredible drink from her vein.

Ah, Christ.

Her blood was a revelation. Hot and sweet and electric on his tongue. The scent of roses and spices filled his senses. He inhaled it deep, savoring the powerful rush of her blood as it raced down his throat and into his body, into his cells.

Into his soul.

He'd heard the bond was a staggering force, but he hadn't been prepared. God, not even close. Every fiber of his being reached for her, connected to her. She fed his wounds, but she fed so much more than that too.

She fed his heart.

He didn't realize how empty it had been until her.

Until now, with Marina's blood flowing into him, joining with his.

He drank some more, then, reluctantly, ran his tongue over the twin punctures to seal them closed.

She groaned softly as he lifted his head from her neck. "I don't want you to stop."

"Oh, love." He grinned, fangs and all. "Who said I'm stopping?"

He took her mouth in an unrushed kiss, letting her taste herself on his tongue. She wrapped her arms around his neck, her naked curves moving against his hardness and igniting a need unlike any he'd ever known. All for her. Always for this incredible woman.

His woman.

His mate.

"I'm never going to lose you again," he said, a solemn vow. He held her close, letting those deep wine-colored eyes drink him in. "I love you, Marina. You're mine. You belong to me forever now."

"Yes," she agreed, emotion swamping her gaze.

He saw the depth of her feelings for him in her eyes, but now, through the connection that bonded him to her, he also felt the strength of her love for him in his blood.

He couldn't resist another kiss. He wanted more. One taste and he was already addicted to her.

He would never have his fill of his sweet, courageous, extraordinary Marina.

But there would be time for more.

Thank God, there would be all the time in the world, now that she was his.

~ ~ ~

His.

Even though she had known it almost from the start, Marina had never felt so sure of anything in her life until the moment Cain had bitten down on her and taken the first taste of her blood.

She was his.

And he was hers.

She saw that promise in his beautiful Breed eyes, glowing bright with amber as he held her against his hardness. She felt it in his kiss, which had always held the power to both comfort and inflame her.

Now, that deep, unhurried joining of their mouths stirred all of her senses, passion exploding through her nerve endings, fueled by the delicious, lingering ache of his bite and the awakening of something powerful and demanding deep inside her.

"Cain." She drew away from his lips on a fevered sigh. Desire flooded her, along with the new craving she could not contain. "Oh, God, Cain. I need . . ."

"I know, baby." His hands roamed her body, leaving fire everywhere he touched. "I know what you need."

He cut off the water, then reached for a towel and wrapped her in it. Her breath caught with amazement as she looked at his unblemished skin.

His *dermaglyphs* surged with color and life, but there was no trace of any wounds.

"Your body is healed."

"Yes." He lifted her chin and kissed the tip of her nose. "That's the strength of your blood. Your Breedmate blood."

She couldn't help but marvel, tracing the healed skin with her fingers. When she leaned down to follow the arcs and flourishes of his *glyphs* with her mouth, Cain's chest vibrated with a low, rumbling growl.

He scooped her up, carrying her out of the shower and onto his bed.

Their bed now.

With the towel moved aside, he covered her naked body with his. Then he entered her slowly, filling her completely. She arched to take all of him, reveling in the totality of his possession of her.

She was his.

She told him so as he brought them both to the peak of an incredible climax. She told him again, as he rolled onto his back and took her with him, seating her astride him, their bodies still intimately joined.

His blazing eyes seared her, fueling the fire that already lived in her veins. "Are you sure this is what you want, love? There's no breaking the bond. It will live in us forever, an invisible chain linking our strongest emotions, both pleasure and pain. You'll be the only one to sustain me, Marina. And once you drink from me, until I take my last breath, there will never be another male for you."

"I don't need a blood bond to understand that." She cupped his cheek. "But that's what I want. Right now, Cain, there's nothing I want more than your bond."

He uttered a strangled curse. "I wanted to wait. I wanted to make this moment special. I wanted it to be perfect for you."

Marina smiled. "We're together. We're home, Cain. What could be more perfect than that?"

With his hand at the back of her neck, he brought her to him for a tender, but passionate kiss. As they parted, he lifted his wrist to his mouth. His fangs sank in, opening his vein.

"Take this," he whispered fiercely. "Take all of me now."

Marina sealed her mouth over the punctures. She inhaled a stunned cry as the first hot taste of his blood raced over her tongue. As fierce as a storm, as bright and jagged as a bolt of lightning, his blood roared into her body. Each spicy, dark taste of him brought a deeper intoxication . . . and a quickening inside her that woke every particle of her being.

But there was something more coming to life within her.

Something more than the sweeping intensity of her desire for this man. Something even deeper than her love for him.

It was Cain.

She felt his desire too. She felt all of the love he had for her. She felt him inside her with every beat of her heart, and with each thundering answer of his.

They were joined in all ways now.

Together forever.

Home, where they both belonged.

And she was right. There was nothing more perfect than that.

~ * ~

Never miss a new book from Lara Adrian!

Sign up for the email newsletter at
www.LaraAdrian.com

Or type this URL into your web browser:
http://bit.ly/LaraAdrianNews

Be the first to get notified of Lara's new releases, plus be eligible for special subscribers-only exclusive content and giveaways that you won't find anywhere else.

Sign up today!

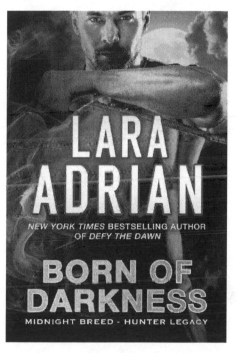

Coming Soon!

Presenting a sizzling, suspenseful standalone
contemporary romance set in Lara Adrian's
acclaimed **100 Series** story world

Run to You

Winter 2018

For information on this book and more, visit:

www.LaraAdrian.com

Discover the Midnight Breed
with a FREE eBook

Get the series prequel novella
A Touch of Midnight
FREE in eBook at most major retailers

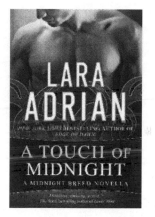

**After you enjoy your free read, look for Book 1 at a
special price: $2.99 USD eBook or $7.99 USD print!**

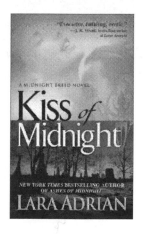

Watch for the next book in the bestselling
Midnight Breed Series from Lara Adrian!

Break the Day

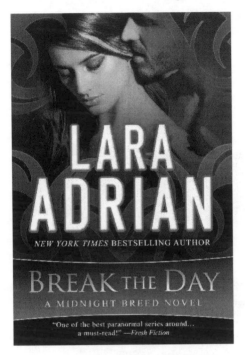

Available Early 2019

eBook * Paperback * Unabridged audiobook

**For more information on the series and upcoming
releases, visit:**

www.LaraAdrian.com

Pick up the latest book in the bestselling
Midnight Breed Series from Lara Adrian!

Claimed in Shadows

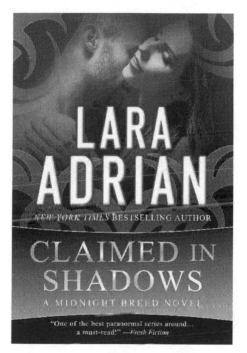

Available Now!

eBook * Paperback * Unabridged audiobook

**For more information on the series and upcoming
releases, visit:**

www.LaraAdrian.com

Turn the page for an excerpt from former
Hunter Scythe's story in the Midnight
Breed vampire romance series

Midnight Unbound

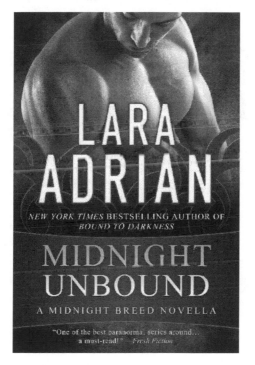

**Available now in ebook, trade paperback and
unabridged audiobook**

For more information on the series and
upcoming releases, visit:

www.LaraAdrian.com

A lethal Breed warrior is called upon by his brethren in the Order to bodyguard a beautiful young widow he's craved from afar in this new novella in the "steamy and intense" (Publishers Weekly) Midnight Breed vampire romance series from New York Times and #1 international bestselling author Lara Adrian.

As a former Hunter bred to be a killing machine in the hell of Dragos's lab, Scythe is a dangerous loner whose heart has been steeled by decades of torment and violence. He has no room in his world for love or desire--especially when it comes in the form of a vulnerable, yet courageous, Breedmate in need of protection. Scythe has loved--and lost--once before, and paid a hefty price for the weakness of his emotions. He's not about to put himself in those chains again, no matter how deeply he hungers for lovely Chiara.

For Chiara Genova, a widow and mother with a young Breed son, the last thing she needs is to put her fate and that of her child in the hands of a lethal male like Scythe. But when she's targeted by a hidden enemy, the obsidian-eyed assassin is her best hope for survival . . . even at the risk of her heart.

~ ~ ~

"It was such an AMAZING feeling to be diving back into the dangerous and sensual world of the Midnight Breed... If you are looking for a fast-paced, paranormal romantic suspense, full of passion and heart, look no further than MIDNIGHT UNBOUND."
—Shayna Renee's Spicy Reads

Chapter 1

Scythe had been in the dance club for nearly an hour and he still hadn't decided which of the herd of intoxicated, gyrating humans would be the one to slake his thirst tonight. Music blared all around him, the beat throbbing and pulsing, compounding the headache that had been building in his temples for days.

His stomach ached, too, sharp with the reminder that it had been almost a week since he'd fed. Too long for most of his kind. For him—a Breed male whose Gen One blood put him at the very top of the food chain—a week without nourishment was not only dangerous for his own wellbeing, but for that of everyone near him as well.

From within the cloak of shadows that clung around the end of the bar, he watched the throng of young men and women illuminated by colored strobe lights that flashed and spun over the dance floor as the DJ rolled seamlessly from the track of one sugary pop hit to another.

This tourist dive in Bari, a seaside resort town located at the top of Italy's boot heel, wasn't his usual hunting ground. He preferred the larger cities where blood Hosts could be hired for their services and dismissed immediately afterward, but his need to feed was too urgent for a long trek to Naples.

And besides, that journey would take him past the vineyard region of Potenza—an area he made a habit of avoiding for the past few weeks for reasons he refused to consider, even now.

Hell, especially now, when blood thirst wrenched his gut and his fangs pulsed with the urge to sink into warm, tender flesh.

A snarl slid off his tongue as he let his gaze drift over the crowd again. Against his will, he locked on to a petite brunette swaying to the music on the far side of the packed club. She had her back to him, silky dark brown hair cascading over her shoulders, her small body poured into skinny jeans and cropped top that bared a wedge of pale skin at her midsection. She laughed at something her companions said, and the shrill giggle scraped over Scythe's heightened sense of hearing.

He glanced away, instantly disinterested, but the sight of her had called to mind another waifish female— one he'd been trying his damnedest to forget.

He knew he'd never find Chiara Genova in a place like this, yet there was a twisted part of him that ran with the idea, teasing him with a fantasy he had no right to entertain. Sweet, lovely Chiara, naked in his arms. Her mouth fevered on his, hungered. Her slender throat bared for his bite—

"Fuck."

The growl erupted out of him, harsh with fury. It drew the attention of a tall blonde who had parked her skinny ass on the barstool next to him fifteen minutes ago and had been trying, unsuccessfully, to make him notice her.

Now she leaned toward him, reeking of too much wine and perfume as she licked her lips and offered him a friendly grin. "You don't look like you're having much fun tonight."

He grunted and glanced her way, taking stock of her in an instant.

Human. Probably closer to forty than the short leather skirt and lacy bustier she wore seemed to suggest. And definitely not a local. Her accent was pure American. Midwest, if he had to guess.

"Wanna hear a confession?" She didn't wait for him to answer, not that he planned to. "I'm not having much fun tonight, either." She heaved a sigh and traced one red-lacquered fingernail around the rim of her empty glass. "You thirsty, big guy? Why don't you let me buy you a drink—"

"I don't drink."

Her smile widened and she shrugged, undeterred. "Okay, then let's dance."

She slid off her stool and grabbed for his hand.

When she didn't find it—when her fingers brushed against the blunt stump where his right hand used to be, a long time ago—she recoiled.

"Oh, my God. I, um... Shit." Then her intoxicated gaze softened with pity. "You poor thing! What happened to you? Are you a combat vet or something?"

"Or something." Irritation made his deep voice crackle with menace, but she was too drunk to notice.

She stepped in close and his predator's senses lit up, his nostrils tingling at the trace coppery scent of human red cells rushing beneath her skin. The rawness in his stomach spread to his veins, which now began to throb with the rising intensity of his blood thirst.

His body felt heavy and slow. The stump at the end of his wrist ached with phantom pain. His normally razor-sharp vision was blurred and unfocused.

Usually, in some dark, bizarre way, he relished the sensation of physical discomfort. It reminded him that as dead inside as he might feel—as disconnected as he had been ruthlessly trained to be as a Hunter in the hell of Dragos's laboratory—there were some things that could still penetrate the numbness. Make him feel like he was among the living.

This particular kind of pain, though, bordered on unbearable, and it was all he could do not to grab the woman and take her vein right there in the middle of the club.

"Come on. Let's get out of here."

"Sure!" She practically leaped at him. "I thought you'd never ask."

He steered her away from the bar and out the club's exit without another word. Although the Breed had been outed to their human neighbors for more than twenty years, there were few among Scythe's kind—even a stone-cold killer like him—who made a habit of feeding in public places.

His companion wobbled a bit as they stepped out into the crisp night air. "Where do you wanna go? I'm staying at a hotel just up the street. It's a shithole, but we can go there if you want to hang out for a while."

"No. My vehicle will do."

Desire lit her features as she stared up at him. "Impatient, are you?" She giggled, smacking her palm against his chest. "Don't worry, I like it."

She trailed after him across the small parking lot to his gleaming black SUV.

In some dim corner of his conscience, he felt sorry for a woman who valued herself so little that she would traipse off with a stranger who offered her nothing in return for the use of her body.

Or, in this case, her blood.

Scythe had been born nothing better than a slave. Had nearly died one. The concept of taking from someone simply because he had the physical prowess to do it pricked him with self-loathing. The least he could do was make sure that when he took he left something behind as well. The woman would be weak with an unexplainable satisfaction once he was finished with her. Since he was feeling an uncustomary twinge of pity for her, she'd also walk away with a purse fat enough to rent a room for a month in the best hotel in Bari.

"This way," he muttered, his voice nothing more than a rasp.

She took his proffered arm and grinned, but it wasn't the coy smile that had his blood heating. It was the pulse fluttering wildly in her neck beneath that creamy flesh that had his fangs elongating. They punched through his gums and he went lightheaded with the need to feed, denied for too long.

They got into his vehicle and he wasted no time. Pivoting in the seat, he reached for her with his left hand, his fingers curling around her forearm. She uttered a small, confused noise as he drew her toward him and brought her wrist to his mouth.

Her confusion faded away the second he sank his fangs into her delicate flesh.

"Oh, my God," she gasped, her cheeks flushing as her whole body listed forward.

She speared the fingers of her free hand into his long black hair, and he had to resist the urge to jerk away as blood filled his mouth. He didn't like to be touched. All he wanted to do was fill the gaping hole in his gut until the next time he was forced to feed.

She moaned, her breath coming in quick pants as he drank. He took his fill, drawing on her wrist until he could feel the energy coursing through his body, replenishing his strength, fortifying his cells.

When he was done, he closed the tiny bite marks on her skin with a dispassionate swipe of his tongue as she twitched against him breathlessly.

"Good Lord, what is this magic and where do I sign up for more?" she murmured, her chest still heaving.

He leaned back against the cushioned leather, feeling the calm begin to move over him as his body absorbed the temporary nourishment. When the woman started to shift toward him with drugged need in her eyes, Scythe reached out and placed his palm against her forehead.

The trance took hold of her immediately. He erased her memory of his bite and the desire it stirred in her. When she slumped back against her seat, he dug into the pocket of his black jeans for his money and peeled off several large bills. He tossed them in her lap, then opened the passenger door with a silent, mental command.

"Go," he instructed her through her trance. "Take the money and go back to your hotel. Stay away from this club. Find something better to do with your time."

She obeyed at once. Stuffing the bills into her purse, she climbed out of the SUV and headed across the parking lot.

Scythe tipped his head back against the seat and released a heavy sigh as his fangs began to recede. Already, the human's blood was smoothing the edge from his whole-body pain. The malaise that had been worsening for the past twenty-four hours was finally gone and this feeding would hold him for another week if he was lucky.

He started up his vehicle, eager to be back on the road to his lair in Matera. He hadn't even pulled out of the lot when his cell phone chirped from inside his coat pocket. He yanked it out with a frown and scowled down at the screen. Only three people had his number and he wanted to hear from exactly none of them right now.

The restricted call message glowed up at him and he grimaced.

Shit. No need to guess who it might be.

And as much as he might want to shut out the rest of the world, Scythe would never refuse the call of one of his former Hunter brethren.

On a curse, he jabbed the answer button. "Yeah."

"We need to talk." Trygg's voice was always a shade away from a growl, but right now the Breed warrior's tone held a note of urgency too. Scythe had heard that same note in his half-brother's voice the last time he called from the Order's command center in Rome, and he could only imagine what it meant now.

"So, talk," he prompted, certain he didn't want the answer. "What's going on?"

"The Order's got a problem that could use your specialized skills, brother."

"Fuck." Scythe's breath rushed out of him on a groan. "Where have I heard that before?"

Six weeks ago, he'd allowed Trygg to drag him into the Order's troubles and Scythe was still trying to put the whole thing behind him. As a former assassin, he didn't exactly play well with others. He damned sure wasn't interested in getting tangled up in Order business again.

But there were only a handful of people in the world who knew exactly what Scythe had endured in the hell of Dragos's Hunter program, and Trygg was one of them. They had suffered it together for years as boys, and had dealt with the aftermath as men.

Even if they and the dozens of other escaped Hunters didn't share half their DNA, their experience in the labs couldn't make for truer brothers than that. If Trygg needed something, Scythe would be there. Hell, he'd give up his other hand for any one of his Hunter brethren if they asked it of him.

Scythe's preternatural ability to sniff out trouble told him that Trygg was about to ask for something far more painful than that.

"Tell me what you need," he muttered, steeling himself for the request.

"You remember Chiara Genova?"

Scythe had to bite back a harsh laugh.

Did he remember her? Fuck, yeah, he remembered. The beautiful, widowed Breedmate with the soulful, sad eyes and broken angel's face had been the star of too many of his overheated dreams since the night he first saw her. Even now, the mere mention of her name fired a longing in his blood that he had no right to feel.

He remembered her three-year-old son Pietro, too. The kid's laugh had made Scythe's temples throb with memories he'd thought he left dead and buried behind him more than a decade ago.

"Are she and the boy all right?" There was dread in his throat as he asked it, but his flat tone gave none of it away.

"Yes. For now." Trygg paused. "She's in danger. It's serious as hell this time."

Scythe's grip on his phone tightened. The woman had been through enough troubles already, starting with the unfit Breed male she'd taken as her mate several years ago. Chiara's bastard of a mate, Sal, had turned out to be a gambler and a first-class asshole.

Unable to pay his debts, he'd wound up on the bad side of a criminal kingpin named Vito Massioni. To square up when Massioni came to collect, Sal traded his own sister, Arabella, in exchange for his life. If not for the Order in Rome—more specifically, one of their warriors, Ettore "Savage" Selvaggio—Bella might still be imprisoned as Massioni's personal pet.

As for Chiara, she was essentially made a captive of Massioni's as well. Sal's treachery hadn't saved him in the end. After his death, Chiara and her son lived at the family vineyard under the constant threat of Massioni's danger.

Six weeks ago, it had all come to a head. The Order had moved in on Massioni, taking out him and his operation... or so they'd thought. Massioni had survived the explosion that obliterated his mansion and all of his lieutenants, and he was out for blood.

Chiara and her son had ended up in the crosshairs along with Bella and Savage, putting all of them on the run. Trygg sent them to Scythe for shelter, knowing damned well that Scythe wasn't in the habit of playing protector to anyone. Least of all a woman and child.

And he still wasn't in that habit now.

Nevertheless, the question rolled off his tongue too easily. "Tell me what happened."

"According to Bella, Chiara's had the sensation she was being watched for the past week or so. Stalked from afar. Last night, things took a turn for the worst. A Breed male broke into the villa. If she hadn't heard him outside her window and had time to prepare, she'd likely have been raped, murdered, or both."

"Motherfu—" Scythe bit off the curse and took a steadying breath. His rage was on full boil, but he rallied his thoughts around gathering facts. "Did the son of a bitch touch her? How did she manage to get away?"

"Sal kept a sword hidden beneath the bed in case Massioni ever sent some muscle there to work him over for the money he owed. After he died, Chiara left the weapon in place. By some miracle of adrenaline or determination, she was able to fight the bastard off, but barely."

Holy hell. As he thought of the tiny slip of a woman trying to fight off a healthy Breed male he shook his head slowly in disbelief. The fact that she survived was beyond lucky or even miraculous, but Trygg was right. The odds of her doing it again were slim to none.

Which was, apparently, where Scythe and his specific set of skills came in. Not that it would take a request from Trygg or the Order to convince him to hunt down Chiara's attacker and make the Breed male pay in blood and anguish.

The very idea of her cowering as some animal attempted to harm her made Scythe's whole body quake with fiery rage.

"So, the Order needs me to find this bastard and tear his head off, then?"

"Just killing him isn't going to get to the root of the problem. We don't think this attack is random. The Order needs you to protect Chiara and Pietro while we work to figure out who's after her and why."

Scythe could not hold back the snarl that built in his throat. "You know I don't do bodyguard duty. Damn it, you know why too."

"Yeah," Trygg said. "And I'm still asking you to do it. You're the only one we can trust with this, brother. The Order's got all hands on deck with Opus Nostrum, Rogue outbreaks, and ninety-nine other problems at the moment. We need you."

Scythe groaned. "You ask too fucking much this time."

Protecting the woman would cost him. He knew that from both instinct and experience. For almost a score, he'd kept his feedings down to once a week. His body's other needs were kept on an even tighter leash.

He'd only spent a few hours with Chiara Genova six weeks ago, yet it was long enough to know that being under the same roof with her was going to test both his patience and his self-discipline.

But the kid? That was a no-go. There were things he just couldn't do, not even for his brother.

He mulled over Trygg's request in miserable silence.

"What's it gonna be, Scythe?"

The refusal sat on the tip of his tongue, but damned if he could spit it out. "If I do this, we do it my way. I don't answer to the Order or to anyone else. Agreed?"

"Sure, you got it. Just get your ass to Rome as soon as you can so we can go over your plan and coordinate efforts."

"What about her?" Scythe demanded. "Does Chiara know you've contacted me to help her?"

The stretch of silence on the other end of the line told him all he needed to know and he grimaced.

"Savage and Bella are bringing Chiara and Pietro in as we speak," Trygg said. "They should all be here within the hour."

Scythe cursed again, more vividly this time. "I'm on my way."

He ended the call, then threw the SUV into gear and gunned it out to the street.

MIDNIGHT UNBOUND

is available now at all major retailers in eBook, trade paperback, and unabridged audiobook.

Although this extended novella can be read as a standalone story within the series, it also connects the Midnight Breed series with the exciting new Hunter Legacy series available now!

Thirsty for more Midnight Breed?

Read the complete series!

. . . and more to come!

If you enjoy sizzling contemporary romance, don't miss this hot series from Lara Adrian!

For 100 Days

The 100 Series: Book 1

"I wish I could give this more than 5 stars! Lara Adrian not only dips her toe into this genre with flare, she will take it over . . . I have found my new addiction, this series." --The Sub Club Books

All available now in ebook, trade paperback and unabridged audiobook.

More romance and adventure from Lara Adrian!

Phoenix Code Series
(Paranormal Romantic Suspense)

"A fast-paced thrill ride." –Fresh Fiction

Masters of Seduction Series
(Paranormal Romance)

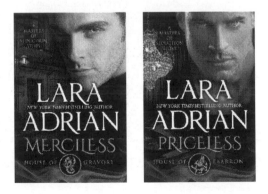

"Thrilling, action-packed and super sexy." –Literal Addiction

Award-winning medieval romances from Lara Adrian!

Dragon Chalice Series
(Paranormal Medieval Romance)

"Brilliant . . . bewitching medieval paranormal series." —Booklist

Warrior Trilogy
(Medieval Romance)

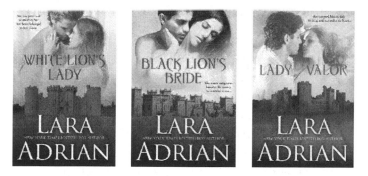

"The romance is pure gold." —All About Romance

ABOUT THE AUTHOR

LARA ADRIAN is a New York Times and #1 international best-selling author, with nearly 4 million books in print and digital worldwide and translations licensed to more than 20 countries. Her books regularly appear in the top spots of all the major bestseller lists including the New York Times, USA Today, Publishers Weekly, Wall Street Journal, Amazon.com, Barnes & Noble, etc. Reviewers have called Lara's books "addictively readable" (Chicago Tribune), "extraordinary" (Fresh Fiction), and "one of the consistently best" (Romance Novel News).

Writing as **TINA ST. JOHN**, her historical romances have won numerous awards including the National Readers Choice; Romantic Times Magazine Reviewer's Choice; Booksellers Best; and many others. She was twice named a Finalist in Romance Writers of America's RITA Awards, for Best Historical Romance (White Lion's Lady) and Best Paranormal Romance (Heart of the Hunter). More recently, the German translation of Heart of the Hunter debuted on Der Spiegel bestseller list.

Visit the author's website and sign up for new release announcements at www.LaraAdrian.com.

Find Lara on Facebook at
www.facebook.com/LaraAdrianBooks

Connect with Lara online at:

www.LaraAdrian.com

www.facebook.com/LaraAdrianBooks

www.goodreads.com/lara_adrian

www.twitter.com/lara_adrian

www.instagram.com/laraadrianbooks

www.pinterest.com/LaraAdrian